SLEIGHT

A NOVEL

SLOANE
KADY

BLACKWEALD

PRESS

Copyright © 2016 by Sloane Kady

Published in the United States by Blackweald Press, Seattle.
217 1st Ave. S. No. 4321
Seattle, WA 98194
www.blackwealdpress.com

ISBN 978-0-9862790-2-7

Printed in the United States of America

Cover Design by Keri Knutson of Alchemy Book Covers and Design

10 9 8 7 6 5 4 3 2 1

First Edition

For Poppers, Gangles, and Bert.
I'll never ask for my heart back.

SLEIGHT

CHAPTER 1

I'm the daughter of two defective people. They came off the factory line dented and chipped. If you could pick them up and look underneath them, you'd see that they're just hollow molds, meant to look like real parents, even sounding like them sometimes, but you know you can't keep them because those chips left sharp edges that will make you bleed, and they're not real, anyway. No one wants a cheap knockoff.

My father was unbearably oppressive. Abusive would be the word to describe him nowadays, but thanks to the archaic thinking of the time, you could hit your kid with leather belts and call it tough love, and slap your wife around and call it guidance. Even when my father showed affection, he held me at a distance. I was part of the scenery—a daughter, a common part of the average American household. My brother was his favorite. They did everything together, until my brother died.

My mother, on the other hand, was neither love nor hate. She just…was. Until she was tragedy, and then she was over.

"Don't be like me, Bryce. Don't ever be like me," is what she used to tell me. I was five the first time she said it. I remember looking up at her and tilting my head like a confused puppy, wondering how something so lovely could be so sad.

My father stifled her, setting in motion the outline society had already laid out for her life. Marriage, kids, cooking, cleaning, and, eventually, death, and then my brother and I went and robbed her of the last traces of independence and passion she had hidden away. Deep down, I think she resented us. Or at least me. She was resigned to her life by the time of my brother's arrival, and anyway, you can't resent your dead son. It's against the laws of nature.

I was the eldest child, the first to have snatched my mother's dreams away, in turn giving her sleepless nights with a colicky infant that refused to breastfeed and wouldn't stop screaming. I guess it's easy to resent your baby when you only had her to salvage the pieces of a marriage that wasn't falling apart but had never been whole to begin with, like my existence could solidify their lifeless union. A pink, screaming sacrifice to the marital gods.

That wasn't my fault, of course, but that didn't stop them from branding me from the moment of conception. "Burden" would have been stamped on my bottom, had I been hollow like my parents. But I'm real. I'm too real, too authentic. I make people feel things they don't like. I expose nerves that have long been buried under the filth and dust of decades of denial. Want to see the truth? Spend a minute walking through the muck with me and you'll crave the platitudes and candy-coated gestures the world throws at your otherwise unblemished feet while you pick my mud from your toenails.

Maybe that's why Mommy Dearest didn't like me around. I asked too many questions. I prodded when strange men came around after my dad left for work and my mother's bedroom door would remain shut, the musky smell of sweat and sex filling the hallway where I would watch her door and cry.

I wanted to know everything. I inspected her: "Why's your hair red and mine isn't, Mommy?" "Why does Daddy sleep at work so much, Mommy?" "Why did everything change after Scotty died, Mommy?" "Why do you have to take medicine? And doesn't that needle hurt when it goes into your arm like that, Mommy?"

I represented everything she wasn't. She had shut down, closed up shop. I was overflowing with life, driven by curiosity. She was a cubic zirconium, and I was a diamond, formed under extreme pressure and dark conditions. I had to unearth my way into life; otherwise I would've died.

My story is sad, I guess. By most people's standards, it's downright horrible. I get that. There's a long list of things that made my childhood the stuff of nightmares, but I don't share all those things. Not because I'm uncomfortable with them, but because they make other people uncomfortable.

The first person who put his dick in my mouth shared the same DNA with me. He said he wouldn't play with me if I didn't do it. I was eight years old, and my brother had just died. Besides, cousins used to marry each other all the time, right?

I'm usually met with a flinch and a disapproving scowl when I tell that story. It's okay to live these things—just don't say these things. Or maybe they're just offended by the vulgarity. My filthy mouth is rivaled only by my dad's, whose repertoire of profanities has a more dated feel. By 'dated' I mean racist and bigoted. But I'm not always crude. Even I have my limits. I don't take the Lord's name in vain, but that's purely out of habit. The Big Man and I parted ways a long time ago. Don't get me wrong, I still love Jesus, but He kind of clashes with my agnostic views.

Like most kids in America, I was raised to walk the straight and narrow path even though my parents didn't. Somewhere along the way, the pearly white road kind of evaporated, like the lines off the little mirror my mother kept hidden in her dresser drawer. When you live a life as real as mine, the mind eventually filters out fairytales. Now I don't know what I believe in. I'm too damn lazy to figure it out and too afraid not to. But if I'm going to believe in an organized religion, I might as well believe in elves. They're little and shiny and they sparkle. Wait. I'm thinking of fairies. I'd like to pluck the wings off the prettiest one and know what it's like to fly, but that would kill her. Taking anything's wings away will kill it. Trust me, I would know. I still have scars from where mine used to be, but my mother cut them off with her sharp edges the day she slipped into the bathtub and went to sleep forever. That's an image no eighteen-year-old girl forgets. Can I still be a diamond if Mommy Dearest killed herself in the john?

You're probably envisioning me as some hellion. Horns and big tits. All hellions have big tits. And they wear red, like proper harlots. But you'd be wrong. Sure, I usually wear nothing but black, I carry a man's name, and I've got the mouth of a drunken sailor, but I'm actually a good person. A really good person. I'm the fool who tells the cashier when they've undercharged me. Once, when some of my high school friends stole a pack of smokes from the gas station, I went back the next night and gave the cashier five bucks and explained what happened. I'm sure the grimy bastard pocketed it. He had the kind of chest hair that screams, *I'll give you herpes in the back of a van and not even call to say sorry.* But who cares. I did the right thing. I also never lie, like I'm incapable of it or something. I give too much of myself, and I love more than I should.

Maybe my parents used to be good, too, or maybe they had potential and I sucked it all up in utero, needing all the light I could get in my dark pressure cooker. If they'd never had me, maybe they would've been diamonds, and I would've been born to one of those Walton families with the plastic smiles and vacant stares. But then I guess I wouldn't be me, and what a fucking shame that would be.

CHAPTER 2

I'm sitting in my dermatologist's office. The office next door is the aesthetic department where Dr. Brackett injects filler, smooths wrinkles, and zaps age spots away. *Swish, zip, zap*—gone. Over here is where all the moly and elderly patients are. That's why I'm here. The mole on my thigh looks a bit ominous, as does the rate at which the SOB is growing. Maybe it's cancer. Melanoma. It'd be ironic, since I live in the cloudiest state in America, as evidenced by my pasty skin. That's what my childhood friend Shana calls it, "pasty." I don't like that word. It makes me feel self conscious, especially when she says it. She's got the tanned skin of a god, that bitch.

I rub the spot on my jeans where I know my mole is. It's genetic. My father had skin cancer. Just another example of his sharp edges doing more harm. I think I'd like to rip it off, but it's got roots, just like family. There's no trimming the nasty nub off the top and hoping the roots will shrivel and die. They need to be excavated.

This office is nice. Really nice. I've never been in a waiting room with reclining leather chairs and footstools, but that's what you get in posh buildings in downtown Seattle. This room smells of cowhide and overpriced cologne from the old men filling the recliners. I don't fit in here, but I sit in the only available recliner anyway and toss my boots on the footstool.

Pass the cigars, ol' chap! Say, pal. Those new Brooks Brothers loafers are the bee's knees!

I can't help but to slip into a transatlantic accent in front of the old timers. I blame it on my pasty skin.

Suddenly I'm aware of all the eyes on me and my wild gypsy hair. I wrap my sweater around my shoulders and swivel my chair around to face the TV. One of those nature documentaries is on, with two fish with giant, alien mouths fighting, or maybe mating. The volume is off, and Dean Martin is playing over the speakers. It's an odd combination, the fighting/mating fish with the big mouths and Dean Martin. All of a sudden, I want a Vegas prime rib lathered in horseradish sauce.

"Bryce Price," the receptionist calls. Yeah, my name is Bryce Price. I told you my parents were hollow. Now shut the fuck up about it.

I stand up while looking down at my boots. I don't want to see all those wealthy men, with their loafers and cufflinks, sniggering at me and my Dr. Seuss name. Bryce Price would like to roll some dice while eating prime rib and rice and drinking vodka over ice. I should've sued my parents. Such bullshit.

~

The tiny receptionist walks me into a room and shuts the door. "What is it we're seeing you for today?" she asks.

I'm dying from the suspicious growth on my leg.

"I have a new mole. It wasn't there six months ago."

"You're certain?"

"Yes."

I probably wouldn't have noticed, but they always say to watch out for irregularly shaped moles, and this one's shaped like Texas. I think I'll call it Walker Texas Ranger. No. Too long. Just Walker.

The nurse passes me a smile and hands me a gown before she walks out, telling me the doctor will be in momentarily. The room is gleaming and sterile. Not like my general practitioner's office, with the beds from the 80s and the crapped-out tiles; mystery fluids dried in hard drops on the floorboards and walls. I might not even wash my hands when I leave this place.

~

I'm just about to grab the strange light thingy on the wall when the door opens and in walks the real Dr. Dreamy. None of that fake *Grey's Anatomy* crap. Damn show isn't even filmed here. Perpetrators.

No, Dr. Brackett is the stuff of fantasies. Strong jaw, piercing eyes, and a five o'clock shadow I'm willing to bet grows in by noon each day. He's made of sticks and stones that can break your bones. I rub the mole again and feel my heart flutter in my chest. I'm such a girl.

"Bryce?" he says, smiling that stupid beautiful smile. "How was your Christmas?"

"Good," I lie. "Ate too many cookies. Gained five pounds." Not a lie. "You?"

He pats his perfect stomach. "Too good. I think I've got you beat by five pounds."

Somehow I doubt that. The man's probably got a Bowflex in every room in his house.

"Even so," he adds, "you can stand to gain a few pounds."

I never know if that's a compliment. Am I sickly? Or did Dr. Hot Pants just compliment me? I look in his eyes and know that it was an insult. This is the kind of man that dates women who look like the cars he drives.

"What do you drive?" I ask, not caring how out of place my question is.

"Um…" He frowns, then grins. It must be expensive, because he looks uncomfortable. "A Maserati. I saved for a long time for that car. Why?"

I look away, suddenly embarrassed to show him any part of my body. I'm not a Maserati. I'm a Ford Fiesta. Maybe a Toyota Camry, on my best day. I'll find a new dermatologist once I leave. First, off with Walker's head.

I flit my hand around dismissively. "No reason. Just thought maybe I had seen you somewhere."

"Ah. I see. So I understand you've got a new mole? When did you first notice it?"

"I don't know. Sometime in the last six months. It's odd looking." I almost tell him that it's shaped like our second-largest state, but I stop myself. That sounds ridiculous. Suddenly I want to be taken seriously. If I can't look like a hundred thousand-dollar vehicle, I want to sound like one. I've got a brain—whether or not I always use it is up for debate.

"It's got an irregular shape and poorly defined borders," I say. "The color isn't consistent, either. My father had skin cancer, so I understand that my risk is above average. And I'm a prior smoker."

"You sound like you've got experience with this."

No, I don't. I sound like I have Google. But I leave his assumption intact.

"You're still young," he says, "but our ears do perk up when we see patients with a family history of skin cancer. The smoking didn't help, but good for you for quitting. Let's have you sit back on the table."

When I recline, the doctor opens the door and the pocket-sized nurse walks back in. She's annoying, with her bouncy ponytail and pink lipstick. I bet she smells like cotton candy.

I had cotton candy body spray when I was younger. I remember dousing myself with it before going on a camping trip with my ex-boyfriend and another couple. We both puked buckets and then had drunken sex in our tent. Fake IDs and crappy booze. Half a dozen showers couldn't wash away the stench of vomit and cotton candy. I had been baptized in cheap body spray and sold my soul to MD 20/20.

"Ready when you are," Dr. Hot Pants says to me.

I blink hard and look up at the ceiling while pulling my gown aside so he can see my thigh. When he touches me, my skin gets goosey. I pretend the scars aren't there and that he doesn't notice them, even though he has to. But he'll play along, a polite member of society, and pretend he's got blinders on.

He makes a sound. "Hmm, hmm, hmm."

He pulls the stubby telescope thingy off the wall and places it on my skin and looks into it. After a moment, he hangs the instrument back on the wall and tells the nurse he needs to biopsy the mole.

"So it looks like cancer?" I ask.

"I can't say with certainty, but we definitely need to check it. It's got some concerning features. Before I biopsy it, let's take a look at the rest of you. Are there any other areas of concern?"

Yeah. Your eyes and your perfect hair and your hands on my body. I feel like a slut.

"No," I tell him, with a shake of the head. Just then my phone rings and all three of us look at my purse, the nurse's face pinching up like she ate something sour. I think I just saw her ponytail droop a bit.

"Sorry," I say, rushing to my phone. "Let me just turn that off."

When I pull it out, I see that I've missed several texts. I glance at the name and swallow hard. Why would he be texting me? Then I see a few words that stand out like they're lit up in neon, and I almost drop my phone on the floor.

"Are you ready, Ms. Price?" the doctor asks. No longer on a first-name basis. I'm trying his patience

"Yeah," I tell him, moving back to the table in what feels like a fog. I sit down and he tells me he's going to check my back. I hear the words, but I don't understand their meaning until his fingers are on me, tracing moles and freckles I only know I have because Shana used to play connect the dots with them when we were kids.

Next, I feel cool air on my breasts and realize I'm exposed. But I don't feel anything this time. Even when he places the light thingy on my ribs and is so close to my breasts I can feel the warmth of his skin, I don't care.

My eyes well up and I wonder what it is I'm feeling exactly. I close my eyes and can still see the text.

"Dammit, Bryce. Call me. Your dad was in an accident."

CHAPTER 3

I drive home in the rain, the water zigzagging across my windshield. It can't make up its mind about which direction it's blowing in. Neither can I. The icy January air usually makes me feel alive, like stepping out of a muggy bar into a crisp breeze, but today it settles into my bones and numbs my fingertips.

The fog is coming in, swallowing the buildings and mountains as it eats its way inland, painting everything in a shade I like to call "Horror Movie Gray." The fog blankets the floor, pine trees jut through the murky clouds at their feet, like fangs reaching for the heavens. This is the kind of place your soul can get lost in. It's not cheap and plastic. It's real and painfully lovely, even if you do hate it six months of the year. You'll learn to crave the sun like an addict craves their next fix. You'll also learn to crave the cold, dark days of winter once you're too drunk on summer heat and your dark, twisted Washington soul is nearly sun-bleached. But what I love most is that no one expects you to smile here.

I could say the weather reflects my mood, but that's cheesy as shit, and it's not true. My emotions are like Southern California on an April morning. They're totally placid. Absolutely nothing particularly special to report, and isn't that the problem?

I should feel something. I know I should. And I think I do, buried somewhere under the years I spent learning to suffocate all my mommy and daddy issues so I could function like a big girl in the real world. I think of all the fault lines running through the West Coast. I'm just another one. The Bryce Fault—no seismic activity in seven years. I'm due for another quake.

I shake my head, trying to rid myself of the memory. Seven years ago, things went KABOOM, and I wasn't in the blast zone—I was the blast. But then I walked out of the hospital a new woman, armed with the tools to cope in society. A shovel to bury my emotions with and a steamroller to make sure they never escape. Since that day, I've kept my trips north of Seattle to a minimum. I was on a roll. Fifteen and a half months since I last drove north on I-5. Guess my streak ends today. Fuck, fuck, fuckety fuck.

~

I stand in front of my closet, eyeing the variations of gray and black draped across the hangers. Everything looks like a uniform. Something dark to help me blend into the shadows, lest the common folk see me and learn of the elusive introvert.

My phone dings behind me again. I don't want to look at it, or the bed it's lying on. I'm going to miss my bed, with its brightly colored floral print that I'd never admit to buying. More than that, I don't want to see the name on my phone. Any name but his. There are people from your past that know you so well, you wish they'd disappear, taking all your dirty secrets along with them. If they were to vanish, your history would cease to exist, and you could start anew.

It dings again, and I make a guttural noise, grabbing a handful of clothes from the closet, not caring which pieces I wind up with. That should be enough for a week. With any luck, I'll be back in my tiny apartment by this weekend, shovel in hand, ready to bury another new memory made with dear old Dad.

~

I'm all packed and have my belongings sitting by the front door. I give my place a once-over, just to make sure all my lights are off and everything's clean. I can't leave my place messy. I don't have a cat to worry about. Maybe I should. I don't see living out my days with someone, so I might as well get cozy with the idea of hair in my dishes and a box of shit in the corner of my bathroom.

Truth be told, I'm devastated by the thought of my golden years being reduced to cleaning up feline crap. And let's face it. I'll probably die old and alone. Before it starves to death, that hairy bastard's going to gnaw my face off and take a nap with a heavy belly. I suddenly think I'm too pretty to die so ugly. Fuck it. I'll buy fish.

~

You'd think people in this state would know how to drive in rain. Anything more than a light mist and the freeway turns into a clusterfuck.

I-5 is packed. No shock there. I turn the radio on and tune into the station with all the classical music. I'm usually a rock 'n' roll, hip-hop, classic rock... Okay, I'm an everything kind of gal. I'm a walking jukebox. But when I'm stressed, I like to listen to classical music. Can't let my nerves get too revved up.

The freeway clears a bit once I pass Lynwood, and I feel my heart start to sputter, like it doesn't know if it wants to pump or give out. The spot where my mole was shaved off burns, and it's pissing me off. It's keeping me from believing this is all a bad dream. I can feel my pulse in the wound, the way you can after slamming your finger in a door.

Someone honks behind me, and I realize I'm driving twenty miles under the speed limit. I feel like I'm dredging toward my hanging. The townspeople will be there at the ready, pitchforks in hand.

Man, how I want to be someone else, anyone else. Like bouncy, pink ponytail girl. If I were her, I'd dress myself in all black and dye my hair black and do black things and say black things, just to see what pretty, bouncy, pink me would look like doing bad, bad things. But I'm good.

~

As I turn onto the highway, crossing the bridge that will disconnect me from my sanity, I can't help but to be stirred by the beauty surrounding me. This place is my lovely nightmare. Mother Nature, so majestic and serene, but she holds secrets in her womb, putrid and rotting. I try to tell myself that what happens in a place doesn't define the land, but I can't separate the two. The ghosts of my past haunt this place, and even the mention of it floods my mind with pictures I've tried to burn. If only someone could remove the pieces of my brain where all my sad stories are kept and stitch them into a macabre quilt, I'd line my father's casket with it when he dies.

Exiting the bridge, I drive up a long hill, passing through a thick layer of fog. I look behind me and see my present life move on without me. I'm in a time machine, in more ways than one. My hometown is an oddity. I didn't know how strange it was until I hightailed it to Seattle. Living downtown keeps you connected to the city's pulse. You've got your yuppies, tree-huggers, metros, artists, tourists, filthy rich, and filthy poor, like one of those mixed bags of candy you buy for Halloween. Nerds and Sweet Tarts and Sour Patch Kids. Reach in and pull out a surprise. You never know what you'll run into in the city, but it's sure to keep you coming back for more. I swear they pump endorphins into the air down there. Walk around Pike Place and tell me you don't feel like you've just entered the mind of an artist. It's America's MSG. Give me seconds and thirds and fourths; I don't care if it's just the chemicals, 'cause it tastes good and makes me feel alive. But not this place.

I'm only thirty miles from downtown Seattle, but it might as well be three hundred. This whole city is built around a large lake, million-dollar homes gobbling up the shoreline, where people flock to water like ants to sugar. Surrounding the lake are beautiful, snowy mountains as far as the eye can see. Giant Snow Caps, clustered in a sea of pines. It always makes me think of Jack London. It's a bit raw and untamed up here, like a dog that knows basic commands but will still bolt when let off its leash. Regardless of how I distance myself, I carry those parts of this place in me. Even after years living in Seattle, city life couldn't rid me of the call of the wild.

~

I pass by the only shopping centers in the city; mom & pop shops sandwiched in with the big chain stores. I see they got a new box store. Another tiny baby step towards modern-day conveniences. Well done. One day you'll graduate from pampers to big kid pants.

To my right is Woody's Bar & Grill, the city's only form of nightlife. A few of the *Deadliest Catch* guys have been spotted there over the years. It's that kind of place: wood paneling, karaoke, cheap beer. The "NOPE," Anti-Obama stickers should tell you where half the city's political views rest. I guess this place is another bag of mixed candy, and we're all cohabitating, gummy bears mixed with chocolaty nuts. You can drive down a residential street and find broken-down shacks right next to homes going for a million dollars. You have your liberals, whose views are on par with Seattle's republicans, and you have your right-wing, gun-toting mountain men who still say things like "he's queer," and "wow-wee, is that there colored folk?" Actually, I'm sure no one here has ever said that. You'd need people of color to actually pass through this place first. I think I'm probably the most liberal thing to come out of these parts.

I'm about to turn left onto the highway when a gaggle of teenage girls walk across the street, one holding a giant blue Slurpee. Three of them are decked out in cheerleading uniforms. I'm in my mid-twenties and still have to suppress my laughter. Grow up, Bryce.

The cheerleaders are wearing red and black, their ponytails high on their heads, swinging left and right with each step. I can almost see their goosebumps from here. What's a little hypothermia when the hairy tribe getting in their pickups outside McDonald's whistles and yells obscenities at you? Attention equals value. Sex equals love. Unwanted pregnancies and gonorrhea before age sixteen equals I-guess-I-should-have-listened. I'm suddenly filled with the urge to jump out of my car, line them up, and slap each one of them. Get your tickets! You can have some sense knocked into you for the low price of FREE.

Instead, I turn left, my head shaking as I watch them in my rearview. They should have more sense than that. They're not undereducated. The reason wealthy people move here isn't just for the lake and gorgeous scenery. This place has some of the best schools in the state, and Washington State's schools aren't anything to scoff at. Whatever. Not my problem. I have bigger fish to fry.

Highway Two takes me a few miles past the lake, and I run into a road that leads me deeper into densely packed trees and older, more modest homes built on much larger lots. The two-lane road swerves and dips, fog settling in the small valleys. I half expect to see Hansel and Gretel skipping along the forest lining the road. The smoke rising from each home's chimney only lends to the idyllic scenery.

I slow down and turn right into the driveway. The little green house sits there, cheerful despite its festering innards. But I see the shutters are just beginning to fall off the windows, and the weeds lining the path to the front door look like my gypsy hair. What the hell's going on? There's no way Sergeant Price would willingly allow this.

I drum my fingers on the steering wheel and watch the house, singing under my breath, because a British bloke once said something about seeing a red door and wanting to paint it black. I grab my old key from the glove compartment and tell myself I can handle this, though the sweat coating my armpits tells me different. I lived with this overbearing man every day of my life and it didn't kill me. But what if I kill him? That's a joke, of course. You have to wear orange in prison, and I've already established that I don't do color.

When I get out, the smell hits me first. It's a shame that I hate it here, because it really is divine. It smells of earth. Mother Nature cooks up her best recipe in this part of the country. Soil, rocks, pines, rain, and cold mountain air mixed together. A northwestern stew for the soul.

I stand on the front porch, bag in hand, and give the red door a quick glance. When I open it, I'm immediately bombarded with the stench of cigar smoke. Whenever I leave here, it seems to take weeks to get the smell out of my clothes, and it never seems to come out of my luggage.

I slip inside and gently close the door behind me. I'd rather startle him than him startle me. My heart starts to gallop, and the spot where Walker was is pounding harder than ever. I want to go home, where people vape instead of smoke, and where grouchy men aren't waiting to toss chunks of putrid, fermenting poison into my northwest stew. I'd rather be back in Dr. Hot Pants's office, with his warm doctor hands on my flesh and his nurse giving me disapproving looks when I admit to never wearing sunscreen as a child.

"Who's that?" my father barks.

Shit. His deep, hoarse voice rattles me. I put my bag in the corner and straighten my hair before entering the belly of the castle. When I walk into his room, I'm immediately struck by how the air changes. It's like Florida in here. I instinctively wave my hand in front of my face and move to the window.

"Don't," my father croaks.

Well, it's nice to see you, too, Dad.

Through the darkness, I can only see his outline in the bed. I don't know what to say. "Yes, sir!" was always a safe bet, but something stubborn in me won't let my lips form the words.

"Aren't you hot?" I ask. "If you're going to smoke like a chimney, at least crack the window."

He reaches over, snapping on the small lamp on the nightstand. When the light hits his face, I try not to react, but it's more than just bruises and stitches from the car accident. He looks like someone else. His pallor gives him a greenish hue, and the loose skin hanging from his neck looks thin enough to read through. By all accounts, my father was always a handsome man. More George Clooney, less Patrick Swayze in his final days. His frame is still substantial. The man always demanded attention when he walked into a room. But his shoulders are starting to slump forward, and his chest no longer protrudes but caves in beneath his pinstriped pajamas.

I hide my shock and ask again, "Can I open the window? It's stifling in here."

"I told Jackson not to call you. I don't need any help."

I'm not surprised. Pride has always been pretty high up there on my father's list. My eyes slowly move to his hands, then his legs, and finally his feet. I think he can't possibly be shivering, but he is, teeth chattering and all.

"What the hell are you looking at?" he says.

I startle, trying to fit my father's voice with this strange man in front of me. He sounds like my dad, he smells like my dad, but he looks like death a few days before it comes knocking.

"Sorry," I tell him, standing at attention. "I wasn't looking at anything. I'm just here to help. Want another blanket?"

"Jackson needs to realize he stopped being a part of our lives the day he walked out on you. Little shit needs to keep to himself."

"You drove your truck into someone's garage, Dad. I'm pretty sure he was just trying to help you." I hate defending Jackson, but I told you I was incapable of lying.

"I said I didn't need anybody's help. Told him the same damn thing this morning, but the little shit wouldn't let me be."

I kind of like my father's nickname for Jackson. Little Shit. It's got a ring to it, but that's not important right now.

"Well, I'm sure a better man would've left you stranded in your smashed-up truck in some stranger's garage, but you got spotted by Jackson. He might be a lot of things, but he's not careless."

"Isn't he, though?" he asks, knowing damn well he's already hitting a sensitive spot. I won't take the bait even though I want to bite the head off that wiggling worm.

I change the subject. "What were you doing, anyway?"

"I was turning around."

"At thirty miles an hour?"

I move in closer without realizing what I'm doing. I'm curious about this doppelgänger. I want to turn him over and see if there's a zipper. Unzip the old man suit and *POP* goes your real dad.

"I was checking my phone."

I stop in my tracks and stare at him. Teenage girls in cheerleading uniforms check their phones and subsequently smash into things. Not my father. He's a member of AARP and the NRA. He goes to church every Sunday and volunteers at the American Legion. He's a Vietnam vet and the meanest son of a bitch I know. He got his first cell phone three years ago. This is not the kind of dude who checks his phone while driving.

I glance at his flip phone sitting on the dresser. "You were checking your phone? For what? Can you even text on that thing?"

He grabs a glass off the nightstand and takes a swig of what I already know is whiskey. I hope he doesn't polish it off, because I'm going to need that later.

The ice clinks in the glass as he suckles at the last drops.

"Are those pain killers?" I ask, pointing at the little orange bottle next to the lamp. "You're probably not supposed to mix those with—"

"Out! Get the fuck out!" he shouts, chucking the glass across the room. I duck just as it shatters on the door trim right next to my head, but it's too late. A shard of glass finds its way to my cheekbone and I feel a slight sting. I reach up and touch my face. This man doesn't look like my father, but he's got sharp edges like him.

"Jesus Christ!" I yell. His skin's no longer green. It's red and inflamed and probably matches my own. Hot anger bubbles in my chest, and I want to spit fire at him. He's seething, his hatred morphing his eyes and lips and chin.

"I said get the hell out of my house," he says, sounding breathy and tired.

I stand up, eyes locked on the man whose blood pumps through my veins, and I feel defective. Fuck cutting out the parts of my brain that hold my sad stories. I want to cut out the parts of me that make this beast my father. But there's only one way to do that, down the hall, in the bathtub.

"Out," he yells.

I turn on my heel, grabbing my bag and making for the front door. I think about leaving it open, just so the old man has to get out of bed and close it, but I can't stoop that low.

"Fuck!" I yell, slamming the door behind me. I can't remember where my shovel and steamroller are. Asshole made me forget all my cool skills.

CHAPTER 4

I drop myself in the seat. When I lean in to place the key in the ignition, something blocks the light from entering my window. I look up and see him. Him. HIM.

I go dumb and feel my jaw working up and down in a silent stutter. A muffled voice reaches my ears. "Can you please open the door?"

I don't want to move. I want to close my eyes, nod my head, and wiggle my nose—pop up in my apartment and crawl under my bright floral bedspread, my one secret pop of color where no one would ever think to find me.

But I do move. I see my hand come up and reach for the handle. No, Bryce! What the hell are you doing, you masochist?

I don't stop. I hear the door unlatch, and then it opens, and then there's a hand. Jackson's hand. He's touching my shoulder while inspecting my face. The second man to do that today, but this one doesn't date Maseratis. You can tell by the depth in his eyes. They're murky and dark, just like the lake—the perfect place to misplace your heart. He's real, like me, and I resent him for it.

"What happened? Are you okay?" he asks.

I can't feel the cut on my cheekbone anymore, or the crater left from Walker. I want him to stop. Don't act concerned. Don't look at me. Don't even see me. I like the shadows. Leave me there to grow mushrooms on my skin and moss in my hair.

"I'm fine," I tell him. And then he smiles at me. That fucker.

He leans on my car, arms folded in front of his chest. His sleeves are rolled up, exposing his muscular forearms.

"Why aren't you wearing a jacket?" is all I think to say.

"Why can't you say hello?"

"I said hello when I called you back."

"Actually, you didn't. And it only took me twelve texts to get you to call."

I hate the way he looks at me, like I'm a child.

"Sorry. I was…busy."

"Right." He slowly nods. "I was just trying to help. Your dad's not doing too well."

"I know. I already saw him."

"Then why're you leaving?"

"He doesn't want my help."

"Yeah, he's an ass. No news there. But he still needs you."

"What do you expect from me, Jackson? I have bills to pay and rent to make. I can't just leave my job because he hurt his back." He only stares at me, his gaze holding me in place. "What?" I say. "Why're you looking at me like that?"

"Maybe I'm being foolish, not being from the big city and all, but last I checked, artists can work from anywhere."

I don't want to tell him that I haven't picked up a paintbrush in over a year. That I sold out to work two meaningless jobs. If he looks closely, he'll probably see the slight tremor from my paint withdrawals.

I look away, across the street, where I see little Mrs. Lorton on her lawn, pretending to water plants. She better turn her hearing aid up if she wants a backstage pass to this sad reunion.

"You still suck at keeping secrets, you know that?" he says.

I snap back to attention. "Excuse me?"

"You. You get all quiet and weird when you have something to say but don't want to say it."

I just stand there all quiet and weird. Little Shit has a point.

"Bryce?"

"I had a mole removed today. It's probably cancer."

He frowns. "Jesus, Bryce. It's probably not cancer. Now can you please stop avoiding me? Are you staying to help him or what?"

Honest Bryce rears her ugly head again. I want to take her in the ring and pummel her.

"I don't paint anymore," I tell him. "But I already talked to my bosses and got the rest of the week off. That's it, though. If he's not better by then, I'm gone."

I try to move past him, but he doesn't budge. He's just standing there, tall and broad, in his perfectly worn jeans and work boots. He smells like lumber. Not like the guys in the city. He rattles me to my core, and I can almost feel myself vibrate when I grab his arm and try to push him out of the way.

"Well, you want me to get my bags, don't you?" I ask. "You want me to stay, so I'm staying. Now move."

"So you'll be here for your birthday?" he asks, moving aside.

"Not now, Jackson."

I'm headfirst, ass out of the car when he says, "I know why you don't want to be here."

I crawl into the back seat and shut the door behind me. He's right, I don't want to be here, and more than that, I don't want to have this discussion with him. It's dangerous when we speak. Just thinking about my last visit makes my cheeks blush. I think about covering my face with the paper bag I left back here from Haggen.

The door opens a crack and I refuse to look at him, but I can hear the smile on his face. I know that tone too well.

"I don't want to talk about it," I say.

He reaches in and I feel his hand on mine. His flesh is hot and calloused. Definitely not like the men in Seattle.

He gently guides me out of the car, and my composure evaporates. He used to make me feel the closest I'd ever be to having fairy wings. I can detect a trace of that magic now. It lies dormant in my heart, only resurfacing when he touches me. What we had was white and shimmery and full of the foolish notions young love ignites in its victims. Then the world got ahold of it and pumped in cynicism and pain, until it was a dark thing. Or maybe I pumped those things into it. Or maybe he did. I don't fucking care. I rip my hand from his.

"Just…don't," I say, putting my hands in my pockets.

His eyes are sad. It's strange to see eyes that soft and broken on such a strong face. I want to glue him back together, but then my pieces will break. It's like one of us can't be whole unless the other is shattered.

He puts his hands up. "Sorry." I can hear his sadness, too.

We both stand there, neither of us knowing what to do.

"So I'll stay for the week," I finally say. "But if he throws another glass at me, I'm gone. If he even looks at me funny, I'm outta here."

Jackson's eyes snap to my cheek, and I see his jaw set into a hard square as a faint flicker of anger passes over his face. "If he lays a hand on you, call me."

I don't need a hero. I don't want a hero. I prefer villains. They can't disappoint you.

"I'll be fine, Jackson."

He repeats himself, firmer this time. "If he touches you, call me. It's not a request, Bryce."

This is when you fall. When you walk away from your strength as a woman and latch on to his back, like one of those little fish that attaches itself to a shark and feeds off its crummy seconds and picks off the organisms living on its skin.

Instead, I swallow my rancid emotions and suddenly remember where my shovel is. I turn around and head for the front door.

"Thanks for the call," I say as I walk away.

"Bryce?"

I slam the door shut.

~

I wait a couple hours before going back into my father's room. When I do, I poke my head in and make sure there's nothing on his nightstand he can hurl at me. Fucking wannabe Babe Ruth. There's only a lamp, but I think I can move fast enough to avoid it if need be.

When I snap the light switch on, my father growls. Literally growls. He doesn't just look like an old man, he sounds like one, too. I think of Walter Mattheau in *Grumpy Old Men*. Only Arthur Price isn't spunky and sassy.

"I told you to go," he says. The bags under his eyes look like saggy breasts, and his words slur. He's too tired to shout.

I walk in and stand over him, feeling his forehead. I've no idea why, but this is what they do in the movies. He feels fine. Clammy, but fine.

"I think you're going to live," I say.

"What the… What are you doing?" he asks, swatting my hand away.

He winces and grabs for his lower back. If I want to take charge, now's the time. I've always been afraid of this man. I have no inspired words about some newfound bravery, but he's also hopped up on meds and is wounded. He's like the linebacker you don't dare go up against unless you know he's playing with a blown-out knee.

"Listen," I say. "I'm here for seven days. I'll leave Sunday, and then I won't be back until you drive your truck into another garage. I'll help you with whatever you need, but I promise, you throw another glass at me, I'll suffocate you with your pillow, old man. You hear me?"

He grumbles and scowls in pain. "Who the hell are you to talk to me that way? You look like your mother. Sound like her, too. All bark."

His words are like a solid punch to the belly. I'm not my mother. She latched on to his back, eating the filthy trash he left behind, cleaning up his messes. I am not my mother.

We make eye contact for a moment, exchanging mutual hatred with matching glares.

"I'm not like her. I'm not like either of you," I say.

"You'd like to think that, wouldn't you, Bryce?"

I turn around to leave, and my father yells at me, more vigorous than he had been moments ago. "I need to use the bathroom."

I grab the doorknob and wait, watching his next move, testing the waters.

"I said I need to use the bathroom, you bitch."

"I'm only here to make sure you don't kill yourself. You can sleep in your own piss for all I care." I leave and slam the door behind me.

Bullshit. I know what I'm here for, and it smells like lumber and fills me with guilt.

CHAPTER 5

I startle from a vivid dream, totally unaware of the time. Winters in Washington are dark. Not Alaska-dark, but you won't see gray skies come up till eight in the morning, and the cloud-covered sun will set before you've even thought about dinner. Go to work in the dark, come home in the dark. The sixty-foot pines surrounding my father's house will mask what little light the sun might offer today. Just a steady stream of darkness, with only our thoughts to entertain us. No wonder we're so introspective in these parts.

I reach for my cell and see that it's too early for a new day—too early for more of my father's shit. Four thirty-one. I close my eyes and sink back into the pillow, but I can hear my father's snores from here, and I wonder if he slept all night in his own urine. I can't tell if I'm feeling a twinge of guilt or if I ate something bad yesterday. Crap. I didn't eat yesterday.

Dreaming here only slightly differs from existing here. I can still taste the flavor of my dream on my tongue. I had been sitting in my father's back yard. It was summer, when the sun doesn't sink below the horizon until ten at night, still leaving an orangey haze in the sky. It was dark in my dream, so I know it must've been late. Warmth from the fire pit brought color to my cheeks that I couldn't see but could feel, and I lapped at a pickle-flavored ice cream cone while it melted and rolled down my fingers, settling into the spaces between them.

My mother sits across from me, wearing a trucker's hat while whittling a miniature totem pole out of white porcelain. I know porcelain can't be whittled, but I know that's what it is, and I also know if I walk into the bathroom, I'll see a sizable chunk missing from the bathtub, my mother's coffin.

I look closer, my face so close to the fire that I think I might singe off my eyelashes, and I watch her fingers feverishly move, carving out faces. I recognize some of them. They're the men I saw come and go while my father was away. One of these is the trucker who used to lick his lips whenever he looked at me and would suck on his teeth when he smiled. He left gifts for my mother. My brother and I used to think it was sugar, until my brother tasted it one day. That wasn't the first time my father hit my mom, but it was the first time he really seemed to mean it.

My mother lifts the totem pole so I can see it. The fire reflects off her wet eyes, and when she speaks, it's my father's voice that spills from her lips. "We all took parts of her away. What's left of her is in the bathtub. But don't go in there, Bryce. Jackson's waiting."

I look behind me and know Jackson will be there in his graduation gown. And he is. He shakes his head at me in slow motion, motioning with his finger for me to come with him, but I'm scared. I don't want to leave my mom.

I look back at her and see that the totem pole is gone. Now she's wearing my graduation cap, the tassel dripping wet, like the rest of her clothes. She reaches out to me through the fire and presents me with a gift. I don't recognize it at first, but then it hits. It's my diploma, but scrolled across it is my mother's full name, Patricia Maryanne Price, and underneath it are two dates, her birthdate and her death date. I begin to scream at her not to leave me, and this is when Jackson pulls me away, as my mother's hands reach out for me.

Then the darkness wakes me.

"One week," I whisper to the empty room. I hate this room. Hate the way it erases all the years since my brother's death and brings me right back to that day. I think if I look at the other side of the room, I'll see my brother's bed still there, and I'll hear him whisper my name. *Bryce? Bryce? What if something's under the bed? If you wake up and see my hands or feet out of the covers, tuck them back in for me. Promise and hope to die?*

I stare through the darkness at the dresser sitting where his bed used to be and tuck my arms and legs tightly to my torso. We thought there were monsters in our house when we were kids. Now I know there are. The worst kind. Memories.

I drift back to sleep and dream of nothing.

~

A sequence of loud bangs coming from the kitchen wakes me. My eyes snap open and I hurtle to my feet.

"What the hell're you doing?" I ask my father when I get to the kitchen.

"What does it look like? I'm making myself breakfast."

I try to take the pan from him but he yanks it away, his movements rigid in his back brace, the one I'm sure he was meant to be wearing yesterday. He's already not complying.

"I told you I don't need your help, Bryce. Got a nurse coming this morning."

I want to dance a jig. "A live-in nurse?"

"No."

I deflate.

He glares at me from under the eaves of his brows. "I don't need a babysitter. I'm capable of taking care of myself. So what do you say you get out of here and let me get back to business?"

Business? My father has no business. He's been retired for two years. As far as I know, his days consist of reading books and taking walks. He's got no friends, as baffling as that is, what with his dazzling personality and all. I ignore the fact that I don't have many friends, either. I'm not like my father. I'm not like my father. I'm not like my father.

"All right," I say. "If you can make breakfast all by yourself, I'll leave. Deal?"

He turns to face the stove without saying a word. I sit down on a barstool and look around, truly seeing the house for the first time since my arrival. Something's different. Plaid couches still sit in the living room. Old school lamps still sit on the same tired end tables. No new furniture, no new pictures. The walls are still bare, except for a few plaques my father received in the Marine Corps. You'd never guess that Arthur used to have a family. He made it a crime to mention my brother after he died. Same with my mother. And he cleaned the house of any traces of their existence.

"What'd you do in here," I ask. "Something's changed."

He sighs, clearly annoyed by my question. He's always been mean, but when the hell did he get so crotchety?

Out of the corner of my eye, I see that the TV is on but the sound is muted. It's the same old twenty-four-incher we had when I was a kid. I used to be the remote, until my father had no choice but to bend at the knee of the local cable provider. I swear he still looks at the clicker with disdain.

Everything in the house is coming together now, as if to show me a picture I'd previously been blind to. This really is an old man's house. It looks old, feels old. It even smells old, like walking into a thrift store and getting smacked with the scent of someone else's history. Only this history is mine.

The walls! That's it. The change is subtle, but I sense it in the way a trapped animal picks up on the slightest changes in its environment. They used to be ivory, but now I detect a delicate whisper of pink in them.

"You painted," I say. It's so unlike my father. Painting is optimistic. It means change, growth, rebirth, progress. It's not meant for the stagnant; those content to spoil in their habitual misery.

"I what?" My father turns around, his face screwed up.

"You painted. When did you do that?"

"No, I didn't."

"Umm..." I look all around. I'm not crazy. I've got paperwork to verify that. "The walls are pink. I mean...not pink-pink, but they're pink."

"Dammit, Bryce. The walls are the same color they've always been."

He slams the spatula down. I don't know whether to sink into my stool or plead my case. I opt for silence. Silence is good. Silence is how my father and I work best. When you say nothing, your words can't be misconstrued and twisted into something ugly.

He picks the spatula back up, and I can see his back brace adjust with every heavy breath. He reaches for the upper cabinet and I know what he's going for before he grabs it. Lawry's and garlic powder. I don't think the man's ever eaten eggs without them.

"You want me to get that?" I ask, knowing he'll say no and probably throw the Lawry's at me. Before I can tell him that he's going to hurt himself, he reaches high above his head and immediately buckles over in pain.

"Fuck!" he shouts.

I rise from the stool and come to his aid just as he snatches the pan off the stove and hurls it into the wall. What do you know? Old men can move fast, and raw eggs know how to fly.

Slimy, yellow yolk sticks to the wall, making the pink pop. At least there's finally something colorful to look at. I think of Easter eggs and want to laugh even though my heart's pounding.

"That accomplished a whole hell of a lot," I say.

My father only stares at the wall, wearing what I think is a sad expression. Maybe he's upset that he ruined the pretty pink paint he won't admit to having. His eyes begin to dart around and his hands shake.

"Are you okay?" I ask. He looks at me, then the wall, then back at me. I detect the slightest shake of his head. "Is it just your back? Let me help you to bed. I'll finish up in here."

He doesn't scurry away when I approach him, but he also won't let me help him to his room. He tries to stand

and groans, raising his hand to keep a distance between us. He looks determined, but the crooked lines on his forehead give away his pain.

"Would you stop being stubborn and let me help you? The sooner you heal, the faster I'm out of your hair," I say.

"Move out of my way before I move you."

I back into the fridge, making room for him to pass. "Fine. Knock yourself out."

He walks away, bent over at the waist, and I watch him disappear into the dark hallway. The slamming of his bedroom door rattles the walls.

Arthur Price is a stranger to me. He's different. His anger is disorganized and sloppy, so unlike the man who raised me. There's a difference between focused anger and untethered rage. My father used to discipline with purpose, his anger—as disproportionate to the situation as it usually was—was delivered with rigid structure and clear aim. Precise and sharp, like a knife. But this man with the pink walls strikes without purpose, leaving jagged lines like a dull, serrated edge.

I hear a slight hiss and realize the burner is still on, its flames licking the bottom of the grate. The heat reaches my hand as I raise my palm to it, and a chill runs down my legs as the warmth hits me. I can see from the kitchen window that everything is coated in frost. I like the way it looks, like sugar. A world so sticky-sweet it makes your stomach ache as you suckle from its bosom.

"Shit."

The fire nips at my pinkie as if to punish me for imagining a world so hospitable. I place my finger in my mouth and suck on my angry flesh, but the warmth of my tongue only makes my skin burn more. I slap at the dial, killing the flame. Does everything that feels good have to burn?

I have to pee like a racehorse, but the yolk is drying on the wall and the kitchen's a mess. The last thing I need is some nurse walking in and accusing me of abusing my elderly father. The sizable dent left in the wall from Babe Ruth and his mighty pan definitely leave the wrong impression.

I quickly grab what's left on the counter and wipe everything down, then I use my fingernail to scrape off the egg splatter that's beginning to harden. The doorbell rings just as I'm about to clean up the last bit of yolk. I stand back and look at it. "Fuck it." It's staying.

CHAPTER 6

It's not until I open the door that I realize I'm still in a pair of boxers and a wife beater. Yes, the boxers belong to an ex. Yes, I'm a cliché. No, I don't care. They're ugly and worn. We get along well.

"Well, someone got beat with the purdy stick. Good morning, Miss Jane Fonda. Is Arthur Price here?" the nurse asks.

I look up at him. Way up. This guy's got to be seven feet and some change. He's a basketball player, not a nurse.

"Girl, it's cold as hell, and you look like you're about to etch glass. Can I come in?"

I follow his eyes to my chest. Suddenly I get the Fonda reference. Hippies. No bra. Hilarious. Did he really just say I was about to etch glass? I think if I were anyone else, he'd be losing his job today. I think I like him.

"Sorry," I say. "Come in. Wait just a minute while I throw something on."

"No problem, honey. I'll just get my things together."

"'Kay. I'll be right back."

I walk past my dad's room on the way to mine and can almost sense the drama to come. Arthur Price is going to lose his shit today, and whoever sent RuPaul is going to bear the brunt of his wrath. Not only is his nurse black, but he speaks with the unmistakable lisp of a very proud gay man. Men like my father should be forced to hang plaques on their front doors: "Contents may explode when exposed to new ideas. Proceed with caution."

I step into my sports bra and pull it up and over my thighs and hips. The puppies have been contained. Not that they're big enough to be puppies. More like the runts of the litter. A pair of jeans, a ponytail, and I'm back in the living room. When the nurse sees me, he looks disappointed.

"Guess the party's over. That means it's back to the coal mines," he says.

A strange sensation comes over me. Something I haven't felt in a few days. Genuine laughter.

I reach my hand out. "Nice to meet you. I'm Bryce."

"I'm Nurse Theo. But just call me Theo."

I like his name, and his smile. You can tell Theo doesn't know how to be anyone other than Theo. Damn it all to hell. Why'd they have to send him?

"I should warn you," I say. "My dad's a handful. You seem really nice, but it's altogether likely he won't give "himself a chance to find that out. I just want to apologize in advance."

Theo props his hand on his hip. If anyone in this room is a diamond, it's him, and he damn well knows it.

"Don't worry your pretty little head. This isn't my first rodeo. I deal with older folks all the time. You have no idea how many cold shoulders I've been served. Besides"—he picks his stethoscope off the table and slings it around his neck—"Alzheimer's patients are notoriously difficult, but it's not their fault. I've seen the nicest people in the world turn on a dime. It's a nasty disease. You just gotta be patient."

"I'm sorry. What? Are you saying my father's got Alzheimer's?"

Theo gives me the how-didn't-you-know look and sighs heavily. "I'm sorry, girl. He didn't tell you?"

All of a sudden the walls are too pink. Everything's too bright. This is when I'm supposed to explain that we're just not that close. *I would've known, Theo. I swear. I'm really not the world's worst daughter.*

"It's okay," he says. "A lot of patients don't tell their children about their diagnosis. Usually denial, or they just don't want to be a burden. I'm sorry you had to find out this way."

"So his accident?" I ask.

"From what I was told, the responders said he was confused. He thought it was his garage he ran his vehicle into. This is all very typical at this stage in the disease."

"Stage?" I'm in a cloud. Theo just looks like a talking head, spitting out bits of information I'm too rattled to understand. "What stage is he?"

He rolls his eyes, not at me, but I'm guessing in response to what he says next. "Alzheimer's is a nasty bird, and you've got some serious learning to do. I can set you up with some paperwork before I leave. I'll make you a list of some books you should get, too, but the Internet is going be your best friend from here on out. I've got some names of good support groups. Now, when we say stages, we just mean where he's at in the disease. Your father got diagnosed with this last October."

"Over a year ago?"

"Yes. Some patients progress slowly, some don't. From everything I read in his file, he was doing pretty well up until a few months ago. His last two accidents were caused by confusion. Once a patient gets to the point where they're a danger to themselves and others, we have to start looking at more in-depth arrangements. Mr. Price is at that point."

"What other accidents?"

"He was treated for smoke inhalation in September. His file says he left the burner on in the kitchen and left the window open. Something blew into the flame and started a fire. Your father said it was a simple mistake, but then again, they always say that. That's why I stress that you've got to be patient. They will try you, believe that. Sometimes they're kind one minute, mean as a snake the next. Fighting with them will do no good. Same with taking it personally when they forget who you are. Gentle reminders and keeping them safe. That's all you can do. Now let's see the man of the hour. I hate to leave you hanging, but the hospital runs a tight ship. In and out, no more than an hour. You're staying here, right?"

"Yeah. But not for long. Just a week." I turn to walk toward my father's room but stop. "Is there anything else wrong with him?"

"That I can tell you about?"

"That I need to know if I'm going to be staying here."

Theo purses his lips and squints.

"I'm not going to rat you out. My dad looks like death. He's lost weight, and he looks…old."

"That's what happens to old folks."

"No. I mean rapidly. And it's not just that. He looks sick."

Theo steps closer, lowering his voice. His Andre the Giant hands are perched behind the small of his back, which he arches like a pregnant woman. "It's not at all uncommon for Alzheimer's patients to forget to eat or bathe. Simple tasks that are no problem for you and me can eventually become impossible. Then there's depression, which is pretty common with patients."

The leftover bit of yolk on the wall is niggling at me. I glance at it and chew my lip.

"This is all part of what I was talking about," Theo tells me. "About needing more in-depth care." He looks at the wall behind me, at my father's plaques. The few, the proud, the Marines. It's right there in their motto. Pride, pride, pride, even if it kills you.

"Oh," Theo says. "He's gonna be a tough nut to crack. Not gonna want to admit when he needs help." He lifts up the badge hanging off his scrubs, the one with the picture of him looking like a hard motherfucker, and says, "That's what I'm here for."

I think about last night. He had to pee, *you bitch*. You wouldn't help him, *you bitch*. He slept in his own piss, *you bitch*. And I wonder if my dad has ever felt guilty for the things he's done, like I feel guilty right now. I hope so, because the clock's ticking, and apparently there's a statute of limitations on his crimes. Pretty soon I'll be the only one left to remember them, and I'm not sure I can carry the weight all alone.

My heart is hidden behind a gate, out of my father's reach. He never wanted the key to the lock. Am I supposed to just open it now, in the wake of hearing that one word? "Alzheimer's." It's like the other bad word, "cancer." They're as powerful as the words "I love you," or worse, "I hate you." Release them and they find their victim and rattle around inside the body like a .22 bullet, tearing everything to shreds.

CHAPTER 7

Theo enters the room first, blocking my view of my father. I don't want to see his reaction to Theo. I also don't want to see my father's gaunt appearance. It means more now than it did before. It's evidence of the ugly beast taking over his brain.

"Hello, Mr. Price," Theo says to him. "I'm going to be your nurse until you get back on your feet. How're you feeling today?"

Theo walks to the right side of the bed, and I slowly make my way to the other side, still avoiding my dad. But I can feel his eyes on me.

"How's your pain level today?" Theo tries again.

The silence stretches on for so long I can't help but to finally look at my dad. His brows are furrowed and he's clenching the top of his sheet with his fists.

"He's here to help," I say. "Just answer the question, please."

The look my father gives me brings me up short. The rims of his eyelids pink up as his eyes get watery. Suddenly he grabs my hand, the lines of his face twisting his expression into one of desperation. Still, I can see something furious behind it all.

Fuck.

My dad clears his throat, swallowing back words I know he wants to say, and I wonder if what I'm witnessing is restraint. When he finally speaks, my back tenses and I hold my breath, waiting for him to expel a flood of insults. I want to sew his mouth shut with the pocket-sized sewing kit sitting on his dresser.

"My daughter's here. I don't need a nurse anymore. She'll take care of me."

I look at Theo, Theo looks at me. Who the hell's supposed to take the reins? I vote for the seven-foot-tall sassy gay guy. But the seven-foot-tall sassy gay guy obviously voted for me, as evidenced by his unwavering silence. Shit on a shingle.

"Dad," I say, no longer sure how to speak to him. "I'm only here for a week, and I have no idea how to help you with your back. I don't even know what happened."

"I hurt it, Bryce. Does it really matter?"

Theo steps up. "Actually, it does, Mr. Price. You fractured two disks. If you don't treat this with proper care, you might wind up in that bed for a whole lot longer, if not permanently. At your age, proper treatment is crucial."

My father's face changes. He drops my hand, whipping his head around in Theo's direction. "You'd have me believe that, wouldn't you? Keep you around and rake in a few more bucks from the insurance company."

Aaaaaaaaand…he's off.

"I don't give a damn what you think I need," he continues. "I won't be preyed upon by you vultures. You can go back and tell Dr. Tann that I won't be needing your services. If I do, my daughter will bring me in." He eases back, his breaths coming slower. "Besides, you're not putting your hands on me, you fucking fag."

"Dad!" I shout. Where's a rolled-up newspaper so I can smack his snout? "Welcome to the twenty-first century. Jesus! It's bad enough that you think things like that, but to say them?" I expect to see Theo's back as he rushes out the bedroom door, but when I look at him, he gives me a small smile.

"I'm sorry," I tell Theo.

"It's my house and I'll say what I please," my dad says, like a petulant child.

"You're right, Mr. Price," Theo says, his hands politely folded in front of him. "If you want me to leave, that's exactly what I'll do."

"Then turn your ass around and get the—"

"Ah, ah, ah. But by law, I have to tell you the risks involved in refusing treatment. So what do you say? Can I keep my job today?"

My father's nostrils flare, he flinches. I can almost see the demon on his left shoulder arguing with the angel on his right. There's no way in hell I'm getting stuck wiping this man's ass after he breaks his back throwing more pans around. Theo stays.

"He was out of bed just this morning, trying to make breakfast," I say. "The old fool didn't get very far, now did "you, Dad? I promise that your bigotry will be waiting for you once he leaves, but hear the man out, otherwise I'm gone, and you and Theo here can spend a lot more time together."

"That's right," Theo says. "I've been looking for some overtime. You worsen your injuries, I'm gonna have all the opportunity in the world for extra hours. See, what's going to happen is that those small fractures, they're going to strain every time you push yourself too hard. All it'll take is just a near fall and you'll find yourself in a chair. Or worse, let's say you have a spell and forget you hurt your back, and you decide you're gonna mosey on out to your car and have yourself a little drive. You get in any kind of wreck, your back is toast, and rehabilitation at your age would be brutal. So I'm fine with leaving. Frankly, this place is messin' with my juju. But I won't leave until you sign something saying that if you break your back and paralyze yourself, or disassociate and have another accident, you were warned. But please do keep in mind that the black won't rub off on you and you can't catch gay. So what's it going to be? 'Cause you're using up all my time and trying my patience, and the good Lord gave Theo only oh so much of it."

"This is how you talk to patients?" my father asks him.

"Mr. Price, I know the difference between Alzheimer's and orneriness."

High-fiving Theo would be against the rules, I'm sure, so I just smile at him. My father's straining trying to look down his nose at him from his position on the bed. It's like watching someone with a missing arm and leg swim away from a life preserver. I take back what I said. My father's not hollow. He's thick—solid stupid all the way through, plated in more stupid. Offer him a hand and watch him sink instead. I want to lend him my eyes so he can look at Theo and see what I see.

"He didn't ask you to marry him, Dad. Answer the man," I say.

Arthur Price's crusty old gears are turning. I can almost hear them squeaking along as he weighs his options. He's standing on the edge of a cliff, while everyone else can see that it's just a baby step toward objectivity, a word that seems to be lost on men like him. I want to shake all the senselessness out of him, but I'd end up breaking something and have to care for him for the rest of my life. Suddenly I'm my mother, and I can't be her—I don't know how to whittle.

My dad's face grows stern, determined. I can't tell if he's going to make the right call or resign himself to a life in his bed.

"Fine," he says. "Just do whatever it is you have to and get me moving again. Once your job here is done, the better off we'll all be. Then the both of you can take a hike."

"Goody," Theo says, giving me a wink. "I was up for a challenge, and paper-cutting my eyeballs just seemed too easy. Now that that's done, let me introduce myself again. I'm Theo, spelled T-H-E-O, not F-A-G. Once you get that down, we'll be right as rain, Mr. Price."

~

I want to run outside like an excited dog and hide in Theo's car when he grabs his keys, but I have to stay and take care of the creature. I'll settle for standing at the window with my paws and nose to the glass, watching him drive away while I whimper. I'd take off my bra again if it would get him to stay, but I know he doesn't bat for that team.

"Okay, Miss Fonda," Theo says to me. I love that he's given me a nickname. I've never had a nickname. I feel like one of the cool kids. "I left my card on the coffee table and some pamphlets. You call Nurse Theo anytime you need anything, even if it's just a question."

He must sense that I don't want him to leave. I'm sure it has nothing to do with the fact that I'm blocking the door.

"Girl, you got this. You'll be okay. Check out the sites I told you about and join those support groups. And use the notebook with him. It's not scientifically proven, but it's Nurse Theo-proven, and in my book, that's almost as good."

"But what if he…I don't know. Like you said, what if he forgets things and takes off or goes roaming the streets? I think it would be best if you came by every day."

"Honey, twice a week is plenty, and we went over this. Your father still has some time, but you need to childproof the hell outta this place, even though it's gonna piss him off. Just do it in increments. Once a Marine, always a Marine, and you don't want to emasculate him in one big swoop. He'll go all Rambo on your ass. Like I said, first and foremost, get the burners taken care of and find yourself a big, strong man to come over and change these locks out so they can be controlled with a key from the inside."

"I don't need a man. I'll change them myself."

Now Theo does high-five me. "Damn right. But you know, you can invite a big, strong man over to fix *other* things. If I looked like you, God knows I would. Put down that *Sex in the City* Carrie Bradshaw hair and sow me some oats while I still got 'em."

I refuse to think about Jackson. Or at least I try not to. Fuck. Not thinking about Jackson is making me think about Jackson. Bloody hell! RuPaul's a bad influence. He can leave now.

"Damn, woman! Don't make ugly faces like that. You're way too pretty for that," he says. "Some man did you seriously wrong."

I open the door and move aside. Theo makes me remember I'm a girl, and that I have sexy Carrie Bradshaw hair (only darker), and that the butterflies that used to live in my stomach never really left. Rats. I need to buy a fly swatter.

I tell Theo goodbye. "All right, you beautiful Amazonian creature. Get out of here and stop planting dirty thoughts in my head."

~

I once read that you can leave a McDonald's hamburger out for months before it starts to decay. Looking at the turkey sandwich I made my father for lunch, I wonder how long it can sit here before it either rots or he gives in and takes a bite. Stubborn old shit. I feel like I'm running a daycare.

"Dad, seriously. Just one bite."

"No."

Every time I move around on the damn chair, its springs moan. The upholstery matches the loveseat in the living room. I wonder if my dad got these from the same old-man store where other old men get their plaid old-man pants and plaid old-man hats and plaid old-man socks. Most old, plaid chairs like these have retired to fleabag motels along Route 66. God, I need out of this house.

"It's been two hours. Would you just take a bite?" Now I'm getting silent treatment. My father won't even look at me. "You're going to have to give me something here. I don't know what you're still pissed about. It could be anything, really. Your injury, my being here, your gay nurse, the end of segregation. Come on, Dad. The suspense is killing me."

Finally he looks at me, his jaw firm. "You're a smartass, you know that?"

"And you're an asshole. Eat your sandwich."

"Not hungry."

I sit back, twiddle my thumbs, shake my foot, chew my lip. There's so much dust covering the one window in here, you can't see through it. It's like a cell. I'm serving a week with no chance of parole. Thank God for cell phones.

I look at Facebook and see that Shana is hiking in Deception Pass with her new boy-toy. Fitting place for them. She's such a bullshitter. She hates the outdoors, but Fletcher—yeah, his name is Fletcher—makes six figures, and apparently that number makes Shana want to get all at one with nature.

I scroll down and see that a few people from work have posted photos. At the storage facility I work at, some guy rented a unit for the day and filled it with balloons. If his girlfriend finds the ring box in the middle of the sea of latex, she wins the ring safely hidden in his pocket. Ugh. People watch too many rom-coms. I won't like that on principle.

The list Theo made for me is sitting on the floor at my feet. I know what I should be doing. I've got a mountain of knowledge to gain and at least twelve sites and four books I should be reading, but I don't want to. That will make it real. Ignorance is bliss, and finding out just how far down the rabbit hole your father's going to fall isn't.

"Eat," I say.

"Go away."

"Man, you're impossible, you know that? How much do you weigh now, huh? Is this about your eggs this morning?"

"No, Bryce. This isn't about the goddamn eggs. This is about privacy. I don't need to be looked after like a child, and I certainly don't need some fag coming in my house, laying his filthy hands on me. You don't know what it's like, being prodded and poked by these people. I'm sick and tired of it. You go your whole life being told to respect your elders, and then you get old and lose your dignity."

"You want people to respect you?" I ask, almost laughing. "You called your nurse a fag today, Dad. Don't you get how fucking disrespectful that is? Hell, it's beyond disrespectful. It's cruel. Are you really that ignorant? So you deserve respect because you're an old white man? But everyone else is just a second-class citizen, right? I mean…do you really not see your own hypocrisy? How on earth do you think it's okay to treat people the way you do?"

"Because I earned the right. I fought for my—"

"Yeah, yeah, yeah. You went to 'Nam. We all got the memo. News flash, Dad. You took an oath to fight for your country and for the rights of its people. All of them. Not just the straight white ones with testicles."

I've never seen this shade of red on my father's face before. If I saw it anywhere else, I might like its severity, but on him it's wretched.

He grabs his sandwich and spits on it before trying to get out of bed.

"Stop it!" I shout. "You're going to hurt yourself." But he rises to his knees before falling forward, crying out in pain. I cradle his torso in my arms, gently easing him back against the pillow.

"My God," I pant. "Is being pissed at me really worth hurting yourself?"

"Leave me alone. I'm still your father. That's still supposed to mean something."

"You're right. That is supposed to mean something. For example, most fathers would tell their daughters that they have Alzheimer's. Why'd I have to find out from someone else?"

"Because there's a lot about me you don't know, Bryce. And I'm not sick. These idiots don't know what they're talking about."

"You ran your truck into a garage you thought was yours."

"Bullshit! I was tired is all."

"And the fire?"

"Fucking hell. What do you want from me? You're not going to believe me, just like they don't. I've been labeled an invalid, and now I get to have my own kid watch me like I'm a ticking bomb."

I'm not the only one unwilling to face the music. We're both in the company of a beast we know nothing about. Right now, his disease is running circles around us, and our feet are cemented in concrete.

I wave the white flag, trying to bring some civility back to the conversation. I lower my voice. I don't know why I can't shake the question. It's trivial, meaningless.

"Why'd you paint the walls, Dad?"

"I already told you."

"Told me what?"

"There's a lot about me you don't know."

CHAPTER 8

I try to remind myself that old, senile people say strange, meaningless things all the time. Shana's grandmother used to yell, "The Yankees are coming!" in crowded stores the last few months before she died. She also told Shana her hair was made of thin strands of glass that would break if she combed them. Then she'd scream when people tried to groom her. But that doesn't mean the aimless ramblings of the old aren't sometimes downright scary, like they really do know something the rest of us don't. As if the closer you get to death, the thinner the veil over your eyes becomes.

There's a lot about me you don't know.

Still. My father didn't seem confused when he said it. Could it be that the man I know as "Dad" really has lived a life I've never been privy to? I mean…all parents have their little secrets. I get that. All kids do, too. There's a lot I never told my father, but it's not exactly like he was all warm and inviting. He wasn't going to make me tea and rub my back while I cried over my first broken heart—which was Samantha Clarkson, by the way. Little dick told me I wasn't her best friend after pig-nosed Rachel Lennus showed up at school with a jumbo bag of Skittles, far more sweet and shiny than little ol' me.

What is there to know about Arthur Price that I don't already know? He was your all-American boy, born and raised right here in Washington State. He married my mother right out of high school and abruptly joined up and caught the tail end of the Vietnam War. I've never been ballsy enough to ask if he was just that damn patriotic, or if his marriage began to decay in record time. I mean, I know it was bad, but not even a honeymoon? Either way, he came home, they knocked out a couple rug rats, and the rest is history. Maybe there was a mistress in my father's past. Might explain the long hours and weekend business trips. After all, the man had to have come up with ways to cope with his wife's drug habit and propensity for random sex with skeevy strangers.

I creep out of bed and turn on the lamp in the living room. The steady snoring coming from my dad's room tells me he's still asleep. He should be after the no-bullshit meds they have him on. Hurt your back, walk away with a nasty new habit. I can almost feel Mommy smiling down on us.

The rain falling on the roof is dreamy. Dark, early mornings with nothing but me and the pitter-patter of water pouring from the heavens. It's one of those small blessings. It's no surprise this place is so breathtaking. Have you ever met a state with OCD? This place washes itself clean every day. That's why it smells so glorious and looks so crisp.

I watch the fog roll in, masking my view of the trees, neighbors, cars. I need tea. This is definitely a tea kind of morning. I wish I could have coffee but the stuff actually makes me groggy. It's a shame, because tea is just coffee's meek, submissive little bitch. Jackson used to drink coffee every day. I'm sure he still does. He used to show up at school reeking of stale brew, his hands still jittery from the thermos full of high-octane caffeine he drank while working with his father before coming to school.

"Morning, sexy," he'd say every time we met between first and second period, when I'd pull away, cringing from his sour breath. He'd always kiss me anyway, no matter how hard I pretended to fight him off. He wanted me. I wanted him to want me. Dammit! Fuck coffee. It smells like shit and reminds you of your first love. I need to stand out in the rain and wash the memory of Jackson off my skin and hair and heart and mind. All the places he touched and changed me.

~

"Dad, wake up. It's almost ten. You need to eat something." His eyelids don't even flutter.

There's a pencil on the nightstand and a half-smoked cigar. I fight the temptation to place them in his nostrils and post a photo on Facebook. See how much fun I'm having up here? Don't be too jealous, 'cause you look horrible in pea-green.

"Dad!" I shout, nudging his shoulder. His eyelids finally part, just thin, crusty slits. He mumbles something about me going straight to hell.

"Hey, old man, I have to head to the store and get those notepads and a few other things. So what do you say you get up and eat something? I made you scrambled eggs, just the way you like them. I even burned your bacon."

His arm comes up fast, knocking the tray out of my hand, sending the food flying. A lump of scrambled egg rolls under the bed.

"What the hell, Dad? Is throwing food in the old-person handbook or something? Shit!"

I think about Theo telling me to keep my cool. Then I wonder if Theo ever had to stand in a dark bathroom and drop his pants and touch his toes while waiting for the leather to strike his flesh over and over.

"Dad, I'm really trying to stay calm, but you're making it incredibly hard. What do you have against people trying to keep you alive?"

He moans while pulling himself up, and his eyes are sleepy and don't seem to be moving in unison. He immediately reaches for his pills, but I snatch them away.

"No," I say. "You need to wait till after you eat. This crap will tear your belly up."

"It's my stomach."

"Yes, and it's also your back that will be made worse if you vomit and strain yourself. If I make you something else, will you stop being such a prima donna and eat?"

He glares at me, his back brace expanding with each heavy breath. "Don't ever call me that." His voice is low and threatening. I'm waiting for him to tell me to grab the leather strap nailed to the wall in the hallway, there as a constant reminder of what will happen if I color outside the lines.

"Don't cut me down just because I can't stand up and throw your ass out of this house," he adds.

I want to defend myself. I want to tell him I'm not cutting him down. That he's changed. He's no longer the alpha dog in the house, which means I have to take the reins. But my inner child tugs on my hand and looks up at me with tears in her eyes. *Don't make him feel bad. He's still your daddy.* Only thing is, she can't see the scars all over her heart and the ashy remains of what used to be fire in her eyes, but I can.

I stand back, looking anywhere but at him. I don't know if I'll cry or hit him if I see the expression I already know is there. He might be weak, but he's still a bully.

Instead I say, "I'm going to make you something else to eat so you can take your pills. I'll wait to leave until you fall back asleep. If you need anything, call my cell. I'll leave the phone and my number on the nightstand."

~

I take the long way to the store. I want to drive around the lake and see the raindrops make craters on its inky surface. I used to think about drowning myself in there. Tie a brick to my ankle and my hands behind my back. No more abusive father, no more crack whore mother. With any luck, I'd find my brother down there and we'd swim together and let the fish chase us while bubbles poured from our lips as we laughed about our tragic endings.

I can't see the raindrops on the lake, though. The fog is kissing the surface of the water, working its way onto the road. I roll down the window and hang my arm out, letting icy droplets pelt my flesh as the wind rushes over the hairs on my arm. My cell phone makes its *ping, ping,*

ping noise, letting me know I've received a text. It's not my dad. The man doesn't text, and I'm not supposed to check my phone while I'm driving. If I die, he'll have to crawl out of bed and eat brittle egg off the floor until Theo comes back tomorrow. But I'm soft, so I pull over and check.

It's Jackson asking how things are going. Most people ask this question as a formality—something we say in order to appear civilized. If you respond with anything more than "fine," most people get fidgety. Not Jackson, though. He's the only person I know who will look you in the eye and wait for a real response. I don't have time for this, and even if he really wants to know how things are, he doesn't want to know. At least he shouldn't. He stopped carrying my baggage around a long time ago.

~

I pull into the parking lot and zip up my raincoat. Ask any Washingtonian and they'll tell you that umbrellas are for pussies and tourists. I check my phone, just to make sure I didn't miss a call from my dad. Nothing. My thumb hovers over Jackson's text. Fire never stops burning you, even after prolonged exposure. You'd think my heart would be too charred to feel anything for him. But they say we replace our cells every seven years. Guess the heart works the same.

I don't know why I do what I do. Maybe I'm a coward. Maybe I'm just a bitch. I text him back, two simple words that I know will bother him more than being ignored.

"I'm fine."

~

I pick up a spiral notebook with a photo of a black-and-white cat hanging upside down from a tree branch. The colors are lifeless, reeking of an era before digital art. In fact, I'm pretty sure I had this notebook as a kid. The caption on the front reads in bubbly letters: "How's it hanging?"

I pinch my nose up like I always do when I see something cheesy. I don't think they're marketing to kids. This is for postmenopausal women who wear seasonal sweaters and banana clips in their permed hair.

I put the folder back and look for something else. If I'm going to get my father talking, it's not going to be with kittens. Black, black, and more black. That'll do.

The store is especially busy for a weekday morning. Moms in yoga pants tote their babies around in overpriced strollers while lookilooing the organic section. I always size them up to see if they're worthy of their skintight attire. Those pants are enough to make me never have children. Not if I have to be indoctrinated and trade my dignity for spandex.

There's an old man searching the cards in the aisle with all the balloons and party favors. I don't know why, but I'm drawn to him. He doesn't look like my father. If anything, he's much older than my dad. The skin on his hands is covered with dozens of age spots, the blue of his veins lit up like neon under his papier mâché skin, and he's wearing one of those military baseball caps with all the ribbons on it. I don't want to stare. I always feel strange about looking too closely at elderly people. Like when your eyes settle a moment too long on someone missing an arm or leg. Does that mean I think of aging as a handicap we're not supposed to notice? It's the media's fault. Aging is distasteful and wrinkles are the mark of the Beast.

The old man is reading a card with a dinosaur on the cover. Probably for his grandson or something. I watch him and I think of my father. Arthur will never go out independently again. His life will soon become whatever someone else makes it. His caretakers, nurses, doctors.

My eyes burn and my throat is tight. The love I have for him and my mom is coated in so many layers of Teflon. It had to be that way. If I had absorbed whatever mud they flung my way, I would've eroded.

~

Only two registers are open and the lines are long. The young man working the register, who can't be more than eighteen, obviously misunderstood his job requirements. Flirting with every young mom who comes in to buy diapers and baby food probably isn't what this place hired him to do. But it's effective, if all the swoony smiles and pink cheeks are any indication. Go ahead and hit me up, little man-child. I'll have your dignity for breakfast and your soul for lunch. For dinner I'll pick off whatever scraps are left on your bones. Being a magician in the bedroom is one of the only things I'm good at. Guess that happens when you learn from a young age what your purpose on Earth is.

I've got two people ahead of me when I hear someone say my name. There's something familiar about it. I turn around and immediately wish I hadn't. It's Roselyn, Jackson's ex.

"I thought that was you, Bryce," she says.

Why are we talking? This is one of those interactions I'm utterly perplexed by. Aside from our taste in men, we've got nothing in common. And what the hell is that thing dressed in all purple, hanging off her chest in one of those baby slings?

"H-hi," I stutter, too busy doing the math to formulate any intelligent thought. She and her little tow-headed child have rendered me speechless. Too many thoughts chase each other around in my head, and all I want to do is pay and leave.

"You know," she says, and I can already see the change on her face, like a cat's back arching before it strikes, "I'm shocked that you'd come back here."

"Back here to my dad's house, or to the store?" It's a valid question. It's just a bonus that it doubles as sarcasm.

"Back here at all," she says, growing more flustered.

"You know, Roselyn, neither of us wants me here, but I don't plan on staying for long, so back off."

"Does Jackson know you're back?"

"What does it matter?" I wasn't prepared for a full assault, and my patience is running away from me faster than I can catch it.

"I'm just looking out for him. Someone has to."

"I'll tell you what, Roselyn. Next time I see him, I'll tell him you said to watch his six."

"It's not a joke, Bryce."

She doesn't know me. She doesn't know Jackson and me, the way we used to be, a unit, a couple. Something you think of as one whole because you just can't imagine the two separated. We were never a joke. Even when we first met, so young it still hurts to think about, nothing about us was a joke. Not like them, one of those couples you point at and say, "I give them six months, tops." She smoked Jackson, but she never inhaled. But there's a plump screamer on her chest that's making me wonder if she and Jackson will always be more serious than we ever were. Suddenly I want to grab my chest and rip out my heart. I've got no use for things that cause me unbridled pain.

"You really should leave," she says. Her eyebrows are high on her forehead, her lips pursed. I'm waiting for her to do the black-girl neck roll. Borrowing from other cultures to try to look hard. I'm stricken with the overwhelming desire to pet her flat, blonde hair and coo. A for effort, Barbie.

"I plan on leaving as soon as possible. Don't fret," I tell her.

Her baby turns and looks at me, offering up a gummy smile. She doesn't sense I'm the enemy. It'll be a few more years before we reckless humans corrupt her.

I smile back because I'm a sucker for a girl with no teeth and the balls to wear all purple. But Roselyn guards the side of her baby's face so she can no longer see me. Her expression is serious; she drops her voice.

"If you ever loved him, get the hell out of here."

I want to slap her. I want to call her every name in the book. How dare she speak to me about love? I know Jackson didn't tell her what happened to us. He would never. If she knew, she'd know better than to speak to me about such things.

"You're out of your depth," I say.

"You ruined him, you know that? You ruined him for any woman."

Her words bring me up short, and I stare at this woman and her perfect baby, at a piece of Jackson's past, and I want to cry. Roselyn was unplanned in the same way all the men I've been with since Jackson were unplanned. But just like with unplanned children, that doesn't mean we don't love them. At one point, this woman meant something to Jackson. Maybe she still does. If the sadness in her eyes says anything, he certainly still means something to her, and I ruined him for her.

I don't want to hit her anymore. I don't want to hurt her back. I just want one more gummy grin from her baby. Something to tell me there's still a reason to smile, even if it's not my reason.

"I'm sorry, Roselyn," is all I can say.

CHAPTER 9

I take a detour home. There are several other lakes around here, all smaller than the one the city's built around. As kids, my brother and I used to swim in them during summer, sometimes stopping at three or four different lakes in a day. Those were the days when we were lucky to get a week's worth of temperatures in the high eighties. Now, summers are growing brutal, especially for this part of the country.

My brother used to run into our room and wake me up. "It's gonna be hot out, sissy. Come on! Come on!"

I was always the babysitter, even though I was just a year older than him. Those were also the days when kids rode bikes and took off on long adventures, only returning home when someone lassoed the sun down from the sky. My father was usually gone, and my mom spent most days passed out on the couch with her soaps on, only waking when some douchebag came by with her fix. We'd throw on our suits, I'd stash a box of crackers in my backpack, and we'd be off. We'd swim all day, only taking breaks to scrounge from the blackberry bushes that grow like weeds here. Hell, maybe those summers explain Walker. If so, the Huckleberry days spent with my brother were more than worth it.

After my brother died, I never swam again. I'd visit his favorite lake and sit on the dock, talking to him for hours, telling him about how things at home had changed but somehow hadn't changed at all. Just varying levels of misery. I'd bring his favorite book and read to him, even doing the voices for each character. I figured the pieces of my brother were left where his best memories were made.

After Scotty died, nothing scared me. I figured I'd lived through the worst nightmare I was ever going to face. I came out braver, and my mother walked around broken instead of just fractured. My father stopped speaking for a while. He even stopped yelling, which told me how hard he was taking his son's death. I can't tell you with any amount of certainty that my parents ever spoke again after the accident. I have no memories of seeing them utter a word to one another. A house full of mimes, each with their hands pressed to the imaginary walls of their very real prison. I didn't know then that there wasn't an escape—that our confines went deeper than the house we all shared as a dysfunctional family. True confines are built with thoughts stripped of hope, and locks are nothing more than our inability to change.

I park in front of Tilquoa Lake, a small bit of water my brother loved most because of its shape. He always insisted it looked like a dragon, but I never saw it. The night of my mother's death marked the end of my reunions with my brother's favorite lake. Every time I come home, I visit all the lakes and say a few words to Scotty. All but this one. I've avoided it for seven years. Haven't stopped by, haven't even driven by. It used to mean something else to me. It used to be the dragon Scotty slayed, and where I became a mermaid and Scotty a deep-sea diver.

I hold my breath and look out the window at it. Now it's shaped like a giant tub, and if I look closely, maybe I'll see a beautiful woman just under the surface, her eyes still open, locked on the gloomy sky above, a pool of vomit floating in her hair. If I jump in, I can be just like her.

I grip the steering wheel and let my tears fall on my legs. My heart is hammering in my chest, beating against my ribs like a toddler with a drum. I run my fingers along my thigh, where under my jeans sit eight faded scars. Eight ways I wanted to die. And eight ways I told Jackson he wasn't enough.

I don't feel Scotty here anymore. He wouldn't be here, wouldn't want to be. I feel my mother. I feel unreciprocated love. I feel my knuckles on her bedroom door as I knock and strain my ear against it, listening to her cries blend in with the animalistic grunting of whatever beast was devouring her body and mind.

Please come out, Mommy. Come play with me, Mommy.

I'm right back to that night, reaching into the water. My beautiful dress is soaked, and Stephen King had it wrong. Blood isn't the most frightening thing a prom gown can be covered in. It's the water and tears and puke your dead mommy's been marinating in.

I can't be here. I need to leave and take Scotty's memories with me.

~

My father's garage is a handyman's wet dream. If I had testicles, I'm pretty sure they'd be quivering right now. The walls are lined with pegboard and are covered with an endless array of tools. I'm no slouch with a hammer, but I have no idea what half these things do.

I see buckets full of smaller tools and reach in, grabbing a screwdriver. This would be much easier with an electric drill, but I don't want to rouse the old man. He managed to get a few bites of lunch down without slinging his tuna at me, so in return I put the TV on rollers and set him up in front of one of those fishing shows that should come with a warning not to operate heavy machinery while watching it. He has no idea what I'm doing, and I want to keep it that way.

~

Inside, I lay the tools and my goodies from Ace on the kitchen table while I adjust the straps on my overalls. I found them in my old closet and figured this was my chance to be Bob Vila for a couple hours. I put one of my father's orange Home Depot pencils in one of the skinny pockets on my chest. I probably won't need it, but it makes me feel like a real handywoman. I stopped at saddling my belt loop with his measuring tape. There's professionalism, and then there's dress-up.

There's a brown rubber band around my wrist. I grab it and throw my hair up into one of those half-assed geisha buns, but it's too heavy and keeps falling to the side. I need a haircut. I need a lot of things. Just when I grab my screwdriver and head over to do my professional assessment of the door, the doorbell rings.

"Who's that?" my father yells.

I look through the peephole and curse under my breath. If I don't answer, he'll just keep knocking, and then Mr. Congeniality's going to haul his broken ass out of bed and make my life harder than it needs to be.

"It's no one. Just watch your show, Dad."

When I open the door, Jackson frowns.

"*No one?*" He looks me up and down.

"No one he wants to see," I say. And it's true. My father loves Jackson like most people love a herpes outbreak. I place my finger to my lips. "What are you doing here?"

He puts his hands in his pockets and gently rocks back on his heels. "You said you were fine, but I know you."

"You came here to ask me how I'm doing?"

"Well, yeah"—he smiles—"but now I'm more interested in why you're dressed like Bob the Builder."

I skulk back, my guard up. How the hell does he know about that show? I think of Roselyn and her baby with the gummy smile. I only know about *Bob the Builder* because of Martin at work. He's always humming the theme song and then cursing his kids for watching it so much.

"Really, Jackson. What do you want?"

"I'm just checking in. I just finished a big project and had the day off anyway, so I figured I'd stop by and see if I can help out."

I ruined him. I ruined him for every other woman. I don't want to damage him anymore than I already have. If I hit him with a dose of reality, he'll bolt. He's good at running when things get tough.

I grab the book I next-day ordered and hold it up. "I'm reading about Alzheimer's. That's what I'm doing, and that's what I need to keep doing, so if you can let me get to that, I'd appreciate it."

His eyes round. "Your dad?"

"Yup. Surprised you didn't know something was up when you pulled him out of someone's garage the other morning."

"He was acting odd, but I thought he must've hit his head or something. I didn't know it was... When did you find out?"

"A couple days ago."

"Jesus. How is he?"

"Well, he's not running naked up and down the street yet, but there's always hope."

"This isn't a joke, Bryce."

I resent his tone. He has no right to act devastated. I'm the one doing all the work and making the meals and changing the locks and reading about something scarier than any horror movie I've ever seen.

"I know it's not a joke, Jackson. I'm getting ready to change the locks because I know how funny this isn't. You know I make jokes about inappropriate things. You used to love that about me."

The hard lines on his face soften a bit. "Still love about you. But...sorry. I was just surprised."

Jackson Eric Landley needs to stop using the *love* word in the same sentence as the *you* word. It's not fair. Once a couple breaks up, boundaries need to be maintained. I don't even care that I started it. I also used the words *used to*, which are totally appropriate. Says so right in the rulebook.

"How're you coping," he asks.

"Fine."

"Bryce?"

"What? You asked how I'm coping. I'm coping fine."

"You just found out your dad is going to be relying on you more than ever, and you're fine with that?"

My head is suddenly light and my vision a bit blurry. My mother and father sacrificed my childhood for their selfishness. I learned to take care of my brother and myself the minute I was old enough to fully understand hunger and what it felt like, and that if I was feeling it, Scotty must have been, too, because the woman who birthed us was sleeping on the job. I used to pick my mother's head up and lay it on a newspaper whenever she'd puke in her sleep, and I'd get Scotty and myself to school and back. Every evening before my father came home, I was the one who cleaned up the house and got dinner ready. If he had ever returned home after a long day's work to see how my mother had left the place, it would've brought hell on my head, or worse, my mother's—whom I still held out hope for, back when I had extra hope to throw away on lost causes.

Now, just when I'm kinda sorta coming to grips with how to be an adult, I'm supposed to play mother again, to the man whose job started and stopped with paying the bills? Hell, I'll send paychecks home. I'll pay extra to Theo if he'll come around every day. That's easy. It's the starting and stopping of life at someone's beck and call, the living each moment to make a home for someone else, the being there twenty-four-seven and never thinking of yourself that makes you a parent. How do I know this? Because I made Scotty my own when I was just a child myself. I answered all his cries, made his meals, dressed him, bathed him, helped him with homework, and I hid with him on those nights when our dad wanted to let his belt do all the talking.

He hasn't hit you yet, Scotty, and I won't let him.
But what if he finally does, Sissy?

"I'm not staying here to take care of that man, if that's what you're implying," I finally say. "I don't even need to explain why."

"No, you don't, and I don't blame you for feeling that way, but someone's going to have to do it. Can you afford around-the-clock care?"

I look away. If Jackson sees my eyes, he'll know the answer. Not that he doesn't already, but at least this way I can pretend.

"Can I help?" he asks. "At least let me change the locks for you."

I can't help but grin. I hear Theo in my head, yelling at me to let Jackson in. Only Theo isn't walking around with the memories of this man's touch etched on his heart.

I nearly slap myself when my eyes linger too long on Jackson's broad shoulders and arms and chest. His fingers are thick and his hands leathery, worn from a hobby I don't need to ask if he still enjoys because I can see it on his skin and smell it in his hair. Architect by day— woodworker by night. His most beautiful design was the one he laid out for our future. We should've known then we were building on quicksand.

I step back so I don't smell his intoxicating aroma. "I'm going to change the locks myself. I'm really okay, Jackson."

"It's no trouble."

Do I mention her—do I not? Do I mention her—do I not? Do I mention her? Oops. No more petals.

"According to Roselyn, it'll cause a lot of trouble."

He shakes his head, looks confused.

"I ran into her today. Her and her daughter." He doesn't falter. "It seems to be her opinion that I need to stay away from you."

"Bryce, I don't care what she said. Why're you—"

"She's only looking out for you. I have to agree with her."

He steps closer. I turn my head slightly away and sink into the house a bit. When he speaks, his voice is low— not angry, but he's certainly not playing with me.

"What Roselyn thinks about you and me stopped meaning anything the day I broke things off with her."

I try to speak, but he's too close, and I'm quickly losing my train of thought. I finally look into his eyes and see a heaviness there. I'm just now noticing that his hair's a bit mussed, which works on him, and the skin under his eyes is dark.

"Are you sure about that?" I ask.

"What's that mean? And don't dance for me. You suck at it."

I stand straight, head high. I can see the faint outline of my resolve coming back together. It's fuzzy, but it's there. "Her baby's very cute," I say. "She looks to be about the right age."

Jackson smiles from ear-to-ear and leans in, whispering in my ear. "She's not mine." He playfully nudges me out of the way and steps inside while I shiver and try to cover my bumpy skin.

"I respect that a woman's got her pride, so I won't step on your toes," he says. "You change the locks and I'll make dinner."

"It's only two."

He takes a seat at the table. "Then I'll sit here and grunt whenever I disapprove of the way you hold the screwdriver."

I'm tempted to call for my dad so he can make Jackson leave. I'm also tempted to rip off Jackson's clothes and have him on the table. I need a shock collar so I can zap myself every time I have an impure thought. He's giving me that smile. The one that means he's getting his way and he knows it. Wind Bryce up and watch her take a sledgehammer to her own heart.

I look down at my overalls and the tools I have lying on the table. I can finish the locks and build my own coffin all before the sun goes down.

"Fine," I say without looking at him. If he looks smug, I'll kill him. "But this isn't a date."

"Bryce Price, I've got my integrity."

"I'm serious, Jackson."

"Of course. I wouldn't dream of it."

CHAPTER 10

A mild zing tickles my tongue when I lick my lips and still taste lemon on them. Jackson's a better cook than I'll ever be. What he can do with a salmon is downright orgasmic.

I tap my foot on the carpet, back in my father's plaid old-man chair. There's no other reason he wouldn't want this fish other than the fact that Jackson made it…here…in his house.

"Come on, Dad. I'm really tired, and we need to start on your first entry." He glares at the black notebook in my hand. "Would you prefer a notebook with kittens? I can get you kittens, or puppies. Maybe some nice tropical fish?"

"This is absurd."

"Absurd or not, it's what Theo recommended, and he's got a hell of a lot more experience than the both of us combined. Besides, it makes sense that writing down your memories will keep you in touch with them. It's a good exercise."

"You and that fucking queen can kiss my goddamn ass."

If the old man were any thinner, I'd break him in half and beat him over the head with his own legs. Or I can just write a journal entry for him.

I came. I did. I hit. I hated. I forgot. —Arthur Price

"Do you feel bigger now?" I ask.

My father screws up his face. "What the hell are you babbling about?"

"You. Do you feel bigger when you talk that way? I'm just curious what it does for you when you call a gay man a faggot. It must be great if it's worth looking like a hillbilly fool. For Christ's sake. You're a college-educated man. You're well read. Deep down, you have to recognize your own bigotry. And when the hell did you start taking the Lord's name in vain?"

There's something under his expression. Something working its way out, like watching a tarantula molt. I can't tell if he's going to yell or cry. I've never seen my father cry. It'd be like watching that nature show in Dr. Hot Pants's office. Seeing the unseen—peeking behind the curtains at something you know deserves its privacy.

"I stopped going to church. They don't want me there, so screw 'em," he finally says, sounding neither happy nor sad. He just says it, like I asked how the weather was.

But surely I didn't hear him right. His admission sounds like a bit of foreign language. I know the words he's using, but together they're jumbled and mixed up, like alphabet soup.

I don't know what to say. It's like when a friend tells you she's broken up with her boyfriend. So I ask what I always do. "Are we happy or sad about it?"

My words seem to rattle him. The clumping together of our emotions; the suggestion that I would share in his joy or pain without ridicule or judgment seems as foreign a concept to him as the thought of him breaking up with the church is to me.

"I'm…I'm fine with it," he finally says, making sure to exclude me from the equation.

"Okay," I tell him. "I won't ask what happened."

"Fuck them is what happened. And fuck you and your liberal bullshit."

His expression is stony again. The slight crack shown in his resolve has sealed itself up, taking with it any chance of finding the real person beneath the weathered shell.

There's a lot about me you don't know, Bryce.

"Fuck me?" I say.

"Yeah. Fuck you. I'll use whatever language I see fit, and I won't apologize for it. The only fool I see in this house is you. Wasting your life away, painting your silly pictures even though you're sitting on a degree most people would give their front teeth for. And that little shit you let in my house. He's lucky I didn't kick his ass out. What the hell is with your generation, forcing heathenism down the throat of anyone with an ounce of morals?"

"You call belittling people having morals?"

"I call it being righteous. A sin's a sin, and I won't apologize for having eyes to see with and a brain to reason with. I won't look at the world with rose-tinted glasses just because it makes you and all your tree-hugging buddies feel better."

"Pretty big talk for a man who walked away from his church. Even when you did go, you were only a Sunday warrior."

"I don't have to go to church to know what's right and wrong."

"So hitting your kid and slapping your wife around wasn't wrong? Not rescuing the mother of your children when she was crumbling in front of your eyes wasn't wrong? I guess when you've committed those crimes, insulting a man just because he's gay seems pretty trivial, huh? God, your self-indignation is baffling."

I get up, throw the notebook on the bed. I don't know what to do with my hands, but I can't unclench them because I'm bound to slap the look of disgust off my father's face. I hate that I've given him this kind of power. I hate that my heart is pounding and I'm shaking, so full of rage it makes me question myself. You'd think I'd have learned by now not to tempt the fates. Discussing the past with my dad is like playing with a jack-in-the-box. *Click, click, click* goes the handle, and that horrid song worms into your ear. You know that fucking little clown is going to explode from the box, but it never fails to rattle you when it does.

I pick up the plate, hold it out to him.

"Eat it," I say.

"I can't. I'm allergic."

"You're not…" I drop the plate and fall back into the chair, my face buried in my hands. I feel tears in my eyes and push hard against them, not allowing them to fall.

I rub my face and take a deep breath. I'm going to try this again, because I'm a damn glutton for punishment.

"Dad, eat the food."

"I'm tired. Let me sleep."

"You slept almost all day and all through dinner. You need to eat so you can take your pill. I get that refusing food is pretty much the only card you can play now, and you have to be in control, but I swear I'll tell them to insert a feeding tube."

"Knock yourself out, little girl."

He knows I hate when he calls me that. I was never a little girl. I was born old. I don't know what youth is.

I look behind me, into the hallway, and that blasted Aerosmith song "Pink" plays in my head. I consider it a massive design flaw that the human brain didn't come with a mute button.

"Why're the walls pink, Dad?"

His fists ball up. "What is your... Why the hell won't you leave me alone about the fucking walls?"

"Eat your dinner and I will."

"I'm not bargaining with my child."

"Why are the walls pink?" I ask again, even though he looks like he's going to spew green vomit while his head spins.

"Shut your mouth!"

"You know what's not as pink as your walls, Dad? A baby's cheeks, a cat's nose, a—"

"Enough, Bryce! That's enough!"

I watch as he glances at the food and frowns. I don't think the man knows how to give in. This is like watching a toddler build with blocks for the first time.

He snatches the plate off the bed and loudly scratches the fork across it as he scoops up a heap of fish and shoves it into his mouth.

I don't have the energy to fight like this every day. Throwing tantrums takes energy I don't have. Now I get why some kids pass out after screaming for so long. I'll have to try that next time. At least I'll get a nap out of it.

I silently pick up the notebook and set it on my lap, waiting for my father's reaction. When he sees it, his shoulders sink and he shoves another bite of rice in his mouth. From where I'm sitting, this looks like acceptance.

I sit back and wait for him to finish eating.

~

My father's got a Rubik's Cube of pillows on his bed, each one angled and perched just so. I arrange them to his liking so he can recline comfortably.

"You good?" I ask. He offers a slight nod. It's been silent treatment for me since he started eating.

I sit down, legs as crisscrossed in front of me as the arms of the chair will allow. I tap the pen on the first page of the notebook and ask, "So what's it gonna be? Any memory you want. Just try to give me as much detail as possible."

My dad stares ahead with an almost fiendish look in his eyes. "I got a story I think you'll like," he says.

"Okay. Shoot. The floor's all yours."

Though he continues to stare ahead at the closet door, I see a disconnected look come over him. He's here, with me, but he's traversing through a memory. Even when he speaks, he sounds different, younger.

"Summer nights in Vietnam were brutal," he says. "You'd sweat so much, your clothes would cling to you like an extra layer of flesh. Sometimes you'd have no choice but to strip down to your skivvies and pray it'd rain, 'cause you knew that was the closest thing to a shower you were going to get for a while."

He instinctively pulls at the neck of his t-shirt. I don't think he knows he's doing it.

"One night, all us boys stripped down and wiped the jungle off our skin as much as we could. Fuck around and don't keep clean, the place would eat you alive. I saw men rot from the things in that place. No sir, I hadn't gone all that way just to get taken out by the jungle.

"We had this new kid in our platoon, Melvin. He wouldn't stop crying. It was his first tour, and boy, you could tell. Looked like a damn baby. No one wanted him by their side. Kid would jump when the wind rustled the leaves, and he was always asking questions but never seemed to remember the answers. And his hands... I remember they looked like a woman's.

"On this particular night, word was there might be VC in the area. We swept the place and didn't see anything. Swept again. Nothing. So first sergeant cleared us. We were all sitting around, some guys were writing letters, others were staring at the stars. Those were the dreamers. You knew they were home. Not in person, but up here." He points to his head. "But not Melvin. He just sat there shaking from head to toe, whispering, 'I can't do it. I can't do it.' That's when I started getting nervous. In that kind of atmosphere, it doesn't take much to get a whole platoon riled up.

"Later, after a couple hours' sleep, I got up and went to my station, and sure enough, Melvin was on my rotation. First sergeant knew I was pissed, but out there it didn't matter. We watched out for each other, whether we liked it or not. And I didn't like it. I resented the kid...the way he stood, the way he spoke, the way he held his weapon. He wasn't like us. Someone like that could get you killed. A moment's hesitation meant the difference between life and death. That pussy would've seen us blown to pieces before using his weapon. Or so I thought.

"We had our asses parked on top of a small hill in this thicket. Sticks and thorns were digging into our sides, the ground felt like sharp rock. Tough shit. That was life. But Melvin started whimpering like a fucking puppy. I tried to talk him down and keep him calm. Kept telling him everything was going to be okay, if he'd just be quiet, but then he was crying, something about his dad being ashamed, and how sorry he was.

"It went on for a while. I tried being nice, tried tough love. Nothing worked. I radioed in, told first sergeant I didn't know what to do with the kid. I hit the button, hit the button, hit the button. Nothing. Just radio silence. That shitheel next to me hadn't picked up on much, but he knew what that silence meant as sure as I did. That's when I saw the change on his face. I'll never forget it. I knew he was going scream, so I reached over and pressed my hand to his mouth and held him down, but it was too late.

"Before I was able to tell Melvin to shut the fuck up, Charlie was on our asses, and this gook fuck pulled me out by my neck. Tiny little son of a bitch with the strength of a bull. He got me down on the ground, trying to work the barrel of his AK toward my face, but I put up enough of a struggle to keep the shithead from blowing my brains to smithereens.

"We kept on like that for what felt like forever, and all I could think about was Melvin. I was about to swallow lead, and all I felt was pissed off. That complete waste of life should've had my back. I certainly would've had his. I was livid, just seeing red, and I tossed that asshole off me and went for my weapon. He reeled around, and I saw the barrel swing in my direction. That was it. As far as I knew, it was over. That tiny Vietnamese prick had a bullet with my name on it.

"I wrapped my finger around the trigger even though I knew my bullet wouldn't beat his, and that's when I heard the shot and my hearing went out. Only I wasn't dead. I didn't know what the hell had happened, but I never fired. I didn't even realize I was yelling. I couldn't hear shit, but my throat felt like I had gargled with sand. That's when I saw Melvin, that bastard, standing there holding his M-16 in those delicate hands of his, gasping like a fish. Wouldn't you know it, that boy put a bullet clear through that gook's skull. A clean shot right through the temple. You could've threaded it with rope. First time firing his weapon in combat and the shitheel was taking home a prize. But he couldn't do it himself, of course. After the shot, he was back to being limp-wristed and useless, but I owed him that much."

I look up at my father. "Owed him what? I don't understand. What prize?"

"His trophy. I still couldn't hear worth shit, but I saw Melvin screaming out of the corner of my eye when I cut 'em off. If I'd been him, I would've taken the set home myself, but Melvin insisted I keep them. Of course I wasn't going to send him home without evidence of his good work for his old man, so I kept one and put the other in Melvin's pocket. Damndest thing was that when I got home, that fucking gook's ear still smelled like the jungle. I bet if you go scrounge around in the storage shed, you'll smell what I'm talking about."

My legs won't move, and my hands won't drop the notebook full of words that prove I stood as witness to my father's horrific tale. I hate him. I fucking hate him, not for what he had to do in war, but for the gleam in his eye and the sickness in his heart, and for giving me this piece himself. It's heavy and putrid, and it's made a part of me dirty that I'll never get clean. No wonder the sun never shines on this dark little house of horrors.

I don't want to be here. My only regret is that my father's illness isn't contagious.

"Why would you tell me that?" I ask. "I know so little about you. Why would you want that to be what I remember? You get to forget. One day you won't know any of this, but I will."

He looks peaceful. Serene, even. "You made me share when I didn't want to. I made you listen when you didn't want to."

The air in the room is suffocating, the smell of cigars nauseating. I stand and back away, not taking my eyes off the man I truly don't know. There's a new bottle of tequila in the kitchen, and my brain needs a bath.

Instead of saying goodnight, I tell Arthur Price I hate him.

CHAPTER 11

How much alcohol can someone drink before they poison themselves? If I don't stop, I'll know the answer. Then my father will find me passed out on the floor tomorrow morning and cut my ears off. Throw them in the shed and let them mingle with his collection of treasures. His wife's mind, his son's life, his daughter's sanity, and a fine collection of ears from all around the world. Step right up, folks, and see the world's most macabre hobbyist.

I grab for the bottle swimming in my vision and miss the first time. I snatch it at the bottom and see that the liquor only comes to about four fingers high. Uh-oh.

I'm unsteady on my feet. I wobble and look down at my stomach, wondering if I really stored that much liquid courage away. In my case, it's liquid denial. My belly protrudes slightly and I poke at it, my bladder protesting with every slight jab.

"Oh…trouble."

I plop down on the barstool and rest my chin in my hand, staring at the tequila. Jackson's salmon is still perfuming the air. It's going to be a shame to puke it all up, but I'm willing to lose my dinner if it means getting drunk enough to block this night out. Really, this is the kind of night that calls for an anvil over the head. How else am I supposed to sleep with that ear just yards away, hidden in a box, listening to my father tell the story of its untimely demise? The least my dad could've done was hide it under the floorboards. It was good enough for ol' vulture-eye.

I'm drunk. My thoughts are dreamy and fall away just before my fingertips can grasp ahold of them, like dark, inky squid darting away from my touch. I'm floating, swaying left and right with the soft current of vertigo. No feelings, no tears, no laughter. Numbness is what I crave. But I can't find it. I'm detached from any thoughts that might explain the aching in my chest, yearning for something I'm too intoxicated to put a name to, but still, like a brainless squid, my body acts on impulse, my hands obeying orders given by my heart and not my mind. Before I know it, my phone's in my hand and my thumb's scrolling along my list of contacts. Right at the top of the J section, I see his name, and my chest burns with a warmth that quickly spreads throughout my body and makes me shiver.

"You're an idiot," I say to myself. "Stupid girl. Stupid, stupid girl." But the message isn't reaching my fingers.

The letters are swimming all over the place. I open my eyes wide and pull the phone a few inches away, trying to wrangle them back where I know they're meant to be, but everything's out of place tonight.

I lazily move my thumb around, punching in letters and emojis. Fucking emojis, like I'm fifteen or something. I don't care. I've always wanted an excuse to digitally flip someone the bird, and who better than the love of my life? No. Not the love of my life. I didn't say that. I don't accept responsibility for anything I say tonight, and I'll later deny having said the things I won't admit to saying because I obviously didn't say them to begin with. Did that make sense?

I read my text back, nod my head, try to blink away the liquid denial. I drank too much, and now I'm overflowing. My tears end up on my cheeks, between my lips, on the counter. They even find their way into my message to Jackson, only they don't look like tears. They look like the letters L and O and V and E. They're ugly, and they're stinking up the place. Better to rid myself of them and make them his problem, because they're too painful, and I've got too many scars from where they dug into me and latched on, thriving off the contents of my heart like greedy little monsters.

I put my phone down and run my hands through my gypsy hair. I need to wash the day off my body. I slip off the stool and stumble my way down the hall, almost tripping over gravity.

Shutting the bathroom door presents more of a challenge than it should. And I thought drinking was supposed to fix all my troubles.

I stand facing the door. I know what's behind me. I can feel it, in the same way you can feel someone watching you. I've taken loads of showers here since that fateful day, and I usually manage well enough, but then there are moments like these, and I swear, if I turn around I'll see her again. I can almost feel the humidity in the air and see the condensation on the mirror. And the smell. Jesus, the smell.

Staring at the subway tiles on the floor is making me dizzy. I close my eyes and scratch at Walker. That's the thing about being home. You don't just go back to your past, you go back to a version of yourself you abandoned long ago, a version that used one kind of pain to numb another kind of pain, and I could easily learn to crave the sting again.

I force myself to drop my hand, because I'm a big girl now, and big girls know that making themselves bleed here won't stop the bleeding there. I turn around, eyes still down, and swallow back the uncanny feeling that I'm going to look up and be transported back to that warm June night, seven years ago.

"Go away, Mom," I whisper.

I put on my war face and look up. Stepping toward the tub, I lean over and see that it's empty, and then I finally breathe.

CHAPTER 12

I hear someone moan and immediately cringe. It's me. It's morning, and I'm still drunk.

Impressive, Bryce.

The acrid taste in my mouth makes me want to vomit. Or maybe I did vomit. When I open my eyes to check the sheets, the dull morning glow burns them, and the *plop-plop-plop* of raindrops on the roof sets my nerves on edge.

"Fuck you, Washington."

When I sit up, the room does this neat trick it learned just for me, and I hold on to the sides of the mattress until the ride comes to a stop. My legs dangle off the bed, just above the floor. I can't remember when I replaced them with lead weights, but there they are, too heavy to move.

I look down and see my bare thighs. I've made it a habit to sleep in long pajama pants. Always. But I'm wearing only my undies, and morning hangovers aren't the time to face such painful memories. I must've stumbled into bed last night and shed my clothes, too drunk to realize I was nearly sleeping in my birthday suit. Happy fucking early birthday to me! I don't want to think about Saturday.

I lean over, yanking my pants off the dresser. Suddenly my legs are more than willing to comply, and I slip into my jeans. Out of sight, out of mind. What scars?

I stand up and open the dresser drawer, pulling out an old Seahawks t-shirt. Not an ex-boyfriend's. This one's all mine, mine, mine.

The antique mirror perched atop the matching dresser is laced with brittle, brown patches, and a long crack runs down the middle of it, separating the reflection of my chest, making my left breast appear to hang much lower than my right, and making my face askew. I touch my cheek, then my stomach. I smash my breasts down and imagine what they'll look like once I've fallen victim to age. They look like my mother's. Only hers fell victim to two milk-suckling leeches. She didn't live long enough to see time ravage her body. Just kids and crack and bad love.

When I pull my shirt over my head, I hold my breath. My clothes always come out of the dresser smelling of history, like the smoky stench left behind after a fire. I throw my hair back and look away from the mirror. I guess I'm pretty. People tell me so. But I kind of hate that word. It's just blah—neither beautiful nor ugly. Just...pretty. Whatever. Let's not harp on it or I'll develop a complex.

~

That old bat across the street is out in her front yard, picking what looks like mushrooms off the grass and throwing them over her shoulder. Doesn't that defeat the purpose?

I blow into my tea, squinting as the steam wafts around my face. I creep back into the hallway and peek into my dad's room. I don't want to wake him. In fact, I wish I had a spinning wheel to prick his finger on.

You know how they say people look serene when they sleep? Not this guy. His jaw sinks back and falls to the side, creating an overbite and a channel where saliva runs from the side of his mouth and down his neck, settling on his pillow. My stomach's too uneasy. I can't look at his pillowcase. I can almost smell the sour stench.

Just as I sneak out of the room, I hear the distinctive cry of an eagle. They're like pigeons here. They're everywhere. Not that I'm complaining. I don't know what I love more about this place: the bald eagles constantly flying overhead, or knowing that wolves run wild through this state. Washington is just untamed enough to keep me aware that I'm an insignificant speck, and if at any point the Earth wanted to, she could shake all of us off like fleas.

When my cell alerts me to a new text, I almost drop my mug. The high-pitched noise is murder on my ears. My phone's on the table, facedown, and a second text comes through before I have a chance to look at it.

I pick it up and begin reading Jackson's first text.

"What?" I whisper. I don't understand.

I scroll up and see a text I sent him last night. Shit! I spit tea on my phone and hold it to my chest, wiping it off on my shirt. I don't want to look again. The scene of an accident is all over the screen, only it's not twisted metal

I'm looking at. It's professions and admissions and words I didn't know I knew how to use anymore.

I look over and see the bottle on the bar. Those weren't my words. Those were tequila's, and I happen to know tequila is both a liar and a traitor.

I go back to the beginning of my text. As much as I want to pretend they're not there, I have to read my words again. I feel like a voyeur, reading something that doesn't feel like mine, something I don't remember writing. So personal, so explicit.

"I thought about driving to your house, but I can't find my keys. That probably means I shouldn't be driving. Plus, I don't really want to bring my dad along to have sex with you. Not him. I mean me. With you. Fuck. You know what I mean. Instead I'll just get in the bath and try to wash you off. I don't know if I hate that I can always smell you on me when you leave, or if I love it.

"Either way, I figured if I couldn't wash off your smell, I might as well immerse myself in it. Because that part was always good, wasn't it? Yours are the only eyes I've ever been able to look into while making love. With everyone else, I look away. But I don't want you to make love to me. I want you to—"

I can't read any more. Ahead I see hazard signs and flashing lights and words like "need" and "you." And is that an emoji?

The heat rising up my chest is burning my cheeks and making me feel woozy. I slam my phone down and let my forehead drop on the table. I'm too hung over to think about what to say to Jackson, let alone how I'm going to obtain a secret identity and flee the country. There aren't enough miles I can put between us to soften the blow of my words. They're just hanging out there, all gangly and exposed, like the twelve-year-old girls you see traipsing around the mall in their booty shorts and crop tops. Just like my message to Jackson: undeveloped and too immature to realize the long-lasting effects of their actions.

Jackson's response was nothing less than what I would expect from a real adult. You know, the ones who deal with their issues without the assistance of firewater and text messages.

"Bryce, can we talk? How about tonight?"

I just birthed a problem into this world, and now it's sitting there screaming, waiting to be dealt with. This is why some mothers eat their young.

I turn my phone off and stare at the door to the garage in the kitchen. I can feel my features harden the way they do when Shana tells me I've got resting bitch face. I can't sit in this house anymore. Not with all my and my father's screw-ups bearing down on me, precariously perched on my last remnants of strength.

The garage calls me, and I get up and open the door. I can't do much about Mr. Forgets-a-lot, sleeping in the room, and I have no plans on dealing with my ex and his intoxicating smell. But I can rid this house of at least one evil.

CHAPTER 13

Across from my father's wall of tools is a small room off the garage. At most, it's a five-by-eight-foot space, fully insulated and closed off with a locked door. He calls it a shed, but it's not. If I wanted to store body parts in my garage, I wouldn't leave the key hanging on the pegboard, but apparently my father's not concerned with someone discovering his nightmarish bits and bobs.

I quietly unlock the door and flip the light on. It smells like cardboard from the small wall of filing boxes to my left, all stacked and organized with precision. On the right are my father's fishing rods.

I prop my hands on my hips and eye the front of the boxes. They have two dates scribbled on them, spanning several years. The box with the earliest date spans from 1975 to 1982. It's as good a place to start as any.

Right away I can see that there's nothing amiss. It's full of papers and envelopes, but nothing even close to resembling an ear. Unless... What the hell does an ear look like after this many decades?

I pick up a small, flat paper bag and look inside. No ear—just dog tags. Three sets, two bearing my father's name and one bearing a name I don't recognize: Danton Scott.

I sit them on top of the box and grab the stubby ladder from the garage and check the remaining boxes, which closely resemble the first. Paperwork, old warranties, receipts. All the photos and keepsakes are probably in the third bedroom, where my mother kept them. Maybe she had planned on putting all the family photos in albums once her world stopped spinning and she could get off long enough to play wife and mommy.

I put everything back except the box with the dog tags. The name stares back at me. Danton Scott.

I pull the lid back again and flip through the stacks of papers. My parents' marriage license is sandwiched between dozens of envelopes, all with my mother's name and our address scribbled on the front. Looks like Arthur was good about writing his young wife while he was away in Vietnam. Maybe there's an ear in one of these letters, pressed thin by the time that separates it from its rightful owner. But probably not. Besides, I've got no desire to wipe the dust off my parents' love letters and weigh down my heart with the echoes of their beautiful lies about always and forever. Theirs was not an unfinished love. It was the stale milk you bring home from the store without realizing you never checked the date. Nope. I've already had enough boy/girl drama for the day.

Maybe that's what I should do. Cut off my ear and send it to Jackson. He can talk, and I'll be the best listener.

I'm just about to toss the dog tags back in the box when I see that the last envelope has a different name on it. It's addressed to my father, from some woman named Abigail Scott, in South Carolina. This is an invasion of privacy. I should feel guilty, but...

There's a lot about me you don't know.

This is wrong. I put the letter back, then pick it up; put it back, then pick it up. The writing on the front looks sad. The letters slant where other women would make them bubbly, and the corners are sharp and abrupt—not at all soft or flowing.

I reach in and pull out a single sheet of lined paper, twice folded. Much like my father's aged skin, the edges of the paper are mottled, the blue ink faded in some areas.

Hand-written letters make me think of a simpler time, when young women lazily swung on porch swings and sipped lemonade from straws while dragonflies flitted about their bare feet. Not Abigail Scott, though. She drank black coffee at one of those retro Formica dining tables, windows and doors sealed tight to block out the sounds of the neighborhood kids' laughter as they scavenged the surrounding woods for bullfrogs and horny toads. All that, just from the jagged lines of her sketchy print. I need to get out more.

Dearest Arthur,

I hope this letter finds you in good spirits. I'm doing my best, but each day presents me with new obstacles.

I took the kids to the beach for the 4th last week and spent the whole day crying. The beach was always Danton's favorite place. We used to take the kids there once a month every summer. They were too little to appreciate it, but that didn't stop Danton from making them sandcastles and collecting crabs for them to watch scurry away. I have no idea how I'm going to express to these kids how precious those moments were. They can't even remember what their father looked like. If it weren't for pictures, it'd be like he never existed.

Enclosed you'll find a set of Danton's dog tags. I know he would've wanted you to have them, Arthur. You were like a brother to him. I still read the letters he sent me, all filled with stories of you and the other men. It broke my heart every day that I wasn't there for him, especially in his last moments, but it brings me some relief knowing you were his family in our absence. I'll never be able to thank you for what you did for my husband. Please know that I will forever be in your debt. Your kindness is unmatched.

My absolute best to you and your wife and children. I think of you often and keep you and yours in my prayers. God bless.

Abigail Scott

I have to take a moment to arrange my thoughts. *Unmatched kindness?* Maybe good ol' Abigail was dipping in the sauce when she wrote this and got my father confused with someone else. I'd be a liar if I said I hadn't been jealous of the military when I was a kid. I know from the plaques on the wall that my dad gave his all to the Marines. Totally dedicated and unwaveringly loyal. But *unmatched kindness?* What the hell did he do that was so great?

Screw it. So Abigail Scott lavished praise upon a fictitious man—someone who was good at his job but who certainly didn't bring that same *unmatched kindness* home with him. I put the dog tags and letter back and slide the box back into place.

The garage is cooler, and I breathe in deep, clearing my head. Time to finally give the last bits of Jose Cuervo an eviction notice.

On the right side of the garage sits one of those huge metal shelving units, and pushed to the back are a few cans of paint. I nudge the tape and tools and brushes aside and see that the smear of paint on the top of the can in front matches the pink walls. The label is hidden under a layer of sawdust. I wipe it away and turn the can so I can read the name of the color.

"Muted Salmon," I whisper.

Salmon's just what we call pink to make it more palatable for big, strong men. You know you're the weaker sex when a color can cripple your sense of masculinity. Then again, those very men are the same ones who can cripple a woman's sense of self-worth. Guess we're all just fragile fools.

I want to pop the lid open and dip my finger in the muted salmon. Catch a nice paint high and torture myself with memories of what I'm missing. My father calls my paintings "silly." He always has. Even when the *Seattle Times* ran a small piece on my work, he balked at it. "The *Seattle Times* is run by a bunch of liberals who wouldn't know a good thing if it bit 'em in the ass," was his response, if my memory serves me.

But maybe my father does get it. After all, he's hiding behind his pink walls just like I hide under my bright floral bedspread. A pop of color to remind you that life isn't always flat. A splash of art to get your blood pumping and your imagination revving. Maybe Arthur's ashamed of his muted salmon in the same way I'm ashamed to admit that I'm a dreamer, because dreaming is for fools and poets. Pragmatism, logic, wisdom. These are the building blocks of a strong individual. Someone who would never throw their pearls into a windstorm just to see where they land. But that's the problem with me. I'm just that kind of fool, dressed in a pragmatist's clothing.

I guess it doesn't really matter, though. Dreamer or no dreamer, I'm still just a leaf connected to a plant whose roots are decaying.

CHAPTER 14

I gently push on my father's door with the corner of the tray and quietly walk in, waiting a moment to see what kind of mood he's in. Mean, angry, cranky? He only comes in three flavors.

He's got his head turned toward the window, a kind of dreamy look about him. The dust on the glass pane gives the light coming through a muted glow. Still, I can see it reflect off his eyes, and that's when I notice that they're nearly void of any sparkle. They shine so dimly that I can no longer see their color. I've only my memory to tell me they're dark brown.

I speak in a soft tone, because the room feels soft, like it forgot the horrible story it was told last night. The air even feels soft.

"Hey, Dad. I made spaghetti for lunch. You hungry?"

He keeps his gaze on the window, and the faintest trace of a smile tugs at one corner of his mouth.

"We used to have blue jays," he says. His voice is smooth, calm.

I put the tray down and sit on the foot of the bed, moving slowly so I don't scare away the gentle creature in front of me.

"Blue jays?" I ask.

"Yes. Tons of them. They loved our feeder out back. The one with the cherub holding the bowl of seeds."

There's something covered in years of overgrowth sitting in the back yard. I vaguely remember seeing a chubby stone statue of a cherub while my brother and I buried one another in leaves each fall.

"Yeah," I say, "I think I know the one."

"I used to stand out there with Patricia before work. She'd fill her pocket with bits of fruit and toss them to the birds. She loved those things."

I'm frozen. I don't even blink. My mother's name sounds strange coming from him. It's a name I'm willing to bet hasn't passed over his lips in seven years. I want to open his mouth wide and see what else is hiding in there.

"She didn't sleep much," he says, still searching the window, as though a memory might be playing out before his eyes. "On the good mornings, I'd wake her up and we'd go out back and feed them. But on the bad mornings, she'd be awake before me. That's how I knew she was going to have a rough day. I'd wake up to her crying and try to hold her, but she said it hurt her skin to be touched. She'd shake so violently the whole bed would "move. I just wanted to take it away for her. That's why I'd leave. Even on weekends when I didn't have to work, I'd go, because I knew she wouldn't use while I was still home, and I just wanted her pain to stop. But then I'd come home and smell cheap cologne on our sheets, and I'd want her pain to go on forever."

My father's words have robbed me of my voice. I don't know what to say, and even if I did, I can't think past the shock filling the spaces in my mind.

I look down at his hand and want to touch it, just to make sure he's real, and maybe to console him, even though I'm entirely sure he doesn't deserve it. I should hate him for being an enabler, for leaving Scotty and me here to clean up all the messes. I should point and scream, "KILLER, KILLER, KILLER," but I don't want to. His admission of love is shocking. Or maybe it's an admission of mercy for a woman he once loved. I can't tell, and, by his expression, neither can he.

I suddenly wonder if he's aware that I'm here, listening to his confession. As if he can hear my thoughts, he turns to me and says, "She made me weak."

Does he expect something from me? Is he waiting for me to absolve him of his guilt? As if merely sympathizing with him will scrub clean his conscience.

I stare at him for a moment, trying to meet him in the middle, where maybe we'll find common ground and I'll finally understand why my well-being has never been as important as his, but something in the air changes in a blink of an eye, and a hardened scowl returns to his face.

"Just hand me the tray," he says. His voice is sandpaper and gravel.

I want to see his moment of honesty as progress, but I feel like I just hiked up a mountain and got kicked off the top. This is what fishing is like. You've got a monster on your line, and just when you're about to reel it in, the line breaks and the damn thing swims off with all the answers you're rightly owed. Worst of all, you don't even know what bait it was the SOB found so alluring.

I grab the plate off the tray and sit it on my dad's lap. I watch his hard eyes and the way his thin, wrinkled lips mash together as he chews through his pasta and sauce settles in the corners of his mouth. Whoever just inhabited his mind is gone. POOF. No afterglow. I can't even sense him anymore.

"Can I ask you something?" I say, getting off the bed and sitting on the arm of the plaid old-man chair.

"Will it stop you if I say no?"

"Probably not."

He fills his mouth to capacity with another greedy bite. I wait for him to swallow before laying it on him.

"So are we done talking about Mom? Was that a one-time deal or what?"

It seems that I've now robbed him of his voice. His eyebrows furrow, and just when he opens his mouth and I think he's going to yell at me, he shoves more food in his face hole.

Seriously? I couldn't get the man to eat, and now he's spooning spaghetti into his mouth faster than a super model at her retirement party.

His bland expression infuriates me, but not as much as Theo, sitting in the back of my head, telling me I can't even get angry. I try to see a victim when I look at my dad. Try to tell myself he's a prisoner of his own mind. But I can't help but take it personally. He dangled a carrot in front of my face and then snatched it back before I could even smell it. I'm over here starving to death, and he's got a swollen belly and sauce stains on his hunter-green pajamas.

"Fine. No Mom talk. Can I ask you something else, then?"

He nods with too much enthusiasm, his head bouncing around like that of a kid who's just been asked if he wants ice cream. His yo-yoing mood is making me dizzy.

I wait for him to take another bite, but he doesn't. He sets his silverware down and rests his hands on each side of the tray.

"What is it?" he asks.

"Who's Danton Scott?"

"Danton Scott?"

"Yes. Danton Scott. You've got a set of his dog tags in a box in the garage."

I consider myself a pretty good judge of character. Reading people isn't so hard, especially when you expect them to lie. They usually don't disappoint. But the confusion twisting the lines of my father's face isn't part of a ruse to throw me off course. He's looking me square in the eye, his right hand slowly opening and closing, as if grasping at an answer just beyond his reach.

I lean forward and speak clearly. "You were in Vietnam together. His wife wrote you a letter. Do you remember?" My hands are damp. Sweat coats the skin between my breasts. "Dad, do you remember someone named Danton? I think he was your friend."

He leans back, frowning as he stares at his plate, seemingly working the pieces around in his head as his index finger moves all over, like he's solving a math equation in the air.

"No," he says, the word coming out slow. "You're thinking of your uncle Jerry."

"No, Dad. I'm not talking about Uncle Jerry. I'm talking about you. You were in Vietnam with someone named Danton Scott."

"That was Uncle Jerry," he says again, with startling certainty. "I wanted to join up with your uncle, but I was told I couldn't on account of my knee injuries. Come on, Bryce. You know I blew them out in high school."

Every kid has a memory of the first time they got lost in a store. The panic that rushes through your body and the way your belly drops when you turn around and see that you're all alone, no adult in sight.

Well, I'm all alone in this house, with only a shell of my father—a ventriloquist dummy; his mouth is moving, but it's not Arthur talking. His illness is running the show now, and it's just us—me and a stranger I don't know how to battle.

"Dad," I say, "Uncle Jerry was the one who injured his knees playing high school football. Remember? You married Mom…Patricia. Then you went to Vietnam."

"I stayed home and looked after your grandmother. My mom was very sick. I guess it was a blessing I couldn't go, but it didn't feel that way at the time. Do you remember your grandma, Bryce?"

I shake my head and look away, hoping my deep breaths will keep the panic on its side of the fence.

"Well, do you?" he asks again. "She sure loved you. She adored little girls. Everything was lacy and ornate with her. If any woman knew how to be a lady, it was Claudet Price. You worshipped her. You used to wear her high heels around when you were little. Even when you'd topple over, you'd just keep smiling."

The saliva pooling in my mouth fights me when I try to swallow. I'm lost. Completely lost. Do I tell him his mother died before I was even born, and that I've never worn heels a day in my life? Or do I nod and smile? I want Shana or Jackson or Theo. I don't care that they won't know the right answer. I just want someone to remind me to breathe.

It's possible to crave fear. I crave the fear I used to have of my father. I crave the familiarity of it, the way I knew to duck behind it and maneuver around it. The fear I feel now is brand new, fresh out of the package, and I don't know how it works. All the instructions are written in a language I've never seen.

"Um…I'll be right back," I tell him. "Just sit tight and finish your lunch, okay?"

He smiles at me and picks the fork back up, uncharacteristically happy to do what I asked.

I run out of the room and rip the business card off the fridge. When I dial and place the phone to my ear, my panting registers back in the earpiece. Five long rings, each one pumping adrenaline through my blood and panic into the forefront of my mind. Then I hear his voice.

"Theo? This is Bryce, Arthur's daughter."

"Hey, Bryce. What's up? You don't sound so good. Everything okay?"

This is just another day at the office for him, so how do I convey that up is now down and left is now right? Nothing is as it was, and I was wrong. I do need a big, strong man to recue me.

"Please come over, Theo," I say. "I don't know what to do. He's saying all these crazy things. He doesn't remember who he is. I know you warned me about this. I thought I could handle it, but I—"

"Okay, okay, okay. Just breathe. That's the first thing I want you to do. This is scary for everyone the first time they witness it. I have a couple other patients before I can get over there. Can you hang until then?"

I look down the dark hallway, where my dad's shell is waiting to tell me stories that aren't true and words with no real meaning. I usually avoid strangers, and isn't that what he is now, a stranger, with a different history, and even a different way of carrying himself?

My pain, my sorrow…it never registered with my dad. It merely flitted through his mind, never solidifying and taking shape. I was always a shadow in his world, something that grew bigger while he distanced himself from me, tending to the moat he built around his heart. So why the hell is this breaking mine now?

I want to reach in and grab my dad's hand and pull him up from the abyss he's fallen into. I hate his memories, I hate his misdeeds, but they're rightfully his, and they make him the man I know and unfortunately love.

"Yes," I say, knowing he can hear the uncertainty in my voice just like I can. "We'll be okay."

CHAPTER 15

Theo told me to get out of the house and take a break while he worked with my dad. I'm pretty sure driving to the bar and having a drink is precisely what he had in mind. If not, fucking oh well. There's a dirty little creature growing in my brain, and it's parched. What I need to do is spend the next forty minutes pretending I'm not in a Lifetime movie.

I pull up to Woody's and watch two men with full-term bellies get off their motorcycles and walk into the bar. I wonder if they planned the matchy-matchy beards and shirts and jeans and leather vests, or if that's all they carry at the other old-man store, the one that caters to those too chicken shit to become Hells Angels but too undomesticated to hold their wives' purses while they peruse the aisles of Bed, Bath & Beyond.

There's always something unnatural about walking into a bar alone. Ask any woman and she'll tell you. It's like that dream you always hear about, in which you're standing naked in front of your whole school. I've never actually had that dream, but it's probably pretty close to what I'm about to feel.

When I open the door and walk in, a dozen or so men all turn and ogle the only woman in the place. One man licks the frothy mustache from his upper lip and then sucks hard on it while eyeing me from head to toe. How I'm not throwing myself at him and letting him break me in half in the bathroom stall is beyond me.

You won't find more of my kind in here until Friday night, when the younger crowds gather around the pool tables and whisper their arguments over who's got the best-looking fake ID. Screw up and gamble on the wrong stud, all you're getting served are mediocre nachos and flat soda. Really get unlucky and you might spend the night in one of the city's finest cells.

I plop down on a stool, not giving a rat's ass about the eyes still reading the lines of my body. I speak their language and even manspread on the stool just to make sure everyone knows I've pissed on this spot and now it's mine. One weatherworn man of maybe sixty tips his cap at me, so I give him a quick guy nod.

"Pick your poison," the bartender says to me.

"Shot of Jack."

A quick rise of his eyebrows and he pours my drink. That's right. I can drink hard liquor, and I won't even let you know how much it burns on the way down. I've swallowed worse.

"Here you go," he says, sliding the shot glass across the bar. "Enjoy."

I pull my phone from my pocket and begin my search for my uncle Jerry. I haven't seen him since my mother's funeral, when my father never said a word to him and I'm guessing hasn't since. I don't have his number, but I know he lives in some bumfuck town in the middle of Missouri. You know it had to be love for him to leave the pristine shores of Orcas Island. If the gods ever stepped foot on this Earth and anointed a place, it's there.

I scroll down a list of names, all similar to his. "Bingo." There he is. Jerry Price of Nuscetti, Missouri. I throw back the shot of Jack and press the call tab. I'd prefer to be tore-down drunk. There's nothing quite like an impromptu call from a sauced-up family member to brighten your day. But good ol' Uncle Jerry will just have to settle for sober me. Not nearly as fun, and a whole hell of a lot less crude, but I still don't pull punches.

"Hello," I hear him say after the second ring. His voice is higher than my father's but there's a similar quality to it.

"Hey, Uncle Jerry. It's Bryce."

"Bryce? Wow. This is a pleasant surprise. What on earth have you been up to?"

That's nice of him to say, especially since we have no relationship. I don't even remember his wife's name. I just know she's shaped like a giant pear and is one of those big, beautiful women who could be a model if she dropped a half a ton or so. His son, on the other hand, I'll never forget.

Come on, Bryce. Just touch it, and then we'll play. We'll do whatever you want to. Here. Give me your mouth. I'll show you how.

"I'm all right," I say. "How've you been?

"Good, good. Can't complain. Tammy is visiting her sisters in Iowa this week, so I've got the house to myself."

That's right. It's Tammy. She'd have to drop more than just weight. That name would have to go, too. You can't be a supermodel with the name Tammy. All the other models will beat you up and send you back to the trailer you came from.

"Ah," I say, fresh out of standard formalities. I'd ask about the weather, but it would be a disingenuous gesture on my part, and who's got time for that?

"Uncle Jerry, can I ask you something about Dad?"

"You mean something you can't ask him?"

This man is blood. He and my father grew up together. There appears to be no love lost, but surely they were close at one time. Still, telling him about my dad's diagnosis feels like a betrayal, and one that won't lead to any good. It's not as though Jerry and Tammy are going to drop their lives and move here to care for him. And you can bet your ass my father wouldn't leave this place, especially for Missouri. The man's got roots on the bottom of his feet. He feeds off the soil and rain.

"More like something he refuses to answer," I say.

Uncle Jerry falls silent for a moment. "Okay," he says. "I don't know that I'll be much help, but what is it you want to know?"

"Dad was a pretty average guy, right? Got married, went to 'Nam, had some kids, then worked a government job on the base. Aside from being a bastard, that's all I know about him."

"So what's your question?"

"Well, am I missing something? Is there anything about him you think I might not know about?"

There's nothing but silence on the other end. Not regular silence, but that pregnant pause that tells you the other person is wrestling with how to articulate themselves.

"Uncle Jerry?"

"I'm here. I just don't know that sniffing around is a great idea. Just let Arthur's demons stay where they are. No good can come from poking the hive."

"So there is a hive to poke?"

"Bryce, drop it."

I consider my uncle's words. I don't know him enough to read between the lines, but the forcefulness in his voice tells me I'm flirting with trouble.

Two men a few barstools away stare at me from the corners of their eyes, each raising their brows. I'm wearing my bitch face again. I can feel it, like armor. How dare a woman be anything other than sugar, spice, and everything nice? I flash them a hard glare, just to let them see the snakes and snails.

I wave and point at my glass. The bartender's quick to fill it. I'm quick to drink it.

"Okay," I say to my uncle. "I get it. Let sleeping dogs lie."

"I really do think it's for the best."

An older man wearing a camouflage jacket walks in, and I think of Mrs. Scott's letter again.

"Oh, hey. Before I go, can I ask you one more question?" I don't wait for an answer. "Do you know who Danton Scott is...or was? He and Dad were in Vietnam together. He obviously never made it home, but his wife wrote Dad this letter, going on about how selfless Dad was and thanking him for what he did for her husband. I guess I just want to know if there's something more to Dad than his anger. My whole childhood, I never dared to ask him why he was so mad. Now, asking seems as "pointless as asking why the sky's blue. He just is, you know? But was he always that way?"

My uncle's voice changes, like he's mourning the death of a friend. "No, he wasn't. That much I can tell you. Things were just complicated for him. There are easy people, and then there are complicated people. As time went on, your father found it harder to cope with his own complications. Some people drink or use drugs. My brother got angry.

"Danton Scott was his best friend in Vietnam. After your father's first tour, we heard all about him. Your mother and I were just glad he had someone over there to talk to, because he sure wasn't talking to us. At least not about anything important.

"To make a long story short, Arthur saved his life and nearly died doing it. It was by the Grace of God that your dad walked away. When Danton got himself killed a few months after their second tour, it hit Arthur bad. Real bad.

"Anyway, when your dad got home he was ticked off. He didn't think the Marines were honoring his fallen comrade. Swore it was because he was black. So your dad went—"

"W-w-wait! Back up a second. Did you just say Danton Scott was black? As in African American?"

My uncle laughs. Good. So I'm not crazy.

"He sure was. Anyway, your dad flew out to meet his wife and kids after he got home. Wanted to thank them in person for their sacrifice and give them a little money to help keep them afloat while Danton's wife found work."

I'm not sure if it's the liquor or the story that's warming my chest. I look down at the bar and hide my face when I feel my eyes get wet. This isn't one of those cool, metro Seattle bars where hipsters knock a few back and bro-mance it over a couple exuberant "I love you, man's." This place smells of yesteryear and mahogany, and its customers are as brittle as the dusty, beaten floors. Cry in this place and they make you take the walk of shame right out the front door.

"Thank you, Uncle Jerry," I say. "I'm gonna go. Honestly, I'm a little shocked right now and don't know what to say. But I appreciate you sharing this with me."

"No problem. And Bryce...your dad...he's more than just his anger. He's just...complex is all."

I quickly wipe my eyes, pretending I'm nursing a tension headache. When I look up, no one seems to notice I'm leaking.

"Yeah," I say, "I'm starting to get that."

~

I walk through the front door and set my purse down. All the fear I felt before leaving the house is back, like I walked through some portal into another world. Grimy shotglasses and torn vinyl stools don't exist here. Just ever-changing shades of reality and whispers of a man on the brink of extinction.

I can hear Theo rooting my father on, "You got this, Arthur. Almost there. Good job!"

When I peek around the corner, I catch my dad as he relaxes into the bed. Sweat is beading on his forehead and soaking the armpits of his shirt. Just as I'm about to walk away, he catches me watching him. At first I think he might smile, but then his lips draw down and he quickly looks away, like he's embarrassed.

I tiptoe back into the living room and sit on the couch, my hands folded on my lap. The posture of someone in an unfamiliar setting. I listen to Theo ask my father a series of questions, all of which he answers correctly, and my stomach untwists just a bit. He knows his name, he knows his birthdate, he knows where he is and that he was born here. But then he trips.

"What's the year?" I hear Theo ask.

My father hems and haws. "I know the damn date. I'm not stupid. It's just not coming to me right now."

I press my palms to my ears and stare at the floor. I try to imagine my apartment and my job and the faces of my friends, but I can't see anything beyond the confines of this house. My memories of such things are slowly being replaced by medical terms and feeding schedules. Freedom is such a delicate thing—as elusive as true love and as difficult to hold on to. It's water in your hands, flowing over the sides of your fingers. You try to catch it with frivolous hopes and impossible dreams.

I look around the living room and can't see a future beyond it, and I resent my father more than ever, because maybe he's not fighting hard enough. Maybe it's easier to live under the weight of a disease you didn't cause than to live under the weight of a past you did. And maybe I'm a product of every woman who's come before me. Does it matter that it's my father I'm giving my job and apartment and life up for? In the end it's all the same. The frame of this house is my bones, the walls my skin, the attic my mind, dusty and full of dark corners, and inside the belly is my father. Look at any street in suburban America and you'll see rows of women, all dressed like homes, neatly compartmentalized, with pristine matching lawns and welcome signs inviting in more needy hands and hungry mouths.

"How you doing, girl?"

I look up and see Theo standing there with his bag. He's smiling, but he looks tired. I shake my head. "He's not going to get better, is he?"

He sits next to me on the couch, his massive hand patting my knee.

"No, he's not. But I think what happened today had more to do with his medication. Have you counted his pills recently?"

He's giving me that look. He knows I don't have the right answer.

"No," I say. "I keep them in the kitchen cabinet. Has he been getting into them?"

"Listen, Bryce. Alzheimer's doesn't make people stupid. If anything, patients get pretty creative when they want something. That's why taking every precaution is so important. Locks on everything, alert bands in case he gets out, maybe even put alarms on the doors. It's possible he forgot you gave him his pills this morning, but he says he remembers and that the two pills just weren't cutting it, so he took another one."

"When? I've been watching him."

"Whenever. Did you use the bathroom or shower or check the mail?"

I rub my forehead. "Okay. I get your point. I'm the worst caretaker in the world."

"No. Not in the world. I'm sure there are worse out there," he says with a playful smile.

Theo waits for me to laugh, but he doesn't know that I'm just an empty house. I can't laugh or cry or love or hate. I just provide protection during the storm, and even at that, I'm failing. I should be condemned.

"Come on now," he says. "You're doing just fine. You did all the right things today. You stayed calm and called me. You just have to be one step ahead of your dad. Easier said than done, I know, but you'll get this down."

"So what happened today?" I ask. "He was hopped up on too much medication? Because it didn't seem that "way. He totally switched his life up with his brother's. Swore he didn't go to Vietnam and that he wasn't even in the Marines. He wasn't just stoned. He even talked about my mo… He just wasn't Arthur."

Theo tilts his head down so we're eye-level and gives me a smile so sad I almost believe we're in this together and he's not just here because it's his job.

"Bryce, I can't tell you how quickly your father's disease will progress, but I can tell you that it will, and it's going to be scary. This is a brutal disease, and it greatly affects everyone involved. You're going to need a support system of your own, girl. I can't stress how important that is. As much as I wish it weren't true, today was a sample of what's in store for Arthur, and for you. The only thing I can promise is that you'll get through it. Having said that, I think the medication really exacerbated things."

"It's too hard, Theo."

"Yeah, it is. Especially if you think about all of it at once. For now, take things one step at a time, and be vigilant about watching him. But he is doing better. Once the meds wore off a bit, he came to. He's still having some difficulty remembering certain things, but we expect to see that at this stage. Remember, patience is key. If you need to get on your knees and pray for some, that's what you do."

I nod my understanding, even though I feel more lost than I ever have.

"Can I ask something without you thinking I'm a total bitch?" I say.

"Hell yes! Anything."

"I'm assuming it'll cost me my firstborn to get him into a home, right?"

There's something in his expression. It's not just his sigh and the way his brows knit together, but it's the way he seems to pull away, as if my insensitivity has stunk up the space around me.

I sit up straight and look him in the eye. "I survived my father once. I don't know that I can do it again, Theo."

His expression eases and something softer exposes itself.

"Bryce, it'll cost you your first *and* second-born."

"Fuck."

"Fuck is right. There's assistance, and there're certainly some more inexpensive facilities, if you don't mind the thought of him living in his feces for days and forgetting to be fed. But sometimes it isn't about love or hate. Sometimes it's just about going to sleep at night with a clean conscience."

The truth in Theo's words is stretching my walls and making my frame creak. I have to open the windows and equalize the pressure before the whole damn place explodes.

"Okay," I say. "I'll work on building that support system."

He smiles and nudges my shoulder with his, though at his height, it's more like his elbow. "You got this, Ms. Fonda."

The vote of confidence is nice, even if I don't believe it.

"Should I go in there?" I ask. "I mean…how is he?"

"Like I said, he's better. Just do what you did before. Be there with him, keep calm, and don't take it personally, no matter what. I don't know if you read about sundowning, but evenings might prove more trying than days."

"I did. I've been reading a ton. But it all kind of goes out the window in the moment, you know?"

"Yeah. It will, until it won't," he says. "Oh, he's been repeating himself an awful lot, though, so be prepared for that. That can happen. Sometimes patients get flustered and impatient and say the same thing over and over. Other times they just seem to forget that they've said it at all, so they'll repeat themselves."

"What's he saying?"

Theo flits his hand through the air. "Nonsense, I'm sure. It usually is. Or maybe it's something about the war. Either way, don't let it spook you."

"Why? What is it?"

"He keeps going on about leaving someone behind, saying 'we killed him.' I'm sure it sounds scarier than it really is."

"Yeah," I stare at the hallway, "I'm sure."

CHAPTER 16

I stand outside the bathroom and listen for a thump. I've made eavesdropping on my father while he takes his morning shower a habit. I can't lose another parent to that damn bathtub. It's like one of those family plots in a cemetery. If Ma and Pa both bite the dust in there, I have to also.

Steam pours into the hallway when he opens the door. He looks at me sideways, mumbling something under his breath as I follow him back into his room and pick up his brace. We haven't discussed his episode yesterday. I don't even know if he's aware that it happened, and I'm sure as hell not going to bring it up, but the look on his face tells me we're sweeping our respective piles of dirt under the same carpet. He looks pensive, like he's walking on tacks.

"You okay?" I ask. "Is your pain bad today?"

He slowly rotates his head around. "No. Breaking your back tickles."

Sarcasm? Well done, Pops! But still…

"Don't exaggerate. You didn't break your back. You fractured it."

"And you'd know the difference? Tell me, how did you cope with your last spinal fracture, Bryce?"

My name sounds sharp on his tongue. I swallow my next words and let them kick at my insides. I know pain, but not much of the physical kind. I know the kind of pain that doesn't tarnish or fade with age. In a hundred years, I'll be dead, but it'll still be here, its presence felt in every place I stepped foot and in the echo of every word I spoke.

My dad winces and cranes his neck up.

"What is it, Dad? Just tell me so I can help you."

"The muscle…in my back. It's seizing up."

I put his brace down and pat the bed. "Come on. Sit down and lift up your shirt."

He frowns, pinches up his lips. He doesn't trust me, but more than that, he hates the back brace. Listening to me is worth another ten minutes out of its confines.

"Come on, Dad. We'll work on your back and see if we can get that muscle loose."

My first day of high school is a blur to me, but I remember going to gym. It was the first time us girls had to undress, and we all stood in front of our lockers, each of us nervously glancing at the girls across from us and to our sides—that elongated moment of hesitation before we succumbed to the inescapable reality of the situation. Shirts flew off at warp speed; pants dropped and were replaced with gym shorts before the brain could register what had happened. We all moved like rods of lightning, dodging the stares of the other girls.

My father's expression reminds me of Sarah Newton's. She stood to my right, too intimidated to move, her eyes darting away the moment she realized mine were on her. We all stood there in our matching blue gym shorts and white tees, averting our eyes while Sarah worked up the courage to get out of her skirt.

"Dad," I softly say, "there's no need to be in pain if you don't have to be."

His lips work at something his brain's not yet ready to say, and his brows knit together as he hesitantly lifts his arms above his head, moving at a snail's pace.

When he sits down, I reach my hands just under the bottom of his shirt and gently pull if off of him. The moment I see his back, a gasp catches in my throat and I bite my tongue. I'm standing to his side and can't see his face. I don't want to see his shame, and he doesn't want to see my shock. I've never seen my father without his shirt on before, and it never even occurred to me till now how strange that is.

"Where does it hurt?" I ask, but my words sound silly. There's pain written all over his skin. Some old, some new. Even the old wounds still ache, maybe not as much as they once did, but somewhere deeper, I'm sure. Scars like these plead for attention. They want to be remembered.

He doesn't say a word, doesn't look over his shoulder. He just points, and I place the meaty part of my palm on the area between his shoulder blades, where I can see a large knot just under the skin. His flesh feels foreign under my hands—the way its ripples and swirls are frozen in place, like an aerial shot of the ocean. It's shiny, like a candle, and smooth to the touch. I try to find a place where his skin remains unscathed, but the fire appears to have licked his entire torso clean. I glance at the waist of his pants and can't help but wonder. Suddenly I want to rip my mother's hair out for ever betraying him.

I gently knead at the spot on his back, only easing up when his muscles tighten and he quietly yelps. Otherwise he seems more at ease. His posture isn't so rigid, and the muscles along his jaw are no longer set. I lean over and see that his eyes are closing. The knot is working itself out, finally allowing him to take deep breaths.

"Did this happen over there? The scars?" I ask.

"Huh? Oh. Yeah. I, uh…I helped a buddy out of a bad spot."

A bad spot? I marvel at those who understate their good deeds and hide their super hero capes under their day-to-day clothes. Not that my father's a saint, but we all have our shining moments.

"Is that what you were talking about yesterday, when Theo was here?" I ask. "You kept telling him you had to leave someone behind. Was that your friend, Danton?"

"Goddammit, Bryce! Are you trying to help me or interrogate me? Just leave it the hell alone."

I pull my hands away and remind myself I shouldn't be stunned.

"Sorry," I say, wrestling my pride down my throat, even though it's dry and makes me want to gag. "I was just curious."

He finally takes a breath, but his shoulders remain tense.

"We need to start stretching more every day," I tell him, trying to peel back the tension. "Sitting in that brace is wreaking havoc on your muscles."

My eyes are drawn to a small spot on the back of his head, where his hair seems to be rubbed clean off. He's been lying around this house for a lot longer than just this week. It's no wonder his skin is beginning to drape around shrinking muscle.

"Once you're up and moving again, we'll start taking walks. Work all these kinks out."

My father stiffens, his head turning slightly over his shoulder. "That might be a while."

"I'm aware."

"Get off."

"What?"

"I want to lie down. Get off my bed. Now."

I move quickly, frowning at him. "What'd I do wrong?"

He leans back against his mountain of pillows and pulls the blanket up to his chest, trying to cover himself.

"You want help?" I ask. "I can help with your shirt."

"No. Just stop fucking babying me."

"If you're just upset, okay. But if I did something, tell—"

"How long do you plan on staying here?"

"I'm going to be around for a while. I know you don't like talking about it, but you're going to need my help."

"Bullshit. Once I'm through with those damn pills, I'll be good as new."

"This isn't about the pills. You've been cooped up in this house for how long? Weeks? Months? You aren't feeding yourself properly, and you're not getting any exercise. With everything you've got on your plate, you're going to have to bite the bullet and accept my help. Besides, it doesn't matter. I already told work, so…"

I can't read my father's expression. He seems to be fighting with himself. I almost look away from his intense stare, but the sudden spark in his eyes captivates me.

I prop my hands on my hips, which I hate doing. I feel like someone's mother, and I'm not ready for a kid. Especially not one that crashes his truck into garages and sets shit on fire.

"Lay it on me," I say. "Give it all you got, old man. You can scream and cuss, but I'm staying." He doesn't move, doesn't blink. "No arguing today? Cool. I'll take small victories."

"How dare you," he finally says.

"How dare me?" My God. Sometimes I want to put on a studded jacket and give him a bear hug. "How dare I drop my entire life to help you out?"

"Who do you suppose is going to support you now, Bryce? Me?"

I cackle, loud and unhinged. It's the kind of laughter that only happens in the midst of hilarity or in the throes of insanity, and nothing about this is hilarious.

I lean forward. "I didn't expect a damn thing from you, Dad. Not even a thank you. I have a little money saved. I had planned on maybe buying a house with it one day, or traveling the world. But who needs that? I guess I'll just squeeze all the culture I can out of the twenty-two-inch boob tube. Ain't life grand?"

"You're an idiot," he says, which astounds me. I didn't think we agreed on anything.

"You have no idea, Pops. This is just the tip of the iceberg, and you're preaching to the choir."

"So you're just going to walk away from everything?"

I shake my head, quietly laugh. "If by *everything* you mean my two dead-end jobs and the box I call home, then yes. I'm going to—"

"Two dead-end jobs? What're you talking about?"

The two deep crevices between his eyebrows merge together. He looks confused, which is no surprise. The man knows nothing about my life. Over the years I've told him only what he needs to know, which is more than I can say for him. I want to tell him I'm slowly dying from some insidious, incurable disease, but he doesn't learn lessons that easily.

Instead I say, "I work at a storage facility and a coffee shop downtown. By most people's standards, those would be considered dead-end jobs. But I have some savings from my paintings."

"You have a degree."

"Yeah. I know. I was there."

"Are you telling me you're not painting at all anymore?"

I look behind me, then back at him. Who is he talking to? Some kids worry about coming out to their parents, others fear what their parents will say when they learn that they have differing religious or political views. And then there's that young girl who hides her art in her closet and spends hours scrubbing the paint from under her nails so her father won't know that she's been sacrificing valuable time to flights of fancy.

My dad called me an idiot the day I told him I was going to art school. He's calling me an idiot now. He's a two-way road, with cliffs waiting in either direction.

"I'm ashamed of you," he says. "You're weak. I didn't raise my daughter to walk away so easily."

"You didn't raise me at all. I raised myself, and wouldn't you know it, I learned that walking away is pretty fucking easy. You should know, Dad. I watched you walk out so many times, I almost forgot what you looked like.

"Besides, why do you care whether or not I paint? You always said it was a waste of time."

The lines on his face draw down and his chest sinks in. I deflated him—poked a hole right in him and let all the hot steam out.

"I never hated..." He balls his fist, then releases it. "I want to write in the notebook."

"Now? If you're gonna to tell me about a time you chopped some guy's face off or ate somebody, I'll pass."

He sits perfectly still, the stern expression frozen on his face. He clearly pronounces each word. "Get the notebook now."

I roll my eyes. I should've outgrown that by now, I know, but I'm sure the answer to why my father's so difficult is back there in my brain somewhere.

"Here," I say, grabbing the notebook and plopping my ass firmly in the chair. "I'm all ears. Oh, sorry. Don't want you getting too excited. I mean, I'm listening."

He reprimands me with a quick scowl before getting right to the topic. "I want to tell you about the first time I met your mother."

"Don't I know this already?"

"If you shut your trap long enough for me to talk, you might just find out."

I pick up the pen and open to the next page. "Fine. I love a good tragedy."

He takes a deep breath, as if readying himself to dive into a pool.

"I first saw your mother on the pier, the one by the library. The edge of the lake was beginning to freeze, and half the pier was covered in a thin sheet of ice. Your uncle Jerry and I ditched school that day and went down there to have a smoke.

"We walked out to the water, and I slipped right on my ass. Went down like a brick. Next thing I know, this girl's laughing at me. I hated that laugh the minute I heard it, because it made me feel small and reminded me of your uncle's laugh. He was just a shrimp still, with these big, wobbly knees and a high-pitched voice. Our dad used to call him Jenny whenever it cracked.

"Anyway, when I got to my feet, I had every intention of turning around and getting the hell out of there, but then she asked me if I was okay, and I froze. Your uncle slapped me on the arm. 'Say something, stupid.' I couldn't tell what exactly he was seeing, but he was in a trance. When I looked up, I got it."

"Love at first sight?" I quietly ask.

"No. It was something else. Something I still can't quite explain. What you don't know is that your mother was out there with her art class. There were easels everywhere, and all these girls wearing smocks. Your mother was standing there in front of this painting that looked nothing like the rest of the girls'. Everyone else was painting the lake and the ducks, but your mother's painting…it looked like another planet. I thought it was the most beautiful thing I'd ever laid eyes on, until I looked at her. She was magnificent. Everything just kind of melted into her beauty, like she could command everything around her and change it at will."

I fight against the tightness in my throat and the sting of my eyes. Listening to my father's words is like witnessing the birth of a child. It's painful and moving, and it stirs in me something I like to pretend doesn't exist.

Looking down at my hands, I wonder if they look like my mother's, if they move like hers did. I never saw her paint, never even knew she had any interest in art. She didn't have time for frivolous things like that. Not when she spent every moment plummeting in and out of various depths of hell, only cresting the top to take a breath when she was so high that she couldn't remember her own name, or that apparently she had once been a diamond as well.

"I didn't know she painted," I say. "I wish I could've met that girl."

The circles under my father's eyes are dark, as if talking about my mother is literally pulling the life out of him. He bites down hard, snapping his emotions in half, and sniffs a couple times. I'm glad. I'm not ready to see him cry. He sees it as a sign of weakness, and right now I need him to be strong, because I feel like I'm made of things that crumble.

"She had lots of dreams, too," he says. "Just like you. She also wanted to move to a big city. She had so much passion. Just being around her got you believing you could be anything you wanted to be. She was a fool. A lovely, optimistic fool, and she had me the moment we met. That's why I didn't want to get involved with her. You know what happens to something special the moment people get their hands on it? It changes, becomes ordinary. Do you remember those yellow flowers Scotty used to pick in the back yard, and you'd yell at him and tell him they weren't going to be pretty anymore?"

I squeeze the pen tightly in my hand and look down at the notebook, quickly wiping away the tears that fall and smear the ink where I wrote half my brother's name before I couldn't write any more. He said it. He actually said it.

"I remember," I whisper. "I just didn't think you did."

"There's a lot you think I don't remember. Just because I get confused about things sometimes doesn't "mean I don't remember anything. I remember those because they reminded me of your mother, of who she used to be. I didn't want to pluck her from the life she had planned, because I knew I couldn't give her what she needed. I knew it the day Jerry pushed me to ask her out. Even the day we married, I knew I was caging a bird, but I was selfish. She was too big for this place, but she loved me. You can see where staying here got her, Bryce. That woman was…everything. She was the whole world, bottled up, and anyone lucky enough to know her knew it. Then she just faded away. I couldn't give her what she needed, so she found it, and then it killed her."

Don't be like me, Bryce. Don't ever be like me.

Suddenly my mother's words have meaning. Maybe through the fog, she knew more than I gave her credit for. But still… "I'm not her, Dad. I'm not some junkie—"

"Don't call her that, goddammit! Don't you ever call her that!"

His fury comes in a wave that leaves as quickly as it came. The redness of his cheeks transition from cherry-red to pink.

"Sorry," I tell him. "But I'm not. I just want you to know that. I'm not her."

"Aren't you? You're back here, and for what?"

"For you. To help."

"That's a crock of shit."

I sit straight, pulling away from his words. It takes everything in me not to stick my fingers in my ears and stick out my tongue in defiance of his ugly little truths.

Nee-ner, nee-ner. I can't hear you.

I grasp at the only truth I can stake my claim on. "I'm here for you, obviously. You think I woke up Monday morning and thought, 'You know, I'm tired of all this "freedom. I think I'll move back home and live with Arthur, 'cause he's swell'?"

"No, Bryce. I know you don't want to be here, but that boy cushions the blow."

"Jesus, Dad! *That boy* you're not so subtly referring to hasn't been a part of my life for years and you know it."

"Just remember why that is. Remember who walked out. If you think he's grown a pair of balls since then, you're as foolish as your mother was. Giving up your damn life for him. Coming back here, rotting away in this house, using me as an excuse. How the hell do you hold that head of yours so high? You're gonna sit here and watch me waste away, just hoping he's attracted to the scent of your desperation?"

"Fuck you," I shout. "Is it so hard for you to accept help that you have to turn this into something ugly and make me the bad guy so you can feel better about why I'm here? I'm not here because you have Alzheimer's, right? I'm not here to wipe your ass once you can't do it on your own, and to clean the slop from your mouth when you forget how to chew. I'm just here for a man. That's a lot more convenient, isn't it, Dad? Tell yourself what you have to, so long as you don't have to face the fact that two women gave up their dreams to be here with you."

My words hang suspended in air. My heart wants to pick them from the space between my father's ears and bury them somewhere where they'll never get out, but my anger sucks up all the oxygen in the room and keeps them afloat.

Every kid fantasizes about unleashing on their parents, serving up on a big fat platter what was served to them. For years I've wanted to force-feed my father the ingredients to his own recipe, imagining the way he would choke on his own hateful bits. All that time I imagined his face, it looked eerily similar to what I'm seeing now. His mouth agape, his eyes rounded in shock, and my untethered rage reflected in them. But in all those years, I overlooked my empathy. I forced it into the corner and made it sit on its hands while I played in my world of make-believe and taught my father lessons I fantasized would turn him into the man he should've been. Now, in the stark reality of the moment, the regret is already invading my brain, planting eggs in every fold of tissue.

My mother made my father weak. My father makes me caustic.

Don't be like me, Bryce.

"I think I'd like to be alone now," my father says. His voice is solemn, far away.

"I'm sorry, Dad. I didn't mean..." But he's gone. Done. Probably trying to figure out how I infiltrated his fortress. Kings never see their own weaknesses.

I walk away hating the smell of lumber and cursing the scarlet letter I was branded with the day I met Jackson. People point and stare at the Humpty Dumpty girl who had a great fall, and the boy who didn't even try to put her back together again. Even if they don't point and stare, even if they don't know my name, they can see that I'm not whole. Long ago, I gave that boy my heart, and the selfish prick never gave it back. He's had it in a wooden box for eleven years, only taking it out when I come looking to take back what's rightfully mine. If I let myself think about why he won't give it back, I'll lose all the other parts of myself I need to keep breathing.

My phone chimes. A new text. And wouldn't you fucking know it? Jackson can sense that the heart in the box is growing hard and weary, and he reaches in and touches it, making it pound furiously against its confines.

I read the six words slowly: "Go on a date with me."

Time to batten down the hatches, board the windows, and fill the perimeter with sandbags. I'm stuck here. I can't flee this storm, but I'm also not going to stand in the eye of it and wait for the other side to swallow me whole.

"No," I text him. And then I cry.

CHAPTER 17

I take a selfie with the plaid old-man couch and text it to Shana. "Does it suit me? I hope so, 'cause I'll be buried in it."

She asks what I'm talking about, and I tell her about my dad, but not the part about me staying indefinitely. Shana's tears would cost me too much today. My phone rings a second later.

"I'm so sorry, Bryce," she immediately says. "I know you have your differences, but still. How're you holding up?"

"I don't know. I think I'm in denial about all of it. Being back here, my dad's diagnosis…Jackson."

"Jackson?" she asks.

The twat does nothing to hide the uptick in her voice. She knows our hearts have gone to battle with each other, yet she holds out hope like a giddy schoolgirl that one day Jackson and I will marry and make all the pretty babies. She's been planning our wedding since ninth grade, when she used to put his name on all three slots when we played MASH.

"Don't get excited," I tell her. "I'm on a strict no-Jackson diet."

"How's that working for you?"

"I don't know, how'd camping with *Fletcher* go?"

"Whatever," she laughs. "You're a brat."

"And you're a butthole."

"Seriously, though," her voice changes, "how're you coping?"

"I'm taking it as it comes. I'm better than I would've thought but worse than I would've hoped. I mean, I'm not carving pictures in my skin, so that's a plus."

"Bryce!" she says in a mothering tone. "Not funny. Don't talk that way."

"Sorry, Mom."

"I'm serious. I worry about you up there. I miss the hell out of you, too. What are you doing for your birthday? Can I come up and bring you a party? Or at least a bottle of wine?"

I can already sense Shana's disappointment. She knows me well enough to know that I need time to process, and that I like my birthday like a high-pressure enema. At this point, growing another year older isn't exactly a cause for celebration. It's a time for deep reflection and a bottle of something that'll leave me aching the next morning.

"You're sweet, and I adore you. But no thanks," I say. "I just need to be alone for this one."

"I understand. What about next weekend? Can I come up and see you then? I'll bring you something from Dahlia's."

"Throw in that bottle of cheap wine and you've got yourself a date," I say, but only because I love her, and I love cheap wine, and because Dahlia's deserts are better than a slow screw against a wall.

"All right, birthday girl. It's a date."

I say goodbye and get off the phone before Shana has a chance to ask how many bridesmaids I want at my wedding…you know, in the land of make believe, where Jackson and I say our vows under the *Twilight* wedding arch, because we live in Washington State and Shana has the romantic maturity of an eighth-grade girl. She still thinks there's a pair of glass slippers out there with her name on them, while I know Converse will be by my side till my dying day. Still, Shana's an angel. You can't find a more loyal friend.

In truth, nothing would've pleased me more on my birthday than to listen to the ramblings of my childhood friend, but I could feel a confession creeping up my throat, and I'm not ready to tell her all the nasty things I said to my father. Shana's too sweet to ever speak that way to anyone, too innocent to grasp all the complexities of my relationship with my dad, and too fortunate to ever be in my shoes. Had I told her about that, and how I turned down a date with Jackson, she would've had a full estrogen meltdown, and I don't have the strength to take care of one more person.

I pick up my phone and scroll through all the texts Jackson has sent me since he called on Monday to tell me about my dad's accident. Look further back than that and you wouldn't know he exists. There are no other texts, no other calls, no other emails. Nada. Before Monday, I had a completely clean slate. Or my phone did, anyway. Now his name sits there, mingling with my friends and co-workers. But his is that one name. We've all got one. It's the name you don't just see but you feel. It's the reason for that momentary catch in your breath and the pesky little butterfly that tries to kill itself by banging against the walls of your stomach. It demands attention like no other, because it's not just a name. It's a story, and if you're lucky enough, you get to be a part of it.

"No," I say, slamming my phone down. My dad is wrong about me. He has to be wrong about me. I hope he's wrong about me.

I smell my arm to make sure I still smell like my body soap and not desperation, but maybe I wouldn't even know what it smells like. Like people who smell like mothballs. They're so used to it they have no idea why people cringe when they walk by. I'd try to wash it off my skin, but this is a smell that comes from deep within, like garlic after a night of heavy Italian food. I sniff again and smell my father instead, and something tugs at my heart.

She was the whole world, bottled up.

Every girl goes her whole life wanting to hear a man speak about her the way my father spoke about my mother. It's as if by professing it aloud, he brought a pulse back to the house. I can feel his love for her, like a third member of the home. It solidifies my conception, but it pulls at the seams of my world. I'm afraid to walk around in case I bump into it and bruise its soft flesh.

I need a distraction. Something stupid to watch so I can't think about the fact that I feel like I've gone into early retirement.

I get off the couch and kneel in front of the small cabinet housing my father's VHS tapes. Yes. Even better. Nothing like watching something old and grainy, with poor sound quality and a disastrous storyline to brighten up your evening. That's what movies are: escape methods.

The tapes are usually alphabetized and lined in neat rows, but now they're scattered everywhere, like victims of a deranged toddler. One isn't even in its sleeve. I pick it up and just then realize maybe I shouldn't be scrounging around an old, single man's movies. I swear, if I see anything starring Bambi or Chad or Cinnamon, I'm going to stare directly into the sun with a pair of binoculars.

I flip the tape over and just see a date. Something whispers in my head, the tip of my tongue grows heavy with the answer.

"Ah, yes," I whisper. It's my parents' wedding date. Just beneath that tape is one titled: "Scotty on Bike." I remember holding the camera as my brother tottered along the road, weaving dangerously from side to side as his little feet kicked at the pedals and the sun glinted off the spokes of his wheels. But I'm guessing my father doesn't. He obviously got into these tapes for a reason. Maybe that's why. He was there, in the background, urging my brother on, but maybe he only remembers that he should remember it. Just like his wedding day. I wonder if these special memories have settled at the bottom of his mind like sediment in a murky lake.

I turn the TV on and push the wedding tape into the VCR and wait for the mechanical munching that tells you it's been swallowed. Most people my age don't know about the power of channel three. Punch the number into the clicker and wait for a magical snowstorm that will take you to the land of long, long ago.

After a moment, the screen goes black and then flickers on, and I can see my mother sitting in a chair, her modest white dress stretching left and right as wavy lines pass through the image in succession.

I sit crisscrossed in front of the TV just as I did when I was twenty years younger and a whole lot wiser, and I watch my mother. Her red hair hangs in long coils over her narrow shoulders. Her face is angelic and innocent, contrasting with the distracting splash of red painted on her lips. She looks like a virgin. Naïve, new, untouched, only I know she wasn't, because my dad plucked her from the ground and made her an ordinary thing. I wish she'd turn around so I could see her stem and compare it to mine.

She's the picture of a young, blushing bride, but when my father reaches for her hand, it seems to accentuate the heaviness in her red-rimmed eyes, and I tell myself I'm just imagining the hesitation in her body language. When my dad speaks, she doesn't look at him, and when he smiles, she flinches, as if deflecting his advances.

"What was going on in your head, Mom?" I say.

She doesn't look like the optimistic fool my father described. She looks like a woman who knew her misery would outlive her happiness. She looks like my mom.

CHAPTER 18

One of my eyes is glued shut with gunk; the other narrowly opens, and I scan the room. The sun's barely up, but still, it's up. That means I slept in. Even my body is fighting against today. It would rather stay tucked in the warm cocoon of sheets than face its twenty-sixth year of existence. Fuck you, January twelfth. And fuck you, early crow's feet, and big, uber fuck you to my barren uterus and my excitable ovaries that seem to fill my brain with a lethal concoction of hormones and stupidity whenever I see tiny humans and their adorable, chunky thighs and pudgy sausage fingers. And fuck babies. Fuck 'em all.

I sit up in bed and groan, stretching my neck all around, and look at the clock. It's almost eight in the morning. I should've had my dad's breakfast started by now, but he'll probably just throw it at me for being such a brat yesterday. Look who has egg all over her face now? Doesn't matter. Men gotta eat—women gotta cook.

I throw on my old gray robe and a pair of thick, fuzzy socks that make my feet look like Frodo's and head for the kitchen, but the smell of biscuits and gravy hit me the second I open my door. It's a fitting smell in the morning. Fatty and homey and American. If your family doesn't warm your heart, the cholesterol and plaque will. No wonder it's my favorite breakfast food.

My dad has his back to me. His jerky movements make the task of cooking look daunting, but he chips away at it despite the back brace. I never took my father for a cook, but he appears to be at home, dare I say, free. That probably has more to do with being out of his padded, horizontal prison than anything else.

Was his menu choice a coincidence, or did he actually remember what today is? I stand at the bar and clear my throat. "Can I help with anything?"

He stops stirring for a moment but then picks back up without looking at me. "No. I just want to finish this." Now he does look over his shoulder, but he still doesn't see me. "Like you said, small victories."

I nod my understanding even though he's not looking. Sometimes you just need to know you can conquer something. Even if it's small, and even if you'll fail at it tomorrow, today's what counts.

I watch my father put the finishing touches on his meal. I can tell by his movements that his pain is worsening, but this is no longer about eating. It's a fight. That's when you know life is getting real. When survival is no longer a matter of instinct but a battle of both the mind and the body. I'm watching a prized fighter go his last few rounds, and the winner-winner-chicken-dinner is going to get a hot plate of white flour and congealed cream and pig fat.

My dad turns around, risking a whip of a glance at me. I want to say I'm sorry again. It's my birthday, and I should be able to do what I want, but his eyes pass over mine so briefly, and I know what that means. Maybe he forgot what I said, or maybe he hates me. Maybe he'll die never hearing my apology, and then I'll be forced to spend the rest of my days listening to emo music while writing "I'm sorry, Daddy" over and over in a tear-stained diary that I'll mail in an envelope marked "To Heaven." Or maybe fuck that.

"Dad, I really am sorry for what I said yesterday. You hurt me, so I hurt you. It was petty, and I should've gone about it differently, but...I guess I'm not that mature."

He stares past me, and I wonder if he sees the dried yolk on the wall. "Mature enough to apologize," he says, then gives a quick half-nod.

He puts a couple biscuits on his plate and spoons gravy over them, then stops and motions to the empty plate beside his. "I, uh...made too much on accident, so eat if you want."

My smile goes unnoticed, but I know what this means. These biscuits are a peace offering/birthday gift of sorts, and who the hell am I to turn them down?

I stand at the bar with my dad because it's easier to stand and eat than it is for him to position himself in a chair. The man doesn't fold. Never has, never will.

He takes a bite; I take a bite. He takes a sip of coffee; I take a sip of water. I watch him while he eats; he pretends I'm not there. He needs my brain; I need his biscuits and gravy. Let's raise a fork to symbiotic relationships.

"It's my birthday," I tell him with a mouthful of food and gravy pasted to my cheek.

He finally looks at me, no smile, no frown, and says, "I'm sorry."

And then I smile.

~

Water runs cold here during this time of year. When I brush my teeth and rinse my mouth, the icy water hits my molars and I nearly jump. "Goddangit!"

Sometimes I want to move to the sun, just for that sheer moment of bliss right before my corneas liquefy and my skin turns to paint. I'm always cold. I'm also always anemic. Tried for years to remedy it, but that's what I get for bleeding like a gutted pig every month. Silly ol' me.

I toss my toothbrush in the cup on the counter and throw my hair in a messy bun high on my head. I don't have any makeup on, and my t-shirt has dried varnish all over it, but I feel like me. This is my skin—low maintenance and understated. I've learned not to get dolled up. I can't pull it off without feeling like a kid who raided her mother's closet. Converse and black boots were made for girls like me. Manolos and Louis Vuittons were made for women with Dom Perignon in their veins and platinum in their eyes. Cut them and they bleed gold, but they don't feel it because they're made of Italian marble. You can't see where they break because they've got sculptors to mend their wounds and smooth their blemishes. Me? I wear scars on my legs and sorrow in my eyes.

~

My dad's still standing at the bar, reading the newspaper. I think it makes him feel normal, like maybe all this will blow away in the next storm and leave behind only the leftover stench of a bad memory.

"How're you feeling today?" I ask.

"Fine."

There's that word, "fine." He might as well have not answered. But I won't pester him. I'm friends with the word, and while it might seem shallow and aloof to some, I find that we get along famously. I don't even mind that it's friends with my dad. I'm not jealous like that.

"Good," I say. "Is there anything you want to do today?"

"I want to read my paper."

Back and forth I rock from heel to toe, my hands in my pockets, my lips pinched to the side. Message received, loud and clear.

"Okay," I say, turning around to go to my room, but then the doorbell rings and my dad and I look at each other. I'm the maid now. This is what I do. Answer doors and phones, cook and clean. But this is still his house. I take a step back and watch. The moment he steps away from the bar, he curses under his breath and grabs his back.

"I got it," I tell him. "Just stay there."

I open the door and see Jackson standing there.

"Ah, fuck," I say, and immediately slam the door shut. It occurs to me that this won't make the gorgeous problem on the porch go away, but it seemed like a pretty good idea at the time.

"Who the hell's that?" my dad asks.

"It's Little Shit."

Suddenly the old man can move with the gusto of a virgin boy on prom night. He barges in front of me, nearly knocking me over, and opens the door.

"What?" is all he says to Jackson, and my bones immediately freeze. I can reject Little Shit, but I don't like the idea of anyone else doing it. I've earned that right.

"Dad?" I say over his shoulder, trying to interject, but I hear Jackson say something, and then the door opens and my father lets him in even though shit stains carpet and gets stuck in its fibers.

Jackson steps inside and my dad positions himself next to me. We stand there in a triangle, both my father and I waiting for Jackson to say something.

"Happy Birthday," he finally says, and my dad snort-laughs.

"Thanks," I say. "I appreciate you coming over here, but do you need something? I know no one's supposed to say it out loud, but this is weird. My dad refers to you as Little Shit, if that's any indication of where his feelings for you are."

"Yeah, I heard through the door," Jackson says. "I was hoping it was a term of endearment, but I'm guessing not."

My dad doesn't bat an eye, nor does he take them off Jackson. I know that look. I've employed this tactic many times myself. He's mind-killing my ex-boyfriend so hard right now. Between Arthur and me, Jackson's probably met every tragic ending the most nefarious mind could fathom.

"Jackson," I say, giving him the what-the-hell's-your-problem look. "Seriously, dude. What do you want?"

"I'm here to give you your birthday gift. I know you hate presents, so I thought of something you can't take back. Something you actually *need*."

Bonne Belle Lip Smackers and *Teen Beat*. Jackson's words take me back to drunken texts and needs that were never met, and heat rises in my cheeks. Using my own words against me, and I know I'm turning a shade of "Not In Front of My Dad" pink, but my girly giddiness grabs hold of the room and rattles the crotchety old man to my right.

"Bryce!" my dad shouts.

"What?" I say, a little too loud, a little too fast, a little too catch-a-grip, Bryce. But all the heat has to go somewhere.

"Seriously, Jackson. What is it?" I ask.

Jackson hides a smile that still reaches his eyes. I fucking hate his smile. Maybe my dad will knock his teeth out and he won't be so pretty anymore. A girl can hope.

Jackson looks at my dad, then back at me. "If it's okay, I'd like to give you a day off. Take a drive downtown, see your friends. Whatever. Just take some time for yourself. That's the best gift I can offer. If Mr. Price here doesn't mind, I can keep him company and help out."

Tupac just offered to hang with Biggie, and I'm over here waiting for Christopher Wallace to pull out his gat and start shooting up the place. I don't know if Jackson's that stupid or that brave, but he should know he's no longer dealing with a man with a full deck of cards.

My dad straightens his back, raises his chin. Jackson relaxes and places his hand on my father's shoulder.

"I think we can agree that Bryce has been working hard," Jackson tells him. "I promise not to get in the way."

Looking at my dad reminds me of the time I watched a rabbit get eaten by a snake. I remember its red eyes and the way they protruded from its skull as the snake hugged it tight, tight, tight.

My father's brows furrow and his jaw squares. "Fine," he growls, now looking Jackson square in the eye, like he just accepted a challenge.

"What the hell is going on with you two?" I ask.

Jackson's Adam's apple thrusts up and down once. His eyes are kind, but they, just like my father's, hide something.

"Nothing, Bryce," he says. "Just go get ready and have a good day."

"Dad?" I say. "Are you sure about this?"

"Yes. Just go."

CHAPTER 19

I blend into a sea of people, basking in my obscurity. I'm standing in a park at Pike Place, staring down at the Alaskan Way Viaduct. Puget Sound is all sorts of beautiful today. That thing I can hardly remember the name of is shining in the sky, making my eyes water and my skin feel warm. Puget Sound is the pretty girl in school the boys look past you to see. Only I don't mind, because she's all mine, and no one else can touch her. Or she used to be all mine.

I need to go to my apartment and grab more things, but I can't bring myself to face my four walls. It might be a shoebox, but it always meant freedom. My wings had just started to grow back, and now I'm trading them in for handcuffs, and they're not even the fuzzy pink ones. They're cold and pinch my skin.

I hold on to the ledge that looks over the viaduct, my knuckles turn white. I don't want to let go, don't want to trade in the sea air for the stench of cigars and the sounds of the History Channel. I could always jump in the sound and wait till my skin turns as gray-blue as the water. Then no one would find me. Or I could just lie right here and let the earth eventually swallow me whole. I'd love to see inside of this majestic beauty. Now I know what it's like to be a man.

I pull out my phone and text Jackson.

"Seriously, are you two all right?"

He responds. "Is there a reason we wouldn't be?" Then he sends a winky face. "Relax, Ms. Price. We're okay. Enjoy your birthday and stop texting. If you wanted my company, you should've said yes to a date."

Ugh. It's really a shame I'm not attracted to women. Life would be so much easier. Then again, maybe I'd be stuck listening to someone's feelings all day and wiping their tears away with the sleeve of my flannel button-down while we listen to "I'm Kissing You" by Des'ree for the hundredth time. Maybe I'll just go buy my cat now and let it live at my dad's house. It'll wear a pink collar and I'll name it Pink and I'll paint its nails pink, and my father will throw his food at it because the cat's a boy, and I made him gay with all my pink this and pink that.

I scroll through Facebook and see that most of my friends are out enjoying the sun today, even if it is only thirty-one degrees. Our bodies are craving sun like a lost soul craves a savior. It'd be easy to meet up and have a drink, but then that would mean breaking up with them, which is really what's going to happen the minute they learn I'm moving up north, which to them is like Kansas or some shit. They'll be too afraid to lose their membership to the Cool Kids of Seattle Club to come visit me. Sleepy towns remind them that they'll grow old one day, but Seattle never ages. Its brittle cracks just get filled in with the anointed blood of metrosexuals and yuppies. I'm not hating. I'm just bitter I have to relinquish my membership.

I shove my lifeline to Jackson in my pocket and turn around. I'm not ready to let go of my city on the sound, but the call of the wild is overriding her siren song.

Just as I look in my purse for my car keys, I bump into someone that smells like the Macy's cologne counter. When I look up, I want to run in the other direction. This is what I get for wearing no makeup and throwing my gypsy hair in a bun.

"Bryce Price, right?" Dr. Hot Pants asks, but he's not really asking. He said my name too fast, smiling at the silly rhyme before he even finished saying it.

"Hello, Dr. Brackett. You look different out of your white coat."

Doctors aren't supposed to go where you go and shop where you shop. It's like when you were a kid and you'd see your fifth-grade teacher at the store.

"Yeah." He looks down at his vintage-style bomber, designed to make him look like a rebel, only it smells like old money. "The white coat makes me look respectable. Please, call me Jonathan."

He'll stay Dr. Hot Pants to me. He's no Jonathan. Jonathans come over and fix your leaky faucet for you and buy you peonies and take care of your pets while you're out of town.

A polite smile is all I can offer. He's far too good-looking to take seriously, and I'm too stressed out to fluff his feathers.

"Well, it was nice seeing you," I say, turning to leave.

"Did you get the results?"

I turn back around and stare at him until it dawns on me. "Oh, no. I've actually been really busy. I completely forgot. I never got a call."

"It's probably in your mail. We mail the results if they're normal."

"So no cancer?" I ask. Had I found this out on Monday, I would've been relieved. Now I can't imagine ever having worried about Walker. It seems so small in comparison to everything going on now.

"No cancer. All clear."

I let that sink in for a moment and then say, "It was shaped like Texas. My mole. It looked like the Lone Star State. Now that I know it wasn't cancer, I wish I'd kept it. I even named him."

"Him?"

Dr. Hot Pants is hiding a smile. He probably thinks I'm being cute and quirky. Probably never had a patient name their mole and speak about it affectionately. Next he'll tell me how different I am, and that he's never met a girl like me before. Then I'll struggle to come up with something witty and instead say the most ordinary thing in the world, in turn leaving him confused and enamored. If my world were intact, I'd be crippled by his smile and silenced by his flirty eyes and verging on obnoxious cologne. But today I don't give a shit. My blues lead the way for carelessness, and carelessness sometimes looks a lot like confidence.

"Yes. Walker was a him," I say.

"You named your mole Walker?"

I nod. "After Walker, Texas Ranger. What else was I supposed to name him?"

His smile widens and he squints, as if trying to figure out where I fit. "I've never had a patient name their mole before. You're…"

"Different?" I say.

"Yes. Definitely different."

And there it is.

"Not that that's a bad thing," he adds. "It's good. I'm going to go out on a limb and say better than good."

And you're not different, Dr. Brackett. You're every cliché. You walked right off the pages of *GQ* and started talking without realizing you're paper-thin and the sun's out. I can see right through you to the homeless woman dancing by herself on the corner. People watch us and think I'm talking to an apparition. But I show you attention because you're beautiful to look at, and sometimes a man like you needs to talk to a girl like me to remember that real things still exist between your glossy, high-end pages.

"So this means I don't need a follow-up?" I ask.

"Right. This also means I'm not your doctor anymore, so it'd be okay to have dinner with you, if you'd do me the honor of escorting me on a date."

The heat rising up my neck is just from the sun beating down on my face. At least that's what I tell myself.

A swift kick in the ass would be too mild a punishment for what I do next, but then I tell myself that this is the last birthday I'll have with my own bed. By now, it's probably forgotten the shape of my body and the smell of my loneliness. It should easily mold to Dr. Brackett's back. No need to worry about mine. I'll be in the driver's seat. I'm still the girl you can leave parked outside your house without worrying about someone stealing her, but if we turn the lights off, maybe we can both pretend I'm a Maserati.

"It's my birthday," I say. "I'm leaving later tonight, but if you want to take me out before then, I'm game. So long as there's cake involved."

"I think I can manage that," he says, with a shit-eating grin. "Your call. Fancy or casual?"

I don't need to ask to know that he doesn't usually ask his dates this question. Casual dinners in jeans and t-shirts is one of the perks of dating a lowbrow princess.

I purse my lips while I think. "Fancy," I finally say. "Dazzle me."

He steps closer and runs one finger along my pinky. "I intend to."

Fuck. And I don't even own heels.

CHAPTER 20

The woman looking back at me in my oval bathroom mirror is a stranger to me. I can see in her eyes that she doesn't know me, either. I watch her, trying to familiarize myself with her shocking appearance. Inside, I'm still casual girl, with my torn skinny jeans and black turtleneck sweater. The woman in the mirror would pass me on the street and at best glare at me from the corner of her eye in contempt of having to share the sidewalk with me.

I pull out all the stops. I'm wearing my one and only little black dress—long on the sleeves, high on the neck, short on the thighs. Should go well with the respectable fuck-me heels I bought downtown. For Dr. Hot Pants's sake, I hope he's into necrophilia. Before the night is over, it's entirely possible I'll kill myself in these shoes.

I put the finishing touches on my makeup while trying not to look at myself. Easier said than done. The man-eater in the mirror is giving me second thoughts about tonight, and the packed suitcases I see behind her carry within them my entire life's plan. Open them up and nothing but ashes will pour out.

"Later," I tell myself. "I'll think about that later."

Tonight is about letting go and playing dress-up and being someone other than the sad girl who loves the man made of lumber in a house full of pink. Tonight is about regrettable decisions and meaningless physical contact that leaves you emptier than it found you.

Deeper, deeper, Dr. Brackett. I think I still have an ounce of self-worth left.

I snap my compact shut and toss it in my travel bag. Looking around my little blue bathroom, I realize how cheery it is. I never saw it before, but now it clashes with my black dress and black fuck-me heels and smoky black eye shadow. The periwinkle walls seem to be closing in on me, trying to birth the dark intruder. I'm no longer welcome here, no longer a part of the scenery. My home can sense that I've betrayed it.

~

I throw my things in the back of my car and wait in front of my apartment, where I told Dr. Hot Pants I'd be. If I let him upstairs now, we'll have each other for dinner, and then I really will be empty. I feel like a pit that needs to be filled. I want to eat rich foods till I'm sick and look across the table at a beautiful man that means nothing to me but sure does hit the spot. I feel more alone than I've ever felt, and I want to surround myself with pretty things that give the illusion of happiness.

He pulls up in his Maserati. Jesus Christ. I'm going to feel foolish just getting in the thing. Maybe it will spit me right out and drive off without me.

Dr. Hot Pants gives me a *Pretty Woman* moment as he rolls down the window and smiles at me, only I know he'll open the door for me. I'm a lowbrow princess, but you can't take the highbrow manners out of the rich boy.

"Good evening, beautiful," he says, getting out of the car and walking around to open my door. I don't want to be unwrapped in a restaurant, so I take off my long red coat and toss it on the seat before I sit down.

The good doctor stutters. "You, uh…look amazing."

I like the way he looks at me. It's cheap and meaningless, but he wants the same thing I do, and in some small way, that's enough for me right now. He's already seen my body, my hidden tattoos, my scars. I've already felt his touch. Our pieces should fit together nicely.

"So where will you take me to be dazzled?" I ask when he sits down and pulls into the lane.

"Will Canlis do the trick, or is that too obvious?"

"It's ridiculously obvious. But no one's ever taken me there, so I say we do it. But you have to order for me."

When he frowns and smiles at the same time, it stirs something unholy in me. Sexy bastard.

"You want me to order for you? Isn't that a faux pas? I didn't know men were allowed to do that anymore."

"They are if a woman asks. I'm assuming you've eaten there. You know what's good. At that price, I'll feel obligated to eat whatever I order, even if it's horrible. So you pick."

His laughter startles me. It sounds too wild and carefree in such a pretentious car.

"Are you always this honest, or did I catch you on an off day?" he asks.

"Maybe it's not that I'm particularly honest. Maybe it's that you're used to a different variety of women."

When he stops at a light and looks into my eyes, I don't look away. I won't lose myself in them or forget who I'm supposed to be. In that regard, he's no danger.

I reach over and touch his bottom lip with the tip of my finger. "Cat got your tongue, Dr. Brackett?"

"No. Just looking forward to getting to know you, Bryce. I'm thinking I might really like your variety."

And then he kisses me in that way a man who truly wants to know the taste of a woman kisses you, and I realize this is unsafe…for him.

~

I hesitate before pulling into my father's driveway. Two men are waiting inside the house for me, each wanting or needing a part of me I don't want to give. At least Dr. Brackett understood the value of my time, and he paid handsomely for it. I think the bill at Canlis cost more than my rent.

I get my suitcases out of the car and roll them up to the front door. I hate that damn red door. Its happiness doesn't match its surroundings. It's lipstick on a pig. Instead, this place should have bars over the windows and solid metal slabs for doors.

When I reach for the doorknob, Jackson opens it, and I already know it's been a long day for him. He looks how I've felt the last week.

"Oh," is all he says when he sees me. His eyes run the length of my body, stopping on my heels. "I see you took my advice and had a good time."

I wrestle my luggage through the door and give him a warning glance.

"Here," he says. "Let me get those."

I follow him in and point to the hallway. "They're fine right there. Thanks."

"This isn't all of it, right?"

"No. I'll rent a truck soon. I just need a minute to come to grips before I make it final."

"I can always help. I've got a perfectly good tru—"

"Jackson." I put my hand up to stop him. "I've got it."

My words wound him. My distance hurts him. He shrinks back, puts his hands in his pockets.

"So how'd things go?" I ask. "I really appreciate you doing this today. I needed some time away."

He nods. "It went as well as it could. We played some cards, had a pretty good talk. He was in quite a bit of pain towards the end of the day, so it got a little dicey, but nothing I couldn't handle. He took his pill and conked out at about ten."

"Yeah. Sorry about that. I didn't mean to get home so late. I should've been here."

He looks at his watch. "Oh. I didn't realize the time. I fell asleep on the couch and then heard you pull up. I guess that means you really did have fun."

He looks me up and down again, this time his eyes linger on my hips and waist and breasts. The doctor looked at me like a new toy. Jackson looks at me with lust and regret. I could think about it too long and make myself lovesick, but he made his bed.

"You look good," he says, his voice sad.

I look down at my silly costume and want more than ever to be back in my usual skin. I'm an imposture, with sore feet and an aching back. Heels are overrated.

"Thanks," I say. "But it's not worth all the work it takes."

He quietly laughs. "It's certainly not the Bryce I know, but you're still stunning."

Now I shrink back, where maybe his words can't reach me. I'm back to the land of reality. The pretty things surrounding me here have venomous thorns.

"Please don't," I say. "I'm so tired. Let's not do this tonight."

"Do what?"

"That. You telling me I'm stunning and looking at me that way."

"What way?"

"Like that, Jackson. Like we're more than just friends. Like there's something between us."

He crosses his arms over his chest and leans his neck forward. "Isn't there, Bryce? Or have you forgotten our history?"

I look away. I'm trying to put our unfinished relationship to rest, and he's trying to give it CPR. It's not that there's no pulse. Its heart is still very much alive, but the damn thing is brain-dead. It just sits there, unanimated and sucking up everyone's energy.

I sit down and tug at the bottom of my dress. I feel exposed, and my dad's words echo in my head. Can I hear Jackson sniffing at my desperation?

"Thank you" is all I can say. "I appreciate you staying with my dad. I needed a night out, but I'm exhausted."

"Please don't ignore my question."

"Of course we have a history, Jackson. But do you really want to get into it? You want to dissect everything that happened? Because I don't."

"Why do we have to dissect everything? Why can't we just be us?"

I drop my head in my hands and sigh.

"Where did you go tonight?" he asks.

My back straightens, my head pops up. "Seriously?"

"Yes, seriously."

We're sitting in a room full of knives, taking turns throwing them at each other. Why do people yearn for pain? What's so romantic about rejection? We like to see the ones we love bleed, and when it finally stops and their wounds begin to heal, we cut out our own hearts and offer to share the pain with them, just to hold on to the familiar sorrow we've come to know as love.

"Why, Jackson? Why do you want to know where I was?"

"Just curious."

"Fine." I stand up and move in close so he can hear my words and feel them pierce his insides, because maybe I am still bitter about Roselyn. "I was on a date."

If anguish is what I wanted to see on his face, mission accomplished. He looks at me like I'm a broken thing. A puppy that won't play with him, a classmate that won't be his friend. I don't need knives. My sexuality is my weapon, and tonight I used it to wound the only man I've ever loved.

"Why?" he asks.

"Why not? I'm young, I'm single, and I'm about to give up my future for this. This house, that old man in there. That's all I've got now, so pardon the hell out of me for having a little fun."

"I'm not asking why you went on a date. I'm asking why it wasn't with me?"

"Jesus Christ. How do you still not get this? We're over. What we had in high school was cute, okay? I get why you look back on it fondly. Puppy love and all that shit. But this is now, and we're not fifteen anymore."

"*Puppy love?* Are you kidding me? Where were you all those years, Bryce?" The green in his eyes catches the light and I feel them on me, trying to pry open the shell I've encased myself in. "Was that all we were to you? Even if you say yes, I won't believe you. We weren't kids playing pretend. I loved you then and I still love you now. Are you going to tell me you don't?"

I shrug. He's using words too evolved for this house. We're apes here. My father and I drag our knuckles and sling shit at one another. Tonight, I'm made of stone. And those tears I'm crying…those are just because I'm already homesick.

"And now you're not going to say anything?" he says. "You're fucking unbelievable. So your text meant nothing, either, right? And your last visit? Was that just a pity fuck for your old high school flame? 'Cause if it was, you weren't very convincing. Maybe you always whisper "I love you" when you come, and ask to be held. Did you do that with your date tonight?"

"Fuck you!"

"Did you cry for him and tell him that you needed him? If so, I certainly hope the poor bastard knows that's just your idea of fun."

"Shut the fuck up, Jackson!"

I yank off my shoes and throw them across the room. Maturity went out the window the minute Jackson walked away from us, and good manners don't come 'round here no more.

"I didn't fuck him, okay?" I shout. "You have no idea how much I wanted to, but I didn't because every time I kissed him, you were there. Even though I beg you to leave and I say mean things and tell you I don't care, you keep my heart on a leash. This guy was nice. He was handsome and rich and all the things most women would lie down and die for, but not Bryce. I ran away from him. And here I am now, trying to be strong, but you won't let me. You don't want me to get over you, but I do. I want to get over you."

Jackson won't let me see him cry. Even in his anger, he loves me too much to put that on me. His hands fall to his sides, he stands tall and breathes in deep. "If you really want me to leave you alone, I will," he says.

And now it's my turn to feel anguish.

His words bounce around the room, kicking at my heart. I try to picture them come to life. Jackson not here. Jackson gone forever. Jackson with a wife that doesn't look like me. Jackson with babies that aren't ours. Jackson going the rest of his days without hearing me say I love him.

The strength leaves my body and I sway. My resolve is no match for my love for him, but my heart is no match for the pain he can inflict on it. If I let him love me, he'd become more than the air I breathe. He'd be my reality, and if he left me again, I'd be the girl in a bubble, with no reality and nothing to ground me. Our lives are comprised of the people we love. Without them, colors drain, foods taste bland, all music sounds the same, the mind no longer dreams, and the soul forgets how to do anything but weep. Asking to be loved and to love in return is asking someone to play Russian roulette. I'd like to believe the chamber's empty, but I can almost hear that bullet whisper my name.

"Jackson," I say, my voice just above a whisper. "I want you to—"

And for the second time tonight, a man kisses me. Only this time I try to pull away. I shove my arms between our chests and push with muted effort until my misery melts into his. Tears run down my cheeks and fall into my mouth, but he only kisses me harder, and even though the voice in my head screams for me to save her from his touch, I close my eyes, open my mouth, and try to taste the leftover "I love you" still on his tongue.

"Don't you want this?" he says against my lips.

I nod yes. "But I can't."

He looks down at me, I look up at him. He frowns, I cry.

"I don't understand, Bryce."

"Nothing has changed," I say. "Years have gone by, but we're still the same, and you're still not strong enough to stand by me."

"Dammit! That's not true. I didn't know what to do back then. I didn't want to leave you, but…I was just a kid, but I'm not anymore. If you'd just let me show you. Nothing's the same."

"Everything's the same," I yell. I pull up my dress and expose the scars on my thighs. Jackson looks. He can see them, but he doesn't feel them still, every day, like I do, reminding me that I'm not shatterproof.

"Things have not changed," I say again. "Take a good look and you might just see a scared little boy running away with his tail between his legs. I'm still that girl. These wounds are still mine, and you're still afraid of what that means. You walked away from us when I needed you most. I sat in that hospital every day, wondering where you'd gone. You were the only good thing I had to hold on to, until it was over, and you weren't even there to end "it. We broke up without you being there. Me, all alone in some room, realizing you didn't love me anymore. And now you're asking me to trust you."

"Bryce, it wasn't like that. I didn't lea—"

"Get out."

"Please don't. Just listen for one minute."

Now he is crying, and I'm crying, and neither of us can be whole unless the other's broken. Jackson's tears weigh too much, and my heart wants to reach out to mend his pain before mending my own. I'm still that girl, and I'll never be safe until she's dead.

"If you care for me at all, leave, Jackson."

CHAPTER 21

No matter how much I scrub at the stain on the carpet, it won't come clean. I drown the rag in a bucket of soapy water and wring it out again. The stain stares back at me, and I want to scream at it. It's old. Maybe older than me. The house is full of stains and marred walls and nicked corners. It's been lived in. It's been died in. The ol' girl's got some mileage.

I keep my eye on that one spot. If I look around and see all the imperfections at once, it'll overwhelm me. But if I'm going to live here, I can't face them every day. If these walls are my skin and the attic my mind, these marks are my blemishes. I want a clean slate so blindingly white that

I won't be able to see anything else for days. At least then I'll know the new stains are mine and not my parents'.

"What the hell're you on the floor for?" my dad asks.

"What does it look like, old man? I'm scrubbing the carpet."

"The whole carpet?"

I look up, frown. "Of course not. Just these spots."

He's watching me. He's hunched over, out of his brace, holding his tray of lunch scraps. In the nearly two weeks since my birthday, he seems to have turned a corner with his back. That's great and all, but it means I'm now the mother of a nearly fully mobile senior citizen with Alzheimer's. I can't even sit down and have the talk with him (no sneaking out, no taking the car keys, and dammit, don't roll your eyes at me) because he'll just forget what I told him.

While his back has improved, I can't say the same for his mind. I've been noticing small changes. To the naked eye, they might not be evident, but to me they're brightly colored orbs in a dark room. The split-second mid-sentence breaks and the dumbstruck look that follows. I don't even know if my dad knows he was talking. The lapses in time, or the trips he takes back to the past without even telling me he's leaving. They're just moments at this point, glimpses of what's to come. I want to put on blinders and sing in the rain.

Bryce, do you take Denial to be your lawfully wedded partner, to have and to hold, in sickness and in health?

I do. Especially in sickness.

"I finished lunch. I'm gonna take my pill now," he says.

"I already cut it in half. It's on the counter."

I watch him to make sure he takes the half-tablet and nothing more. "Are you still hungry?" I ask.

"No. You gave me too much. You always give me too much. Wasteful. It's an epidemic with your generation."

"It's only wasteful if you don't finish it. You can keep trying to hold on to that swimsuit body of yours, but I'm not going to take you to the lake come summer and watch you oil yourself down and parade on the shore. We've got morals in this house."

His old-man lips mash together and his brows droop over his eyes. He knows I'm funny. I don't know why he won't just laugh. Stubborn donkey.

"What're the stains from?" he asks, sidling up beside me and watching me scrub the floor. Suddenly he's a drill sergeant and I'm a grunt.

"No idea, Pops. Do you know?" I stop and look up at him.

"Stop it, Bryce."

"Stop what?"

"Testing my memory. You do it all the time." He walks away and leans against the back of his recliner with the permanent head indentation. "Besides, even if I didn't have Alzh… I wouldn't remember how those stains got there anyway. Taking care of the house was never my job. I only asked because I thought maybe you wised up and killed that little shit the night of your birthday and hid his body in the garage. But I'm guessing those aren't blood stains."

I drop the rag and gawk at him. A joke? Did the crotchety bastard just make a joke? This is the closest we've come to having a normal interaction. Not just since I've been back, but ever.

"Well, well, well, Dad. So you do have some sass in those pants after all, eh? I always wondered where my twisted sense of humor came from. Think I found the "guilty party." I pick the rag back up. "But no. Sorry to tell you I didn't whack Jackson. Maybe another time. You're the only one storing body parts here."

I quickly lift my eyebrows and clear my throat.

"About that…" he says. He picks at the fabric on the couch.

I plop on my butt and rest my forearms on my knees. "About what, Dad?"

"There's not a whole lot to do in my room. It'll drive a person stir crazy laying in bed all day."

"I bet."

"That night Jackson was here and you two were hashing it out, I heard you."

Puppy love, anger, and sex, oh my! If I were more bashful, I'd crawl in a hole and only come out once my dad's memory was completely wiped clean.

"You heard everything?" I ask.

"Don't worry, Bryce. I was never under the impression you were a saint. But I'm talking about what you told him, about not trusting him. About how you're still the same, and how he still can't handle it."

What my father says next takes effort. I almost want to tell him to breathe and push. *Push harder, Dad. I can just see its head.*

"I'm prou…" He hesitates. "You did the right thing."

So close but no cigar. A bitter taste is left in my mouth from all the things I want to say but won't. I won't tell him it's good he's not proud, because he shouldn't be. What kind of woman walks away from love? What kind of woman spreads her legs for the man of her dreams but not her heart? But I do say, "Well, it shouldn't be the right thing, Dad. I shouldn't be that same girl. Something should've changed by now, but I guess I'm not saying anything we both don't know."

"I don't follow."

"Us, Dad. What looks different today from five, six years ago? We're both still emotionally stunted and alone. I use meaningless sex and sarcasm to keep people out, and you use racism, bigotry, and ugly plaid furniture. Nothing about this is the *right thing*."

"Women always have to overthink everything. Love means nothing, Bryce. You hear me? It's worth two handfuls of shit and a free ride to nowhere."

"What the fuck does that even mean?" I get up, throw the rag down. "Seriously. What's with old-man analogies? Why can't you just say love is useless? Or, here's a novel idea. Why not just tell me what happened to make you feel that way? You might be making a good point, but instead I'm too busy trying to figure out what handfuls of shit and free rides to nowhere have to do with anything."

"What I'm saying is that love doesn't always mean a whole hell of a lot. Sometimes we fall in love with the wrong people, and no matter how much we want to be together, it doesn't matter, because the cards just got stacked the wrong way and no amount of crying about it will change a goddamn thing. You did the right thing is all."

"How come you're talking about this like you understand it? You got to be with Mom. You married her. It's not like you never even got the chance. You did, and then you went and fucked it up."

"You're absolutely right. So maybe I know what I'm talking about and I'm not just the idiot you think I am. You don't know everything, kid. Not about me, not about your mother, and certainly as hell not about who I've loved."

The brakes squeal like a pig. I'll sue my dad later for causing me whiplash.

"What?" I say.

His eyes grow wide. His knuckles go white as he grips the back of the chair.

"What do you mean *who you've loved?* Was there someone else, Dad?"

"Of course not."

"But you said—"

"I know what I said, and I'm telling you you're reading into it. My back hurts. I need to lie down."

"You know, Dad, lies will get you nowhere. They're as useless as two handfuls of shit and a free ride to nowhere."

He keeps his hands fisted, his body language guarded.

"Why do you hate Jackson?" I ask. "It certainly can't be because he made me cry. I mean…if I wanted to be with him, if I wanted to be happy, what would be so wrong with that?"

"Sometimes people just see too much of who you really are, and then they can't ever see you differently."

"I still don't know what that has to do with you."

He slowly shakes his head. "We let him into this family. He was there on one of the worst days of our lives, and then he walked out."

"He was eighteen."

"He was your rock."

"And you were Mom's, but that didn't stop her from loving you when you screwed up."

I look away and stare at all the stains on the floor, mocking me. No matter how hard I try, I'll never have a clean slate. Even though I canceled on Shana last weekend, I hope she brings two bottles of wine tomorrow night. Enough to make me forget Jackson's face and my father's words, and maybe a little extra to pour out for my mom. The carpet could use another stain, and if you can't beat 'em, join 'em.

CHAPTER 22

I put the finishing touches on the guest room for Shana. Clean sheets, a fluffed pillow, and one mini bottle of whiskey I found in the kitchen cupboard. She's going to need all the booze she can get after I tell her I'm moving here. We always promised to grow old together and sexually assault the male nurses in our retirement home. I'm being dramatic, of course. I won't grow old here, but I need to wallow in my depression. It's the only company I have right now, and it's loyal as fuck.

I spray some air freshener around to mask the smell of Old Spice, stale smoke, and the cod I made for lunch. Now it just smells like a cheap motel room a hooker got tag-teamed in. Not nearly up to Shana's five-star standards, but she loves me, so she'll suck it up, buttercup.

I pick up the cleaning supplies and head out of the room when I hear what sounds like a fist go through the wall and my father scream.

"Dad?"

I drop everything and run into his room. You always think you'll know what to do in a crisis, but I freeze and try to make sense of my dad's contorted face and the awful screams pouring from his lungs.

I snap back into action and lunge into the heap of thrashing arms. "Dad, Stop! You're gonna hurt yourself. Stop! Now!"

But he can't hear me over himself. He's got pipes on him, and my eardrums buzz and kick at my brain.

"We left him I'm so sorry we left him I need to go back we need to go back. Help me go back and get him please Bryce help me!"

I try to wrap my arms around him to keep him from injuring his back, but his adrenaline is pumping and my fear is a hindrance.

"Dad, you have to stop moving. You're going to hurt yourself. You're okay!"

But he screams and screams and begs me to go back for *him*, the man who haunts my father even as he sleeps and wakes up crying and shaking and pleading, covered in sweat and what I think is urine.

"He wanted me to tell you but I can't Bryce you'll hate me and I'm so sorry I can't tell you!"

My arms are stretched as far as I can spread them. Acid tears through my muscles, demanding that I stop, but if I let go, he'll break something, and I'm stupid because I'm going to get hurt, but so long as he doesn't. I love too much.

"Dad! You. Have. To. Calm. Down."

And then he arches his back and something loud crunches—a horrible sound that makes me think of chewing on ice. Unadulterated fear ruled his screams, now agonizing pain rules his cries for help.

"Oh, fuck!" he yells. "Jesus, it hurts. Fuck, it hurts. God…"

"Stop moving, Dad. Just don't move!"

He finally hears me and looks in my eyes. I've never seen my dad scared. Maybe the night my mother died, but I don't remember that. He's a cat being held in water, and I know by the tears streaming down his face that I'm his rescuer, and he needs me to save him. Only how?

I nod quickly, look him up and down. "Okay. Just take some breaths with me. Can you do that?" He doesn't move, doesn't speak. "In"—I breathe with him—"and out. Again. In…and out. One last time. In"—he finally blinks and eases his death grip on my hands—"and out. Good, Dad. Just keep doing that. I'm going to look you over."

I can't see anything through his clothes. I don't even know what I'm looking for, but I think it makes us feel better. Or at least him. My mind is still somewhere in the hallway, and my heart fell to the floor and scurried under the bed, thumping loud enough to drown out the screams.

I try to pull my father's blankets back, but my hands rattle. Not shake. Rattle. I don't know how I can still move them after he crushed the bones, mashing them together like marbles in a bag.

"Where does it hurt, Dad?"

"Don't know," he pants. "My back, I think."

I figured as much. "Okay. Gotta be honest with you, Pops. I don't know what I'm looking for, so I'm just going to make you as comfortable as I can. Luckily you have an "appointment with Theo today." I look at the clock. "You've got less than an hour to wait. Let's just get some pillows wedged around you, okay?"

Fear like my father's holds you tight and doesn't like to let go. You've got to kick it in the balls and run like hell. But my dad's immobile. He's under fear's thumb. It's present in his wild eyes and the way they skittishly track the room, looking for the monster responsible for his nightmare.

I adjust the pillows around him so that he can relax if and when the panic abates and his muscles loosen. Right now they feel like stones under his skin. I sit next to him and take his hand. He's too frightened to pull away—I'm too alone to let go.

"What happened, Dad? Do you want to talk about it?"

He closes his eyes, swallows hard.

"It's okay," I say. "Just relax and breathe how I showed you. You're okay now."

~

I see Theo's car pull up, and I open the door just as he's about to knock.

"Hey, pretty girl," he says. "How're you?"

I move aside and open the door wide.

"Been better. How're you?"

"It's Friday. I think that about sums it up. So what's going on today?"

"Can you sit for a minute?"

He looks at me sideways and takes a seat on the old-man couch. He clashes with it. I sit on the recliner. I don't clash enough.

"My dad hurt himself pretty badly today. I didn't want to drive him to the ER and possibly do more damage."

"What happened?"

"He was taking a nap while I got some chores done, and next thing I hear screaming. I ran in the room and he was thrashing around in the bed, just totally out of control. I tried to keep him from moving too much, but he just lost it."

"From what? Do you know?"

"A bad dream, I think. You remember that stuff he kept repeating that day?"

"Sure do."

"It was more of that. But he kept begging me to take him back to get him. Whoever the hell *him* is. He was bawling his eyes out and just kept asking for my help and saying how sorry he was."

I look at Theo and wait for him to say something. He's the Alzheimer's Whisperer, after all. He needs to tell me it's okay and chase the boogeyman off.

"It could be so many things," he says. "It's impossible to say what. It could've just been a recurring dream. It could be a memory from the war, or maybe something he's repressed. Sometimes patients forget to keep their own secrets. They don't remember that they never told anyone, or they forget that they're not supposed to tell anyone, and things kind of trickle out. Or it's nothing you'll ever figure out. But you'll break your head trying, I guarantee you."

I zone out on Theo's oversized shoes. They're so clean and white. They pop against his skin and make him look like some luxurious shade of exotic cocoa. My own skin's still blotchy and red from my father's hands.

"Maybe I'm just being paranoid, Theo, but I can't shake the feeling that it means something." I look at him and wait for him to disagree. I want him to disagree. I want to be the dumb girl with her big ideas.

He shakes his head. "You can't go looking for answers every time he says something confusing. He's going to say a whole bunch of crazy stuff, and you're going to learn at some point to let it roll off your back. I told you last time it's probably something from Vietnam. Did you ask?"

"Yes. But he wouldn't tell me. It's not nothing, though."

"How do you know?"

"I don't know, I just do. And it can't be a memory from the war. Earlier, he said something like, 'He wanted me to tell you, Bryce, but you'll hate me.' That can't be about Vietnam."

Theo stands up, which means I stand up. I can't look up at the guy from a seated position without straining my neck. He's all serious and no fun right now, but he's still a giant teddy bear.

"Listen," he says, "people have pasts. It's hard to look at older folks laying up in bed, too sick to remember their owns names, and remember that they were once young and lived their lives, doing God knows what with God knows who. If he's remembering something from his past he never wanted you knowing about, you need to respect that."

"But—"

"Even if he's the one spilling the beans, you need to respect his privacy. Remember what I said. He's not stupid. If he wants you to know, he'll tell you. But right now *I'm* telling you that it's probably nothing. Tomorrow he could wake up and forget you exist. Won't make you "any less real. When patients get confused, sometimes they voice every thought in their head. Gotta learn to roll with things, girl."

I nod, then shake my head. "Yeah. Maybe you're right."

"So let's take a look at him. How's he doing otherwise?"

"Subtle changes," I say.

"That's the name of the game."

Theo follows me down the hallway. I open my dad's door. "Hey, Dad. Theo's here. You ready to see him?"

My dad's still wedged in all his pillows, facing the door. The room smells of urine and sweat and embarrassment. My father wouldn't let me change him. Guess my words from our last fight are still too fresh.

"Hey, Mr. Price. I heard you had a bit of an accident. Let's take a look at you and get you feeling better," Theo says.

Theo ducks under the doorframe and waits for the man with the scowl to mark the commencement of the exam with a grunt of compliance, but my dad does no such thing. Instead, his hand moves. He's still shaking, but he seems to be moving with intent. Before my brain can process what's happening, he reaches out for Theo's hand.

"Thank you," my father says, his voice raspy and cracking from stain.

"You're welcome, Mr. Price."

And then my father finally breathes easy and lets his guardian angel with the gleaming white shoes and giant gray scrubs do what he was hired to do and take just a little of his pain away.

As for me, I guess I have to believe in miracles now.

CHAPTER 23

I take my father's tray away and sit it on the floor. I can see through his shirt that his stomach is bloated from the heavy meal I cooked him. Hurt your back and pee your pants, you get any meal you want. I actually enjoyed cooking—he actually enjoyed eating. Maybe we're getting better at this whole symbiotic thing.

"Whatever Theo did earlier helped a lot, huh?" I ask.

"For a while."

Theo worked his magic on my father's pinched nerve. Now if my dad would've just let him help him get out of his wet clothes instead of insisting on doing it himself, he wouldn't be in as much pain now. But that wasn't going to happen. Theo has man parts that only like other man parts, and straight men always think all gay men want them here and now, hot and heavy. But my dad's a product of his upbringing, and Rome wasn't built in a day. He shook his hand. If there is a God, She did her work for the day. I can only assume God's a woman. Who the hell else would put up with seven billion brats screaming ME, ME, ME all day? If God were a man, he would've gone out for a pack of smokes thousands of years ago and never come back. Then again, maybe he did.

I look around, hands on my hips. "You want to write in the notebook?" I ask.

"Not really."

"Wanna watch some TV?"

He shakes his head.

"I'll watch with you. Even if it's that woodworking show."

"I'm not in the mood for TV."

His fire got snuffed out long ago, and he's not even smoldering anymore. Nothing like screaming like a scared child and pissing your pants in front of your daughter to chip away at your dignity. But it's more than that. He doesn't seem to even care, and I'd rather deal with a mean old bastard than one who doesn't care.

"Hey, Pops. How about you let me shave you?"

"What?"

"Not you"—I wave my hand along the length of his body—"but this." I touch his cheek. He might be a brittle, crotchety man, but everyone likes to feel pretty. Just ask a dog after it's had a bath.

"What do you say? Can I get rid of this Unabomber beard you having going on? I think you'd feel better, and God knows I would. You're starting to scare the hell out of me. If you look this way tomorrow, Shana won't sleep here."

I might need to bring in a team of scientists to confirm it, but I think I just saw my father smile. Suddenly I have daddy issues and feel all warm and Hallmark-y inside. We're like one of those Campbell's Soup commercials, and I want to call him "Papa" and give him Eskimo kisses.

Enough, Bryce. Have a little self-respect.

"So what's the verdict?" I ask.

He hems and haws, then says, "I think that'd be okay."

~

I come back with a tray full of tools I've never used. My father's got one of those old-school setups with the brush and beard soap and a serious razor that makes me think maybe I shouldn't be shaving a damn thing. I sit the tray down and read the back of the beard soap.

"There aren't instructions," I say.

"Men don't need instructions."

"Oh, yes. That's right. Silly me. Of course you don't. So it's like building a dresser from IKEA." I place the bottom of the jar on his forehead. "So this goes here, then?"

He swats my hand away and takes the brush from me. "You dip the brush in a little water and lather it on the soap. The rest is pretty self-explanatory."

"Ooooooooooooh. Phew. Glad you told me. God knows what I would've wound up doing had there been instructions. I could've taken half your face off."

"Yeah, well, try not to. You ever done this before?"

I get serious. "No. What if I cut you?"

"Then I'll bleed, and then it'll stop."

He's matter-of-fact tonight. My jokes and irresistible wit only pull him so far from his shell.

"Okay, Pops. Here goes nothin'."

I dip the brush in water and place it in the soap, just like he told me. Next I move the brush around in small circles, starting at his cheek. The brush dancing over his neck tickles me just watching it. Before long, a thin layer of creamy snow covers his face from below his eyes, all the way to his neck. Instead of looking like the Unabomber, he looks like Santa with an eating disorder.

"All right. I think we're ready to get this show on the road, Pops."

He offers no words of encouragement or even an "atta girl." He just closes his eyes and relaxes into the pillow.

I start at his cheek and slowly pull up on the handle of the razor, feeling a slight tug when the blade meets the base of each shaft of hair.

"That doesn't hurt, does it?"

"No. Don't overthink it."

I pull harder and feel each hair catch on the blade. It sounds like I'm shaving sandpaper, but my father's resting easy, so I guess this is normal. I pull the razor over his cheekbone, easing in pressure when I meet the crown of his cheek. I touch the skin left behind and stubble bats at my fingers. It makes sense that he'd be rough even after having a razor blade taken to him. He's prickly to his core. I'm prickly to my core. But I'm still not ready to be like him.

When I get to the area under his nose, he draws his lip down, sucking it into his mouth to smooth out the skin, and gets shaving cream in his mouth. This must just be a guy thing. Boys are weird.

I make baby strokes in this area and work delicately around his lips. My father emerges with each stroke of the blade, and out comes an older version of a man I can't remember ever being so close to before. This is the first time I've touched my father's face. Growing up, I thought he was made of stone. Now I'm painfully aware of his flesh and blood, and how it means mortality.

I shake the blade around in the cup of water and wipe it down. My father's face is clean. Only his neck remains covered in hair. I do nothing to quiet my gulp. I want him to know I'm scared. I'm sure it's just a symptom of having watched too many horror movies, but one slip of the razor and I'm afraid we're going to have a little elevators-in-the-Overlook-Hotel moment right here in this room.

I place the blade at the bottom of his neck and pull up, but he stops me. His hand rests gently on mine, swallowing it whole.

"Like this," he says.

He moves my hand along at the slightest angle, and I immediately feel the difference. This is my first time off training wheels, and my first time jumping in the deep end, and that one time I shot at an empty Foster's can with my friend's .22. I fell off that bike, I panicked under the water, and I almost dropped the rifle. My dad's hands should've been guiding me, as they are now. These hands were meant to keep me safe and carry me on shoulders and hold me when I fell and scratched my knees. They should've held my little heart until it had grown strong enough to hand over to Jackson, and then maybe I wouldn't have had to cut myself to remember I was still alive.

We reach the tip of his chin. He can let go now. I've got it. But he doesn't. He lingers a moment longer than he needs to, because maybe my skin is just as foreign to him.

And then he holds my hand. It's only for the briefest moment. If I blink, I'll miss it. But he does, and somewhere in me that little girl is writing "I love you, Daddy" with hearts all around it in chalk on the sidewalk outside our house.

His hand falls away and I position the blade back at the bottom of his neck and begin the process again. It's too quiet in here, and my hand feels cold now.

"Hey, Dad. You know I'm always here, right? I mean…if you ever want to talk about anything."

"Sure."

He's locked up tighter than a safe.

"I have a question," I say.

I can see his chest freeze as he waits to be bombarded.

"What's your favorite color?"

"That's it? That's your question?" he asks.

"I just realized I have no idea what it is. That's something every kid asks their parent, but I never did."

He stares at the ceiling, looking contemplative. "I guess if I had to pick a color, I'd say orange."

Funny. Not pink?

"Orange?"

"Yes."

"Hmm."

I never took my dad for an orange kind of guy. I would've guessed moss-green, or maybe plaid. I know that's a pattern, but it should be a color option for him.

"What's yours?" he asks.

My dad wants to know my favorite color. I feel like I'm five, and I want to show him all the colors of the rainbow.

"Oh, shit." I cut him. I got so excited about making small talk that I cut his neck. "I'm so sorry, Dad. I'm an idiot. I shouldn't have tried to do—"

"Bryce?"

I stop dabbing his neck and look at him.

"It's okay," he says. "It's just a nick."

I get quiet and just want to finish the one job I had and somehow screwed up. Red was going to be one of my favorite colors, but not now. I pick the blade back up and move at a snail's pace.

"You were about to tell me something," he says. "Your favorite color."

I maintain my focus this time. "All of them."

"That's impossible."

"No it's not."

"Then why do you always wear black and gray? How does an artist only wear two colors?"

Hundreds of people have called me an artist, but never my father. I like the sound of it. I want to pull the string on his back and make him say it again.

"I don't know," I say. "I guess I don't see myself as being worthy of bright colors. Only happy people wear brights."

"And you're not happy?"

This is when I realize we're in the middle of our first meaningful conversation, and our knuckles aren't even raw. He's my dad and I'm his daughter, and he wants to know if I'm happy.

"I am right now," I tell him. "Does that count?"

He looks away, but it's okay. He already cried once in front of me today.

"Why, uh...why'd you stop painting?"

"I don't know."

Another stroke of the razor, but my dad grabs my hand and stops me. "This can wait. I want to know," he says.

I drop the razor and slump in my chair. "Because it just became easier to not feel anything instead of feeling everything. It might just look like paint to some people, but for me it was a door, and when I needed to kick all the pinned-up shit out, I'd open it. But I don't tap into that part of myself anymore. Now I don't even know if I can. Besides, it's not like anyone noticed when I stopped. My art wasn't going to change the world or anything."

He points to his closet. "Open the door and grab the blue accordion folder on the top shelf."

"What's in it?"

"Just do it."

I get up and open the door. Above my father's coats and old uniforms is the pregnant folder, bursting at the seams. I pull it down and bring it back to my seat.

"Okay. Open it?"

He nods.

I undo the elastic strap and pull it off the circular tab. The moment the pressure's released, the top flap flies back and the file splays open on my lap, exposing several different compartments separated by clear plastic. I immediately know what I'm looking at. Every flier for every art show I ever did, every online article someone ran on me, the *Seattle Times* article…they're all nestled in the crammed folder. I flip through the other compartments and a slight gasp escapes me. Every drawing I thought he threw away, every little painting I secretly created in my room and hid under my bed are all there. Pieces of me my father kept and held on to.

"I don't know about anyone else," he says, "but I noticed."

"But I thought you…" I can't articulate myself while trying not to let him see that I cry as ugly when I'm happy as I do when I'm sad. "You never wanted me to—"

"I said and did a lot of things, Bryce. You wouldn't understand why. There are things I've always wanted to tell…" He looks around like he just caught himself in the middle of a close call. "I just want you to know that I noticed. But I…I'm in a good bit of pain. I don't think I'm making much sense. I just want to rest now."

I hold the folder to my chest. I want to scream at him, but I can't find my voice. It's trapped between the drawings pressed to my chest. He opened the door and then slammed it in my face right when I was going to tell him I needed him. Why do both my parents hide behind doors and leave me all alone?

I wipe my eyes and get up, trying to grab the tray without putting the folder down.

"I do want you to do what makes you happy," he says.

I look into his eyes and will him to keep going. *I'll be quiet, Dad. I won't interrupt, Dad. I'll be good and let you say anything you want. Just don't stop talking, Dad. I feel like I could know you, and you could know me, and maybe we'd find something to like about one another. And if not, I still love you.*

"Good night, Bryce."

~

I don't know exactly what my father was getting at, but I leave his room with the smell of lumber in my nose and the hankering for a slice of heartache. Suddenly I want to be around a man who's filled with too many words and wants to say them all to me. I need to know I'm not the only one who's starting to feel things I've never felt, because maybe my heart is making room for the possibility of a father who's disappearing before my eyes.

I text Jackson.

"Can we talk?"

I tap the screen with my finger, chew my lower lip. My phone chimes.

"Can I apologize?" he asks.

"The mechanic called and said my dad's truck will be ready soon. My dad managed to hurt himself today, so his nurse is coming back again on Monday. Can you drive me there while he has his appointment? I'd really appreciate it. We can do the talking and apologizing stuff then."

"Sounds good."

CHAPTER 24

The air has a bite to it. We might not always get snow, but the fog will make you forget there's a ground to hit when you fall in love with this place. Washington is flavored gray and lasts on your tongue like a harsh burn. It hurts good and leaves you wanting more. Sometimes you need something icy, with all the good looks and the deep, dark thoughts.

My arms are chilly and my skin is prickly. And I just shaved my legs. Crap.

I yank the comforter high over my head, but now cold air envelops my feet. Must've forgotten to turn the heater on before bed.

"Dammit."

I open my eyes and can just make out the outline of my door. It's open. I wrap the covers around myself and haul my tired body out of bed, sliding my feet across the floor in the dark. The leg of the bed is waiting to stub my toe. I'm on to you, fucker.

I slide my left foot forward again and hit something on the floor. It's too dark to see what it is, but when I reach down and feel it, I know what the oddly shaped items are. Chapstick, wallet, crumpled receipts...my purse, open. I didn't leave it here. I didn't leave my door open, either. And where are my keys?

A slight movement in the air brings with it more cold. Too much cold, too concentrated.

"Oh, shit."

I leap from the ground and peel around the corner into the hallway where my heart stops. I locked it before bed, but the front door is wide open, like the mouth of a monster I'm afraid swallowed my father whole.

"Dad?"

I rush into his room. His back brace is lying on the floor, his sheets are strewn about. He's gone.

"Fuck! Dad?"

I run into the living room and out the front door. I don't remember grabbing my phone, but it's in my hand.

"Dad?" I yell again.

I run around the back of the house but can't see much of anything through the fog. Once I get closer, the slate-gray sky sheds just enough light for me to see the top of the bench and the cherub covered in overgrowth. I'd hoped my father would be back here, feeding imaginary birds and talking to his dead wife, but he's nowhere.

I hurry back around to the front of the house, ice crunching under my bare feet as I run through the frost-covered grass that meets the road. My skin burns, but it doesn't register as pain. I'm too afraid to feel anything other than fear. I look left, then right. More fog. Just an endless, murky sea teeming with my father's natural predators, like cars and ditches and lakes and vast miles of forest.

"Dad?"

I don't think. I just dial. Two rings.

"Hello?"

"Jackson, it's me. I don't know what to do. My dad's gone. He took the keys from my purse while I was asleep and got out. He didn't take my car, but I can't even get into it to go look for him. He walked off somewhere."

"How long ago?"

"I don't know. Could've been three hours, could've been twenty minutes."

"Did anything happen last night? Did he say anything?"

"No. Nothing out of the ordinary. He's been having these bad dreams lately, about leaving someone behind or something. I think he had another one last night. He was whimpering a little, but then he went quiet. That's all. Nothing else happened."

"I think I might know where he is," he says. "Just stay there. I'm on my way."

"How would you know that?"

"Just stay there, Bryce!"

He hangs up, and I don't follow orders. I go left and take off down the Hansel and Gretel Road with the curves and dips and valleys. There's a long white wooden fence that runs along it for miles, and I follow it so I don't drift into the lane and get smacked by a car.

"Dad? Arthur? Dad?"

~

I run for what feels like hours, calling out my dad's name, but it's only been twenty minutes. Time warps when you're in a crisis. Seconds blend into minutes, and minutes blend into hours, like a big block that's lost all meaning and does nothing to pull you from your panic or propel you through it. It just leaves you wading in it till something comes along and rips you out.

My pace goes from a steady jog to a hurried walk as my lungs fight back. I wish the fog were thicker so I could swim through it. I still can't feel my feet, but that's because they're completely numb. There's something dark on them that I think is blood. I'm leaving crumbs behind for my dad to follow.

I pick up the pace again and hold my arms under my breasts to keep them in place. I can't get warm. Can't stop shivering.

"Dad? Arthur?"

What if he doesn't know his name? What if he has no idea where he is? My heart does somersaults in my chest and makes my stomach roll. My dad can't die on my watch. I'm supposed to be his mind. I'm supposed to protect him and watch out for all the things he doesn't realize are now a danger.

I see Theo's expression when I tell him I lost my father.

I just looked away for a minute. Just a little sleep to get me through the next day.

I hate myself. I hate my father. I hate that I love him, and I hate that last night he showed me lovely pictures and said lovely words. He noticed. All along, he had noticed.

I scan the road from left to right and back again as I jog faster, shredding my feet to bits, which I don't understand, because I'm a diamond, and diamonds don't break.

The sun is slowly rising, and instead of slate-gray, now the sky's just gray.

"Dad?" I scream into the wild. Forest sits on both sides of the road, trees flicker in my peripheral vision as I rush past them and think I see my father, but it's just another tree trunk.

Ahead I see lights. Two of them, coming closer. They look like eyes floating through the fog, slowing as they approach. As it nears, a hunter-green hood emerges, and then the large body of a truck follows, like a beast appearing from the mist.

I wave my hands around and nearly collapse. Suddenly I have no energy.

Jackson rolls down his window. "I found him, but he won't come with me."

I gasp, out of breath. "Where? W-why won't he come?"

"Get in. I'll take you."

I pull myself into the truck and wave for him to go. He turns the heat on, aiming all the vents at me.

"I told you to stay put," he says. "You could've gotten hit out here."

"How'd you know?"

"Know what?"

I slap the seat, hard. "Dammit, Jackson! How'd you know where he was?"

I wait. I watch. I lean forward in case he's talking so quietly that I can't hear him. But his mouth isn't moving, and he won't look at me.

"Jackson?"

"It's... I had a hunch."

"A hunch? Did you seriously just say that? What the hell's going on with you two? That pissing contest on my birthday, and now this. My dad decides to take a moonlit stroll to God knows where, and you're telling me you had a hunch?"

"It's not my place."

"What the fuck does that mean?"

"That means it's not my place," he yells. Jackson never raises his voice at me. I've only heard him yell one other time, but I don't remember if it made me feel small, like it does now.

"I'm sorry," he says, "but there are some things I'm not at liberty to discuss."

His words are drenched in regret so thick I can't see through it to make out their meaning. He's nothing but serious words and a stiff posture and a tone too formal for us. I want to show him my scars to remind him that we're past formalities.

"Look at me," I tell him. But he won't. Not even a blip of movement to indicate that he's considering it.

"It's foggy," he says. "I don't want to hit something."

I sink into the seat and shiver harder than ever, even though the vents blast me with desert air. I'm so tired all the sudden. My voice is soft and weak. I resent it.

"Please tell me what's going on, Jackson."

"It's not my story to tell."

We crest a small hill and Jackson slows the truck down. His headlights shine in the small valley below, and just off the side of the road I see my father on the ground.

"What's he doing?" I ask.

"Just sitting there. He won't move."

I touch the handle when the truck stops, but I can't open the door. I watch my father out the window. He looks like a pile of skin and bones. Like one of the toys you press the bottom of and the animal crumples at its joints. Something broke him out here. Some story it's not Jackson's place to tell.

I'm afraid to open the door to more unanswered questions. The man sitting on the ground with tears in his eyes is more honest than I thought. He was right. There is a lot about him I don't know.

I look at Jackson. He should be ushering me out the door, but instead he's staring ahead.

"Still afraid you're going to hit something?" I say.

"What?" His neck snaps around, his eyes finally find mine, only they don't look like his.

"You said you couldn't look at me earlier because you didn't want to hit something. So why're you avoiding me now?"

He always loves me with his eyes. Even when he doesn't tell me he loves me, I know he does, because he looks at me like I'm something that might just be magic. But now he looks at me like I'm sharp, like something that could hurt him. These aren't pictures I want to remember. I look away.

I step out of the truck and kneel down next to my father. "Dad, you scared me to death. You can't just take off like that. What're you doing out here?"

He grabs both my hands without taking his eyes off the road. I can feel him tremble, and something inside of me now breaks for him.

"I want to go back," he cries. "I'm sorry. I'm so, so sorry I didn't save you."

He's not talking to me. I can tell by the invisible force holding his attention in the road. When I look out, I see nothing but black asphalt. I think he's talking about my brother, but he didn't die here.

"Dad, are you talking about Scotty? You couldn't have saved him. It was too late, and it wasn't your fault."

"Why couldn't it have been me?" he asks. "I want to go back and trade places with him. I would change so much about that day. I'd change it all."

I grip his hands tight. I know what it's like to need an anchor to tie yourself to when your mind kicks up memories you're not prepared to battle. And isn't that the way of the mind, to betray the heart without warning or hesitation? We think we've moved on, and then something yanks us back. A song, a picture, a fucking smell. We're constantly setting out to destroy ourselves, one memory at a time.

"Come on," I tell him, urging him up, but he's a boulder. I can see the roots on his feet cracking the asphalt as they grow deeper and wider. "It's freezing out here, Dad. Let's get home and warm you up."

"Not with him."

My father's throwing daggers with his eyes. If Jackson doesn't roll his window up, he's going to get hurt. I try to pry my father's talons from my flesh.

"I understand that you're having a really rough time right now," I say, "but I'm only asking that you let him take us home."

"No."

"Dad, please. I can't walk like this anymore."

He looks down at the blood between my toes.

"Come on," I say. "Get in the truck for just a minute."

"I can't leave him again, Bryce."

Desperation does have a smell. It smells like blood and mud and fog and pine trees. It's all around my father.

"Please," I beg. "Why're you out here?"

"Because"—he looks at Jackson—"I don't want to forget."

"Forget what?"

He drops my hands, as if I've suddenly burned him with my cluelessness.

"You've got to give me something," I tell him. "I don't know what's going on. But I'm freezing, and I need to get you home. Please."

I wait for the earth to shake and rattle as he moves and picks up one foot. His movements seem strained, each step towards Jackson's truck monumental in effort. When he gets to the door and I open it for him, he stares inside, glaring at the man who doesn't dare look anywhere but straight ahead.

CHAPTER 25

I get out first and help my father out of the truck. His whole body seems to be trembling now, and he looks confused.

"Just go inside, Dad. I'll be right there."

I watch him walk in the house, forgetting to shut the door behind him. God, I'm tired.

"Thank you," I tell Jackson.

He looks at me now, but just barely.

"No problem. You need to get inside, too. Get yourself warmed up, and clean off your feet before they get infected."

I nod, stretching my toes and prying apart the dry, caked on blood.

"The day I came back, you told me I always get weird and quiet when I'm keeping something from you. Remember that?" I ask.

"Vaguely."

"Well, you've been weird and quiet since you picked me up. What happened with you and my dad? Did he tell you something the day you stayed with him?"

"Something like that."

"And you don't think you owe it to me to tell me what the hell's going on?"

"Why do I owe you anything?"

"How can you think you don't?"

"Because I made a mistake when I was a kid?" he says. "That's why I owe you? Because I was in over my head and thought the best thing to do was walk away, because I knew the last thing you needed was one more person to take care of and explain things to?"

I pinch up my toes and let them burn to distract me so I don't cry. Now that he's seeing me for the first time all morning, I want him to stop looking and talking and making me hurt.

"I'm sorry," he says. "I'm incredibly sorry that I fucked up so monumentally. I really am, Bryce. But when the hell are you going to let me off the hook for not knowing how to deal with the fact that my girlfriend hacked herself to bits? That was a long time ago, and we were so young."

"Old enough to know better," I say.

"And young enough to not know what the hell to do about it."

He runs his hands through his hair and down his face. I can hear his stubble scratch his hands as they glide over his jaw. One night with me will age you. Jackson doesn't just look tired, he looks older, beaten, like he lost, but I don't see how when I didn't win.

"Bryce…you like to say I'm the same person, that I've not grown or changed. If I didn't know better, I'd say you have to keep me in that role because if you didn't, you might have to admit that I've grown, and suddenly we'd have potential. But *you're* not ready for us. *You're* the one who hasn't changed. *You're* the one running now. I mean…Christ. Look at us. We're out here chasing your old man down in the middle of the night, you're half-naked, bleeding from your feet, and I've never been more in love with you than I am right now. What the hell's wrong with me? I'm not being facetious. I'm really asking. What the hell's wrong with a man who loves a woman who doesn't want to be loved?"

Some words sting, others break you. I try to find my own words, but they've fallen through the cracks Jackson put in my heart. He's wrong. The words are right there. Three easy words. You. Are. Wrong. But they can't make their way past my lips, the gatekeepers keeping me and my bullshit in check.

I walk away, because I'm the woman afraid of love and the big, bad man trying to give it to her. I hear Jackson's door open, and I try to run to the front door, but my feet betray me, and his hand is on my shoulder, spinning me around. He's too close. I can't survive his words at close range.

"Stop running away from me," he says. "Just tell me that I'm wasting my time. Tell me you don't love me enough, and that nothing will ever change. Put me out of my damn misery and I swear I'll never bother you again, 'cause fuck if this isn't tearing me apart, Bryce. I've loved you since I met you, and I don't see that ever changing. If

"I'm going to have to get through life pretending I don't need you, let me start now."

I want to breathe him in and swallow his tears and let them infect me with his kind of vulnerability. His words give no regard to their inherent weakness, nor do they falter in the face of possible rejection. He's ten times the person I'll ever be, and instead of just loving him with every fiber of my being, I also envy his strength. His chest is splayed open, his heart exposed, and he's never been more powerful.

"I can't tell you to leave," I say. "But you can't stay."

"You can't have your cake and eat it too, babe. Stop holding me at a distance. It's all or nothing."

Can he be right? Did I get my lines crossed? If I go into my closet and reach up into the dark shelf above, will I find a box with Jackson's heart in it? I thought he had mine, but here it is, in my chest, breaking more every second.

I only know how to play the victim. I'm the one whose world gets shattered by the hands of a big bully. Not the other way around.

I look at my hands and suddenly wonder what they've done. Then I look into Jackson's eyes and see it. I'm the conductor of his heartache, our heartache. I've spent years painting beautiful pictures for other people, but I refused to ever keep one for myself. The only man I've ever loved doesn't owe me anything. I owe him back the years I robbed from him, the hours he spent waiting and hoping, the minutes he spent loving me. And this moment. Don't I owe him back this one, too? The one when he tells me he loves me, and I tell him to walk away.

Why do we move mountains for those we care so little for, but we place thick glass between ourselves and the ones we love? You can see me, but you can't reach me.

"An apology seems too small," I say. "I didn't realize, Jackson. I'm sorry...but I—"

"Just can't?"

He comes close, so close I can feel his breath. He's testing me, daring me, giving me one last chance to come to my senses. So I kiss him. I bury my fingers in his hair and stand on my toes and despite the pain, I kiss him and forget that this moment will never stop hurting for as long as I live. I'll never breathe again once he turns and leaves, so I better fill my lungs with as much air as possible. Once it runs out, I'll suffocate.

He moves me backwards until my back hits the house. Our lips never part, like they've made a pact our heads weren't in on. We taste each other's yearning and swallow back words that will only make this moment sting more.

Can he taste my love? Can he feel it on my lips and breasts and hips, where he leaves his mark so that any other man will know I'm his, his, his, forever and ever?

He kisses my neck and I wrap myself around his body, and I wish we didn't fit, like we were made for one another. I hear him cry in my ear, and I close my eyes and let my own tears fall with no regard for what they say about me.

I, too, am weak. I, too, am vulnerable. But please stay back, because sometimes I break into sharp pieces, and just like my parents, I cut the people I love.

His tongue is my tongue, his arms my arms, his legs my legs, and our hearts? For a moment I forget they aren't one anymore. Even my skin is his, and his mine. There's no telling where I begin and he ends, which is going to make this ache all the more.

I shove hard and push him away, making room for my friend of misery. She'll braid my hair while I plot her death, but I'll still let her keep me company tonight.

"It doesn't have to be this way," he says.

My breath catches in my chest with every cry. All I can do is shake my head.

"Bryce, don't do this."

"I told you before"—I step inside the door—"I'm the same girl I was, and she doesn't know how to love in a way that doesn't hurt."

"That's not true, Bryce. Listen to yourself. You sound like your father."

I stiffen. "You're right."

If I look at him, I won't close the door, so I look down at the blood coating my feet and remember the last night we were together. I don't need someone to bleed with me just to prove their love.

"I love you, Jackson."

"Bryce, wait."

"But I can't."

CHAPTER 26

I listen at the door to the sound of Jackson's truck taking off down the road. Goodbyes don't always sound the same. The sound of his engine blending into the silence is the loudest goodbye I've ever heard.

I wish tonight was make believe, but the blood I leave on the tile of the small entranceway tells me my wounds are real. The ones I can see and the ones I can't. Someone always walks away from a battle wounded and bloodied. I'd love to say, "You should see the other guy," but I don't want anyone to see what I've done to Jackson. The scars I left on him don't make him ugly, they make me ugly.

"Dad, where are you?"

"Out here," he says. His voice is far away.

The back door at the end of the hallway is just cracked open. I slip a pair of fuzzy socks on without cleaning my feet, and I grab our jackets and head out back. Jackson's got all the good advice. "Go inside, Bryce." "Clean your wounds, Bryce." "Don't get an infection, Bryce." But bathtubs are bad for my health, and being in this house feels dangerous. Especially this morning. I can sense my mother calling me. If I get into the tub to clean my feet, I might just decide to wash all the dirt away, and there's only one way to be that clean.

I open the door and see my dad sitting on the bench, staring into the fog.

"Can I join you?" I ask.

He moves over and makes room for me. Doesn't take much. I still could stand to gain a few or twenty. I can't eat, can't sleep, but I make up for it in liquid calories. I'm disappearing in this place. Every day I lose bits of what makes me who I am. I haven't laughed in weeks, and the last time I truly smiled was...well...I'll have to get back to that later. Even my sarcasm has taken a hit, which I resent. It was my armor. Without it, I'm just a turtle without its shell.

"Here," I say, holding up his jacket. "Put this on before you get hypothermia."

He lifts his arms without taking his eyes off the wall of fog in front of us.

"What're you doing out here, Dad?"

"Watching?"

"Watching what?"

"The fog."

I look where he's looking. The air doesn't move, the fog doesn't drift. It's as if someone pressed the pause button on the world around us. I wish. I'd kiss Jackson and say "I do" and love him for all the days of my life, and then run away just before pressing play.

"You see something I don't?" I ask.

My father cocks his head to the side and squints. "Not a goddamn thing."

He grabs the edge of the bench, squeezing with all his might, like he might fall off.

"Dad, you gotta tell me what's going on. What happened this morning? Why were you out there like that?"

"Why'd you call him?"

"Jackson? Because I was terrified. It was that or the cops. I wasn't really thinking. I just reacted."

"You were terrified?"

"Of course. I had no idea where you'd gone. I kept thinking I was going to find you dead, or never find you at all."

He sighs, his eyes still glued ahead. "Would it be so terrible?"

"Come on, Dad. Self-deprecation doesn't suit you."

"I'm not pitying myself. I'm asking a legitimate question. Surely death would be kinder than this. Disappearing this way."

I pry his hand off the bench and hold it tight. "We're going to get through this," I tell him. "I won't waste my time or yours by telling you it's not scary, but you're not alone. I'm not going anywhere. Hell, after a couple more weeks with me, you might just be thankful your memory sucks."

He laughs, but it's too heavy to be happy. I flinch when he pulls away, but then he takes my hand in his and looks at me. A broken man's eyes look different than the eyes of a whole person. Their function is no longer to show him the world around him, but to rid him of his pain with every tear shed, and to close out the agony at the end of each difficult day, when maybe sleep will transport him into a world where memories abound and life tastes like the nectar of the sweetest flower.

"Do you think someone like me deserves mercy?" he asks.

"If you're talking about God and redemption, you know we have much different—"

"I'm talking about you."

I shake my head. "I don't follow."

"Do you remember that little dog you had? That little hairy thing that used to bark whenever you left for school?"

The little hairy thing that used to bark when I left for school, until my mother opened the door and let it out.

"How could I forget? I came home and found it hit in the road."

"So you remember what I did for it."

"Stop being morbid, Dad. That's my thing, and you're not funny enough to pull it off."

"I'm not being funny."

I throw his hand away and get up, searching his face for something to tell me I've misunderstood, but we're already deep in the middle of a silent discussion I don't want to have. I'm not merciful. That's God's job—not mine. I'm small and human and petty, and I want to keep all the things I love, even if they are broken.

"No," is all I can say.

"Why?"

"Because I'm not"—I look around, lower my voice— "I'm not a murderer. And because as much as I might not like it, you're all I have left. Don't put this on me. How dare you."

"How dare I? How dare you! How can you sit in this house and watch me rot away? Look around, Bryce. What am I sticking around for?"

"For me."

"Is it worth the trade-off?" he asks.

"What trade-off?"

"You, trading your entire future to give me one I don't want and won't even remember to thank you for. You, walking away from everything you care about just to watch me waste away. You, winding up like your mother, and it being my fault."

"I call bullshit. Mom chose this life. She didn't have to stay. She wasn't a victim. I watched the video of your wedding. The look on her face, the way she hesitated before every word. She could've hauled ass and got the hell out of Dodge, but she walked right up to that alter and said 'for better or for worse.'"

"You really don't know what you're talking about," he says. "You know nothing about my relationship with your mother."

"I know she was unhappy, but instead of leaving, she shot up and snorted her way through each day and made me the mother. And now you're asking me to put you out of your misery because you feel guilty."

"Damn right I feel guilty. I should feel guilty. I'm not trying to take more regrets to the grave."

"No, no. Of course not. You'll just put that on me. You can cling to your religious hypocrisy all day long, Dad, but asking me to kill you is still suicide, and that's not going to earn you any points with the big man upstairs."

"This isn't about God. I've got no problem admitting that I'm scared to end it."

"Then don't."

"But I'm more scared of living this way." He grabs my hand. "I'm scared to death of everything, Bryce. My mind is unraveling, and there's not a thing I can do about it. Having you here watching doesn't help."

"That's no reason to—"

"My own son," he cries. "I don't even remember how my own son died. You said his name earlier, and I've spent all morning trying to remember how my little boy died."

His agony grounds me. I'm wearing a straitjacket stitched with his sorrow, and suddenly all I want to do is squash his pain and make him sleep and never wake up. But my hands are better than my morals, and they won't wield the final blow.

"I can't, Dad. Whether you get why I want you around or not, I can't."

"Then at least tell me how it happened. Scotty deserves to be remembered, or else it's like it never happened."

Inside me live secrets that could break my father's heart. It's not power—it's a curse. Arthur wants to hear a story of the worst kind. *Shatter my soul and tell me sad things.* But one day—maybe tomorrow, maybe in a year—he'll get to forget that once upon a time there lived a boy with the sweetest smile and love so big it didn't fit in this house, and that's why he had to leave. It's a burden to know such loss, but if my father wants it, it's his burden to carry.

I sit down and let him hold tightly to my hand. He's going to need it when he starts to fall apart and I cry in his open wounds.

"Do you remember our old neighbor, Tom, the one that had the baby-blue T-Bird Mom used to drool over?"

He nods. "I think so."

"He used to have those huge trees on his property that Scotty loved to climb. He'd get so high, none of us could figure out how he'd managed it without scaring himself stiff. It always scared me. I used to tell Mom to yell at him, but she left that to you.

"Scotty and I came home from school one day, and the trees were gone, chopped up in slabs on Tom's lawn. You don't remember Scotty crying?"

I didn't need to ask. My father listens with virgin ears, hanging on every word.

"No," he says.

"Later that day, when I was getting dinner together, Scotty went out back here and climbed one of our trees, the one that used to be over there." I point into the fog, where I can't see the stump but if I look hard enough, I can still see the outline of my brother's body lying on the ground.

"I couldn't tell what I was hearing at first," I say. "It was so quiet. Sometimes I think I must've left him out here crying for hours, but I know it couldn't have been more than a minute.

"I heard Scotty cry. No thud, no landing. Just a slight whimper. When I ran out here, he was lying"—I blink hard and clear my throat—"he was lying right under the tree. I thought maybe he broke his legs or his back. I was afraid to touch him, but then Mom came out and screamed. I told her to leave him alone and call nine-one-one, but she kept howling about him needing his mommy.

"When she picked him up, his eyes kind of…went back in his head, and I…I remember thinking that wasn't normal. But who was I? I was just a kid, even though Mom kept yelling at me about how it was my fault because the tree was rotten and I should've known better than to let him play in it.

"You came home and Mom told you he just *had a spill.* A fucking *spill.* I remember watching her and thinking she looked like a scared kid. She didn't want to get caught. She hadn't been watching her son, and now everyone was going to know it—not just me.

"I tried telling you guys that he didn't look okay. He didn't eat at dinner, and he kept falling asleep, but Mom insisted I was being dramatic. For all I knew maybe I was, so I shut up but kept an eye on him.

"Every night when we went to bed, Scotty and I would play this game where we'd make up these elaborate futures we were going to have. Scotty always said he'd have a pet dinosaur. No matter how many times I told him that was impossible, he insisted he'd have one. That night, I told him I was going to be a doctor, and I'd make a medicine that would take pain away. That way, next time he hurt himself, he wouldn't be so sad. I waited for him to tell me what a good idea that was, but he just asked me to be quiet. He said he was tired and wanted to sleep. 'Be quiet, sissy.' Those were the last words he ever said to me."

Now when I look into the fog, I see all the years since then, all my brother's lofty goals and absurdly optimistic dreams. They settle at my feet, piling around my legs. They're so beautiful and shiny, if you can see through the years of dust that weighs them down. It's a shame they won't get used.

I try to move my legs, but I know Scotty's deserted dreams are part of what's kept me from living out mine. Why should I be able to be a doctor or astronaut or a painter or even happy when my little brother only became a memory?

"And he never woke up," my father whispers. "The next morning, he never woke up. I"—he swallows loud—"I remember now."

I touch his shoulder. We do that to remind each other we're not alone. A simple touch—it's supposed to release endorphins and bring us contentment, but I do it to hold on to the pieces of my father before they, too, are buried in dust.

"Why was the tree out here?" he asks. "If we knew it was rotten and Scotty liked to climb, why'd we leave a hollow tree around?"

I look into my father's wet eyes and will him to remember. I don't want to say these words. They taste foul and make me gag, but I'd rather keep them to myself than spit them out and make my father sorry he talked about a son he's refused to mention for years.

"We just… I don't—"

"Was it my fault? I can't help but feel like it was my fault."

"It was no one's fault."

"Then tell me what happened?"

My lips part, my voice breaks up the quiet. I'd hold my hands over my mouth and lock the truth inside if I thought it wouldn't break loose while I wasn't looking.

"You were going to cut it down the weekend before his accident, but you had to go away for work."

His face contorts. I can't tell if he wants to cry or yell or scream or hit me. He's every emotion you never want to have.

"I didn't have to work," he sobs.

"What?"

"I didn't have to go. I wanted to. I needed to get away from your mother and the two kids I had failed so… I could've stayed, and Scotty would be here." His voice trembles under his tears. "It's my fault he's dead. I took your brother away."

My heart sits on its edge. It could fall in either direction. I could hate him forever. It's not like it would be hard. Or I could look at him and see a person just like me. An average fuck-up who destroyed everything, including himself, without ever setting out to. I see Jackson and I hear Jackson's words and I'm sorry for Jackson's pain, and I know I'm just a person who destroyed everything, including herself, without ever setting out to. I hate myself for it. I hate my father for it. But we're just human.

"It is not your fault," I say. "How many parents plan to teach their kids to swim or to look both ways before crossing the street but never get around to it? Most of them are just lucky enough to never come to regret that they got busy or forgot or put it off. You were an asshole, Dad." His head cocks up. "A serious asshole, but you didn't deserve to lose your son. You deserved to have him grow older like me and resent you for being such a dick. Not that he would've. You two were always close. But still"—I bend down and start to button up his jacket—"it's not your fault. Shit happens, and that's why Scotty's gone. You told him to stay out of that damn tree. I remember you saying it. But that child was just too wild and beautiful to keep his feet on the ground. He wasn't like you and me. We're built to wade in the mire."

He moves his arms so I can button his jacket the rest of the way. "I thought you said you weren't like me?" he asks.

I stop and look up at him. "I think we're more alike than either of us care to admit."

If I look closely, I can see his lips fighting against his pride. Man versus beast, Arthur versus Arthur. A smile tugs at the corner of his mouth, making his tears look out of place.

"I always thought it'd be Scotty," he says.

"Hoped, you mean."

"At one time, yes."

The little girl in me needs him to say more. She loves her brother best and always will, but she's scrawny and malnourished and needs some of the sun he's soaked up, even in death. She waits with bated breath and holds my hand while waiting to see if my dad finally calls her number.

"But I think I like you just fine," he says.

I nod and set my jaw. My father sounds strong, his brevity lending to his strength. I try to be the son he lost and manage my emotions without the water and the works and the snot and the blubbering. Just two strong people pretending they're not having an exchange of the hearts. But then he reaches down and gently takes my chin between his thumb and index finger and looks into my eyes as I try to keep from crying.

"I didn't love your brother more, Bryce. I was just raised in a time when daughters became their mothers and sons became a father's best friend. To be any other way meant something was wrong with you. I was afraid of how alike we were, and what a dreamer your brother was, just like your mom. I excluded you because of what it would've said about me if I hadn't."

"Whose opinion were you so preoccupied with?"

"Everyone's. And that's the most exhausting preoccupation to have."

I close my eyes and curse the warm tears spilling from them. How can he trust me to be strong when I can't contain the shattered girl living under my skin, pushing everyone away so no one knows I'm as delicate as my father's pink walls and as fragile as his future?

"Bryce," he says, forcing me to look at him. "If you don't cry, I won't get to know what makes you you. If you don't mind, I'd like to get to know my daughter before it's too late."

I open my eyes and let him see the parts of me I always believed he thought were ugly, and then I tell him I love him with my tears.

CHAPTER 27

"Hello there, you gorgeous specimen!" Shana says.

I don't even have the door completely open before she's cramming herself through it, holding a paper bag up to my nose.

"Three of your favorite Dahlia's pastries, my lady."

My mouth immediately waters. I snatch the bag away and step back to get a better look at the shiny girl from the city. She's like stepping into the sunlight after being in a dark room. She looks like an expensive toy, with silky hair and shoes that could kill a man. The pastries smell great, but when I lean in for a hug, Shana smells even better, like faraway lands and exotic foods. If this were *The Silence of the Lambs*, I'd wear her.

"You look amazing," I say. "Now I get why men who've been incarcerated lose their minds when they finally see a woman. The only woman I see is the neighbor, and her idea of dressing up is wearing slippers that match her house dress."

"Ah"—Shana flutters her lashes—"don't be silly. You know these are my grubby clothes. And you look great."

Ah, don't be silly. You know you're a total liar, Shana. But I love her anyway. I can almost smell the store still on her new clothes, and that leather jacket is a force to be reckoned with. Nothing's getting through that thing. Shana made sure of it. Over her dead body will "back home" permeate her clothes and seep into her skin, where it might devour all her hard work of the last few years.

"Thanks, Shana. You always were a good liar."

"I'm not lying. You have a real earthy vibe. It suits you."

I reach in the bag and snort. "Earthy, frumpy. Whatever. You brought me a chocolate croissant, so you can say whatever you want."

It would never occur to Shana that I've always looked this way. It's the environment that's changed. In the city, my carelessness was edgy and rebellious. Here, I'm just another county fair princess whose Keds match the color of her minivan and the siding of her three-bedroom rancher. I'm just missing the two kids and a dog named Spot.

Shana throws her stuff on the couch and touches my hair. "Is he asleep?"

"Yep."

She tilts her head and looks sad. "How are you, hun? I've missed you so much."

I nod, using my lips to rein in the unruly bite of croissant I'm wrestling down my gullet. "Been better," I try to say, but Shana's frown never leaves her face.

"Your dad's got dementia. Obviously you've been better. But how're you?"

"Alzheimer's," I say.

"Aren't they the same?"

"No, actually. But I'm all right, all things considered. I thought I'd have my head in the oven by now, but I'm coping. I only wake up drenched in sweat a couple nights a week now, so the outlook's okay."

"So *okay* that you don't want these?" She reaches in a larger paper bag and pulls out two bottles of wine.

I hold the croissant to my chest and feign tears. "They're beautiful, Shana."

"That's what I thought," she says with one of those perfect winks I can't pull off without looking like I'm stroking out.

"Oh, and I almost forgot." She puts the wine on the coffee table and reaches back in the bag, pulling out a bottle of tequila. "In case we decide tonight's no night for child's play, I brought reinforcements."

"Shana, if I could get over the whole you having a vagina thing, I'd marry you."

"And I'd say yes. Now get me some glasses."

~

Shana and I sit on the floor in front of the couch, a pizza box splayed open on the coffee table in front of us. I can see her eyeing the remaining slices, but she's too busy counting calories to take another bite. I, on the other hand, can eat to my heart's content. Plaid camouflages unflattering areas, and I don't have any anyway. All those fad diets were wrong. A dysfunctional past and a sick father is the ticket to staying thin. Rotten insides, broken soul, fractured heart. But as long as I'm thin.

I smile when I glance at Shana's stomach. The girl really doesn't eat carbs. You can tell by her bloated belly and the glassy look in her eyes. Wine she can handle. Saturated fats and cheesy crusts, I think not.

She's slouched on the floor, crumbs on her emerald top, the lipstick wiped clean from her mouth. She glances at me sideways and makes a guttural sound.

"You're such a dick, Bryce."

"Yeah, you would know, expert."

"You're so skinny. By tomorrow morning, I won't fit in this skirt."

"Just relax. Tonight we leave Seattle in Seattle. Up here, ladies eat and age and drink the men under the table. If tomorrow you're fat, I have some lovely sweats I can lend you. But I'll want 'em back. They're my best ones."

She looks like she might be sick. "Ugh. That's not even funny."

"What? All of it, or just the part about the sweats?"

"The sweats. No…all of it. Being here, back where we grew up." She looks around the room, then back at me. "You're stronger than me. How can you stand it?"

"I look at it like a job. Clocking into the coffee house, punching in at the storage facility, being here on call twenty-four-seven. They're all just jobs. Eventually my shift will end."

Shana turns to look at me, her elbow on the couch, holding up her head. "You've been here for almost a month. When do you clock out?"

My best friend is beautiful and she smells exotic and she has dark, mysterious eyes, but unwrap the packaging and you'll find a few parts missing. She stares at me with equal parts cluelessness and annoyance.

"Seriously, when're you coming home, Bryce?"

I pour her another drink and tell her to chug. She lets out a sloppy giggle and complies, but then she's back to business.

"Okay. You want me liquored up for some reason. Now tell me when you're coming home."

"I'm not coming home, Shana. At least no time soon."

Her head straightens, her brows lift. "What are talking about? You hate it up here. Of course you're not staying."

"I do hate it here, but my father's got Alzheimer's. I don't know how much you know about it, but he's very sick, and he's not getting any better. This isn't a let-it-pass kind of situation. This is a see-it-to-the-end situation."

"The end?" she asks. Shana's so pretty. Shana's so oblivious.

"Yes. The end. My father's end. He's starting to lose his memory. He crashed his car into a house he thought was his, he lit his kitchen on fire, he doesn't remember the date or sometimes the year. The other night, he took off while I was sleeping and we found him crying on the side of the road, like four miles from here. I can't afford to put him in a nursing home. Even if I could…"

"Even if you could…? Don't tell me you're going soft for the guy. He was such a tyrant, but now that he's sick, you're going to move up here and stop your life to take care of him?"

I think about the last few weeks and all the things my father's shared with me. The bad, the good. How do you quantify the value of a man's life to someone who sees him as just a monster? I can't. I won't even try, because

Shana's not wrong. But neither am I. Where in my father I used to see anger, I now see weakness, and where I used to see a tyrant, I now see someone so scared of expressing himself that he's made his life a prison sentence and the air in his lungs a burden he must carry.

"Shana, all I can tell you is that I understand things a bit clearer now. I'm not making excuses for my dad. I don't make them for myself, so he won't get that luxury, either. But I've learned some things. When you're a kid and you look at these abusive, angry, fucked-up parents, you spend every day wondering why the hell they choose to be so miserable. Why would anyone want to be that unhappy and that cruel to the people they love? Like it's a choice your parents are making. It doesn't occur to kids that parents don't know better, or that they're more lost than even you are. We think our moms and dads have it all figured out, so if they're horrible to us, it must be a conscious choice. But that's bullshit. I didn't know until coming back that my dad was and is more lost than I've ever been. I don't know what caused it, but he's so scared, Shana. You sit in a room with the guy and you can feel his fear. He was a horrible father, and it breaks my heart to say that probably won't change, but somewhere inside him is something good."

Shana plays with the hem of her skirt and glances up at me quickly. "Well now I feel bad. I've spent this month wanting you all to myself, and here you are, learning all these important life lessons." She takes a long sip of wine. "Am I a bitch if I say I still think it stinks that you have to be the one to sacrifice everything?"

I hate to see people drink alone. I knock the glass back and finish my wine.

"Not at all," I tell her. "It is unfair. I drink a lot. I also don't think about the future. If I ever caught myself "hoping my dad would hurry up and kick the bucket so I can get the hell outta here, I'd never be able to live with myself. Luckily that hasn't happened yet, but I don't want to tempt it, either."

The room falls silent. Shana looks around with a curious expression.

"Sorry," I say. "Little too blunt, I guess."

"No, no. It's not you." She points her little finger at the wall. "Did you do this?"

"The pink walls? No. That's all my dad, and they're not pink. They're *salmon*."

"Salmon, my ass. That's pink. What's up with that?"

I sit back, arms over my chest, and stare at the wall with my exotic friend. "I haven't the foggiest idea. The old man won't tell me. Loses his shit every time I ask."

"It reminds me of something," Shana says.

"Brain matter?"

"No."

"The new skin under a scab?"

"No."

"A clam box?"

She rolls her eyes at me. "Seriously? Are you like five?"

"You're giving me too much credit. I didn't know what a clam box was when I was five."

"You're a pervert, Bryce."

"And you're a little bit of a slut."

Her laughter blends into mine, and for once this house does something other than weep.

"That's why we love each other so much," she says.

"Yeah. That, and you bring me sweets and liquor."

"Not that you needed any more, from what you've said. So how else have you been keeping yourself busy, "other than drinking?" The arch of her brow tells me we're not talking about crocheting or tapestry work.

"No one has been keeping me busy, Shana. How about you? What's up with you and Nature Boy?"

"We broke up. He wanted me to train with him to climb Mount Everest, but I had to wash my hair that day."

I laugh-snort. "What? You didn't want to find yourself?"

"Nah. I'd rather have pretty hair."

I raise my glass. "A fine head of hair it is, my friend. And I don't blame you. The water's always warmer in the shallow end of the pool."

She tips her glass and gives me another wink.

"What's up with Jackson?" she asks.

I pour another glass for myself. "The wedding's next month and our house is in escrow. We'll be house poor, but we needed that fourth bedroom for the twins."

She glares at me from over her glass. For a minute I think she'll spit her wine at me.

"I should hate you," she says. "Here you have this perfect guy who just fawns over you, even when you dress like that—"

"Hey! You said I looked earthy."

"I was being nice. You look like my mom. And still, I bet Jackson looks at you like you're the only woman on Earth. Am I right?"

"Kinda. Sure. Yeah."

She taps her wine glass on mine. "Hence, I should hate you."

I skulk away into the kitchen and open the second bottle of wine even though my glass is still full. I'm going to need a lot of truth serum if Shana and I are going to get out of this alive. She'll hang me if I don't start spilling all the good details soon.

I come back into the living room and top off her glass. All my secrets pour from the bottle. Once they escape and hit the air, they start to decay and stink up the joint.

"I went on a date with the dermatologist who removed the mole on my thigh. We almost had sex, but he kept turning into Jackson, so..."

"What?"

"And I don't have cancer."

You know it's serious when Shana puts a glass of merlot down. She pats the spot next to her and snaps. "Get over here and tell me everything, or else I'm not your friend anymore."

I sit down, shrug. "There's nothing to tell, or I would have told you. I had that mole I was telling you about forever ago removed. My doctor was super hot. When I came down on my birthday—"

"And didn't call me—"

"Yes, when I came down to get some things from my place, I ran into him. He asked me out and I said yes. It was fine, he was fine. That was it."

"And?"

"And nothing. I left him with a case of blue balls and came back here to argue with the perfect guy who fawns over me."

"He was here? With your dad?"

"He was, and it didn't go well...between us, I mean."

Shana gets quiet. I get quiet. I know I've burst her bubble, even though it's not my job to keep air in it.

"What, Shana? You look all pensive."

"It's just..." She flits her hand through the air and shakes her head. "You two are just... Did you both sustain some kind of brain injury together? Maybe you swapped a brain-eating amoeba as kids or something? I "mean, you are aware that people are walking around everyday, searching for someone who will love them the way you two love each other, yet you aren't together. You hold what happened over his head, but it wasn't his fault."

"Sorry I have trust issues," I say. "I swear I don't do it on purpose. I'm not opposed to being happy. I just…get in my own way."

She sits up straight and faces me. "It's your father's fault. If it weren't for him, you guys would still be together."

"My dad's an asshole, but I can't blame him for this one. Jackson had a choice, and it wasn't the right one."

"Yes, it was. Maybe you and your dad need to have a little chat about what happened back then."

"What're you talking about?"

Her split-second moment of hesitation kicks at my gut. It's these little cues that tell us life as we know it is about to change. I hate these pauses. Hate the weight they carry and their bloody need for attention.

"What, Shana?"

"Jackson said we shouldn't tell you. He knew your dad was going to be all you had when you got out of the hospital, and he didn't want you hating him. Not after everything you'd already been through."

"Shana, you couldn't beat around the bush more if you tried. What the hell are you getting at?"

She looks at me like people always do when readying themselves for the blow they're about to watch you take.

"Jackson went to see you in the hospital. As soon as they would let people visit, he went, but your dad saw him in the waiting room and told him to leave."

"I know you've always wanted us together, but painting the past with pretty lies isn't going to change what happened."

"I'm not lying! Go ask him. Wake him up and ask him if he told Jackson to leave because he didn't want him there."

"That's impossible," I say. "Aside from the fact that my dad actually liked Jackson up until then, there's no way you wouldn't have told me this sooner. Not our biggest cheerleader. You've been picking out our kids' names since high school. You would've said something."

"Really? Well, then ask yourself how many times I've broken my word to you. Then ask yourself if you're the only friend I'm loyal to. Jackson begged me not to tell you. At the time, he had a good point. We knew you'd need your dad. And Jackson… I don't know what happened to him after that night, but he changed. He thought your dad was right, so he left, and I kept my word. But now you don't need your dad. He needs you, and you need to know the truth, whether Jackson or Arthur like it or not."

And there it is. The blow, and the gaping hole left in my chest. I try to piece myself together, but the bits of my past that acted as glue aren't even real. They're lies, and they won't fit with the truth anymore.

One hand on the coffee table, one on the floor, I try to ground myself in the moment so I don't float away. The last seven years were built on heartache orchestrated by my father. Same old story—nothing new. My father opens his mouth and out pour lies that make me bleed.

I try to speak, but what's there to say? Shana touches my shoulder and gives me the same smile you give a child who's just learned Santa isn't real.

"I'm sorry," she says.

But I pull away, because I love her but I hate her right now, and maybe I could rip all those exotic black strands of hair from her head. She still wouldn't hurt as much as I do right now.

"I'm trying real hard to tell myself I shouldn't hate you for keeping a promise to Jackson," I say. "But I can't forgive you right now, either. I can't believe you'd lie to me all these years, Shana."

"I get that. I really am sorry. If I had it to do over, I'd make Jackson tell you. We really were just looking out for you. I didn't know what the hell to do back then. I was just following his lead."

"Maybe that's true, but I needed the truth. You see what good keeping this from me has done."

"I do. We were wrong."

I grab the tequila off the coffee table and drink straight from the bottle. I don't care what they say about wine before liquor. They can go fuck themselves. Those pussies just can't handle their drink. And I want to be sick. Maybe I can purge myself of Shana's words.

I take another swig and wipe the liquid from the corners of my mouth. "Swear to me you'll never keep anything from me again," I say, wiping away what I refuse to believe are tears. I'm too angry to cry. "Right here, right now, swear it. I can't afford to lose trust in another person. Your loyalty to me overrides everything else. Promise me, Shana."

She tries to take my hand, but I won't let go of the bottle.

"You have my word," she says. "I'll tell you the truth, always, no matter what."

I nod.

"So I guess that means I have to tell you what these walls really remind me of," she says.

I slam the bottle down. "What?"

"A hotel my parents took me to when I was little and we vacationed in Victoria. It was a monstrosity. The whole damn thing was pink, just like this."

"So?"

"So we saw your dad there that weekend. He wasn't alone, Bryce. Well…we didn't actually see him with anyone, but my mother spent the whole ride home talking about how obvious he was being, and whispering to my father about your poor mother, and no wonder why she was never seen in public. They said I wasn't allowed to tell you. I honestly forgot about it till now."

I pick the bottle back up and say, "I guess me and the old man are due for a little chat."

CHAPTER 28

I listen in the hallway to the sounds of Theo and my father chatting like they go way, way back. I even hear my dad laugh, which stirs in me a kind of madness I probably have no right to. I'm trying to rise above it and all that happy horse shit, but why should he have a moment's happiness when I've been the dartboard for all his lies? So what if you leave holes in Bryce. Just fill her up with another tall tale.

The picture keeps running through my head. Jackson showing up at the hospital. Jackson being told to leave and never come back. It's enough to make *me* want to leave and never come back. I want to be done with being good, but it grips me in place and plunges its grimy probes into my conscience. I just wish the aliens had been courteous enough to abduct me from this quaint little hellhole.

I walk past my father's room and hurry out the front door. Saturday night with Shana left its mark. Until yesterday, I'd forgotten how to walk in a straight line. I've definitely purged the poison from my system, but my legs still feel rubbery and uncertain.

This is my father's fault. Had he not turned Jackson away all those years ago, I'd have a ride to the mechanic's right now and wouldn't be walking five miles in the mist that hasn't stopped falling from the sky for the last two weeks. I hate this state right now. I want to move to Key West and be a sunny person with a sunny smile and sunny skin that smells like coconuts and salty air, but I'm too swarthy for anything other than damp pessimism, and my gypsy hair doesn't like me enough for humidity.

I start heading down the street, kicking a small rock along the way. If I can manage to get it all the way to the shop, I'll paint kitty ears on it and name it John Gunther. My cat collection's gotta start somewhere, since I really am going to end up all alone.

I have my hood on, head down, and give my rock another good kick, sending it across the lane closest to me and into the opposing lane, where it settles in the middle of the road. I stop and stare across the street, looking both ways, but there's a vehicle coming, and I'm happy John Gunther is made of minerals and not soft tissue, so he won't go splat under the big truck that looks just like Jackson's. Shit. That *is* Jackson's.

I turn and walk in the other direction, but I can hear his engine slow and his tires chew the gravel as he comes to a stop.

"Bryce?"

I walk faster, because somehow outrunning a truck seems as realistic as outrunning the question, *Why didn't you tell me you came to the hospital?*

"Bryce?"

If he says it three times, I have to click my heels and go back home.

"Bryce, stop."

Wouldn't you know it? Jackson's home.

I stop and turn around, looking at him from under my hood. His window's down, and he's wearing a dark-blue baseball cap that hides his eyes and the same tan Carhartt jacket every man in the Pacific Northwest owns. I can almost smell his rugged pheromones from here. It's this kind of nonsense that makes a woman want to mount a man like a horse and have his beautiful babies, even if she does only wind up becoming a mere speck in his cosmos.

"Get in the truck, Bryce. Let me give you a ride."

"You told me you were leaving. For good."

"And I meant it. But I also told myself if I drove by and saw you walking, I'd break my rule just this once."

"Aren't you supposed to be working?"

"I took a late lunch so I could drive you."

I can tell from here that he hasn't shaved in a few days, and I wonder if he did it to torture me. My biological cuckoo clock has bells and whistles and one of those damn birds that pops out of the house and screams, "DO IT, DO IT, DO IT." I want to pluck him clean and wear his little birdy beak around my neck for all to see, but something warms in my chest when I look at Jackson and already know that I'd fit perfectly beside him in his truck. Not too tall, not too short, not too big, not too small.

I shove my hands in my pockets and watch my breath billow around my lips as I speak. "It is cold."

"Then what're you still doing out there, dummy?"

I will not smile, I will not smile, I will not smile.

I walk across the street and open the door. Jackson offers up a polite smile and nods his head, motioning for me to climb on. I mean *in*. Climb INNNNNN. Jesus, Bryce. Keep your dick in your pants.

I get in and shut the door, staying as far away from him as I can. The taste of him still lingers on my lips, and I want seconds and thirds and forevers. I hear him giggle and want to point at him and tell him what a girl he is, but he even makes giggling sound inherently masculine. I give up. I'm just going to sit here and pretend he's not amazing.

"You mad at me?" he asks.

"Nope. Wasn't mad at you the other night, either. You were the one making absolutes."

"Do you not get why?"

I nod, look out my window. "I get why, Jackson. You made some valid points."

"I'm not trying to argue."

"Nor am I." I look at him to show him there's no hidden intent behind my words. "I'm being serious. You made some good points."

He looks at me suspiciously.

"I mean it. I completely appreciate where you're coming from."

"Okay," he says, looking back at the road. "And I completely appreciate where you're coming from as well. I have every intention of respecting our new boundaries. I just couldn't let you walk all the way there in the rain. Plus, I should be there."

"Why?"

"Because it's a mechanic."

"And?"

"And you don't know what you're looking for. They'll see you coming a mile away."

"I know what I'm looking for. Does his truck look like a truck or a crumpled piece of paper? Okay, looks like a truck. We're good."

"My point exactly," he says with a lift in his voice. "It's not whether or not the outside looks good. You need to drive the thing. See if anything seems fishy. They see some looker stroll up in her cute little rain boots and they'll never take you seriously."

"You're a sexist pig, and my boots aren't cute."

"Hah!" he laughs. "I'm not and you know it. But they are, and you don't know anything about engines."

Jackson could probably dismantle an engine in the dark. God knows that's what he did to me. But the old man never let him rebuild me, and now my gaskets and hoses and plugs are lying on the floor at Jackson's feet. If only I could tell him to suit up and get his hands dirty, but I don't know how to tell someone I'm not whole without them.

"How's your dad?" he asks.

Doesn't he mean *the enemy*?

"I thought we were making headway. The other morning, after you left, he shared some things with me. Kind of made me look at him differently, you know? He's talked more to me lately than he ever has. He actually talked about my mom and my brother. Can you believe the guy actually kept a file full of my art?"

"I can."

I wait for him to elaborate, but he goes quiet.

"Anyway, it was all bullshit."

"How so?"

"I just…I found out some things about him. Lies he told. Big lies. The kind that change things forever."

The truck speeds up, and Jackson takes his hat off and turns the heat down. "Warm in here," he says, wiping his forehead and gripping the wheel.

"Yeah." I eye him. "Anyway, I just need to stop investing myself in him. I'm here for a job. No more, no less."

He adjusts his seatbelt, curses under his breath.

"You okay?" I ask. "You're acting strange. You're not prying, which is totally unlike you, and now you're all sweaty and agitated."

"I'm not agitated. My seatbelt was just tight."

"Right."

"I'm not, Bryce. And I didn't pry because I'm keeping my distance. I told you I meant what I said. This…us…I'm respecting what it is."

"And what is it exactly, Jackson? We're not friends, but you just felt guilty and decided to give me one last lift before never seeing me again? If so, let me out. I don't take rides from strangers."

"Truth?" he asks.

"No, lie to me."

"Fine. Truth is, I don't know what we are, Bryce. I haven't known that for a very long time. We're just…an anomaly."

"Great. What every girl dreams of."

He slows the truck down and pulls into a parking lot with a dingy shop tucked in the corner and my father's beige Ford parked out front.

"Look," I say. "No more dents."

He rolls his eyes, and we get out and stand next to the truck. I look down at the puddles and at Jackson's soaked leather boots.

"Who's the dummy now?" I ask, playfully kicking his foot with my cute rain boot. He takes a step away from me. Uh-oh. His expression tells me I've crossed one of those boundaries he was talking about.

An old man with grease for skin emerges from under a hood and asks Jackson what he can help us with. He sounds like he gargles with glass, and one of his front teeth matches the gray sky.

"I'm here to get my father's truck," I say, asserting my dominance, but the old man doesn't bat an eye in my direction.

"Where're the papers?" he asks.

I pull them from my pocket and hand them to him, and he tells Jackson he's a pussy just with his eyes.

"I'll go get the keys," he says.

"Thanks," Jackson tells him. "I want to take it out for a spin before we leave."

The old man mumbles something and walks away with a limp that makes him look like he's doing the shimmy with every step.

Jackson lifts the hood and stares down at the engine while I stand across from him, doing the same.

"The fuel injector looks good to me. Maybe a little tightening on those lugs. Don't wanna lose our chassis in the road," I say.

Jackson leans forward, hands on the side of the hood, doing his best not to laugh. "Do you have any idea what you just said?"

"Not really, but I had you fooled."

He bends down and pulls on something. "Mess around if you want to, but I'll tell him you said you want your lugs tightened."

"And how do you know I don't? He looks like an experienced man. Maybe I want someone who knows how to tighten a lug."

Ol' dancing shoes limps back out with a set of keys and a folded sheet of paper. "I guess these belong to you, then?" He holds the keys out to me.

"They can go to him"—I point to Jackson—"he's going to test her out."

Jackson catches the keys when the old man tosses them to him.

"Anything else?" the man grumbles.

"Yeah," Jackson says. "The little missy here says she wants her lugs tigh—"

"No!" I shout. "We're good. Thanks. That'll be all."

The man limps back inside, adjusting his junk as a farewell.

"Jackson!" I come around to slap his shoulder, but he moves away, laughing at me.

"What? I was just trying to get your lugs tightened. I thought he was dreamy."

"Shut up!" I shout-whisper.

"I saw you undressing him with your eyes, Bryce. It's okay. Nothing wrong with a May-December romance. Just go easy on him. I think his hip's bad."

"Yeah?" I arch one brow. "Jokes on you. How do you think his hip got that way?"

He grabs his chest and feigns a heart attack. "How could you betray me so soon?"

I stomp my foot in a puddle, sending greasy water onto his jeans and sexy timber-man jacket. "Just hurry up and go test drive the damn truck so I can have a moment with ol' Studs back there."

"Fine." He gets in the truck, revs the engine. "But you better use something. He won't be around much longer to pay child support."

I kick the tire. "Go!"

He puts the truck in gear and gives me a small salute. "Yessum."

~

Jackson pulls back in with the beige beast ten minutes later. He puts it in park and gets out, handing me the keys. "She sounds good. Should get you home in one piece."

It's all fun and games until someone gets hurt. I jokingly look around to make sure my May-December romance isn't watching, and I go to hug Jackson, but he leans back and takes my hands instead.

"I'm sorry, Bryce. But I can't. I wrap my arms around you and it's that much harder to let go."

"Then why'd you kiss me the other night?"

"You kissed me."

"And you kissed me back."

He nods and lets go of my hands, putting his in his pockets. "I shouldn't have done that. It was wrong."

"It felt pretty right to me," I say.

"Of course it would. You don't mind a quick fling, but I want commitment. I know I'm breaking some guy code by saying that, but it's what I want."

Now I put my hands in my pockets, where they can't take off with my last sliver of dignity and wrap themselves around Jackson's leg so he can't leave me alone forever.

"So this really is goodbye?" I ask. "We're never going to see each other again? You're missing out, you know. I was going to bake you cookies for rescuing me today and bring them by your place later."

"Won't your boyfriend back there get mad?"

I try to smile, he tries to smile. We both lose at masking our sadness.

"That's nice of you, but don't worry about it. I won't be around tonight, and your cookies would probably suck, anyway."

"What? Got a date or something?"

I wait for him to tell me no, but he looks away, and all I hear is the blasted squealing of that wrench thing I don't know the name of. Suddenly I'm the girl on the outside looking in at Jackson and his date—a woman I know nothing about but am convinced is tall and thin and blonde and has the tits of a Greek goddess and the legs of a gymnast, and most of all will love him so unabashedly that he'll forget my name and what I look like, and that we taught each other what it meant to be loved.

Now I understand Shana. I'm already planning their perfect wedding and imagining their lovely children, only I don't want an invitation. May it rain on the day of their putrid nuptials, and may their children be cursed with unibrows and low IQs .

Did I not love him enough to leave my mark all over him, like a cautionary road sign telling other women to turn around? I expected a lot of things today, but I didn't expect to be gutted in front of Murphy's Mechanics. I've held my breath for the last seven years, and now, when I finally come up for air, the surface is frozen solid. I can see Jackson, but I can't hear him or feel him anymore. All I can hear now is my phone ringing in my pocket.

"You gonna answer that? Whoever it is called twice," Jackson says. "Bryce?" he claps, and I shake my head.

I grab my phone and turn around so he can't see that I'm still drowning.

"Hello?"

It's Theo on the other end, only it's not the Theo I know. This one is rushed and panicked. "Bryce, you need to get back here, ASAP."

"What's wrong? Is he okay?"

"He's tearing everything apart. I can't calm him down."

"Shit. Okay. I'll be right there."

I grab the keys from my pocket and get in the truck. I haven't driven a stick in years, but today's no day for whiners.

"What is it?" Jackson asks, holding on to the open window.

"I don't know. My dad's freaking out or something. I gotta go."

"But...I—"

"I don't want to leave it like this, either, Jackson. But I have to get back."

The words are on his tongue. He wants to tell me to call him if I need him. He can't stop recusing me, and I can't stop falling without him.

I put the truck in reverse but hesitate. "If you want to help me," I say, "don't go on that date tonight."

"That's not fair, Bryce."

"Fuck fair. Just don't go."

And before he can pull the trigger and tell me "tough," I leave the parking lot and head home.

CHAPTER 29

I can feel my father's rage before I even get through the front door. His screams make it all the way to the driveway.

I open the door and walk into a storm. My father's a tornado, all the debris left in his wake looks like pieces of his home, but they're now causalities of whatever war he's waging with himself.

I step over couch cushions and walk around a toppled end table. I can hear Theo's pleas, followed by the crash of something being thrust against the wall.

"Dad!" I stand in the doorway to my father's room and wait for him to turn around, but he's on autopilot, like someone programmed him not to stop until the walls are no longer standing and the roof is blown off. He's tossing items off his dresser and knocking over any furniture he can get his hands on before Theo blocks him.

"Help me out here," Theo yells.

I walk in and duck. My mother's porcelain goose flies into the wall next to me and falls to the floor in pieces.

I stand, block my face. "Dad! Stop throwing shit! What the hell's wrong with you?"

But he can't hear me over his own voice.

"Where is it?" he screams. "What'd you do with it?"

"No one touched anything. Stop it!"

Theo's eyes are round and protruding. He looks at me and just shakes his head.

"Grab him!" I say.

Theo holds his hands over his ears, trying to block out my father's strained voice. "I tried, but I can't risk hurting him."

"Then I'll do it."

"Don't, Bryce. He's a lot stronger than you right now. Just let it play out."

I have no time for Theo's opinions. Short of a tranquilizer gun, it's going to take an act of God to stop my dad. That or me.

I sidestep around broken glass and splintered wood, dodging my father's arms as they fly with gusto and no precise aim.

"Dad, look at me," I yell. He glances over his shoulder but doesn't see me. "At least tell me what you're looking for and I'll help you find it."

He shoves me out of the way and goes to work deconstructing the other side of the room as Theo shouts at me to get back.

"I can't lose that, too," my dad cries. "Where'd you put it?"

"Put what?" I ask.

"The box! The box the box the motherfucking box! Where is it?"

I grab my head, pulling my hair at the roots. "For fuck's sake. I don't know what you mean. Please stop!"

He reaches up to grab a frame off the wall, and I see an opening and grab his arms from behind, trying to fight against his madness and the six-inch advantage he's got on me.

"Let him go," Theo orders. "He's gonna hurt you."

My dad fights back, yanking his arms forward, so I pull back again, spinning him around with all my strength.

"Dad…stop," I gasp, but before I can see what's happening, his cocked arm rushes at me, and I don't even feel the pain of the punch over the shock it delivers. He throws me to the floor and my head slams on the edge of the bedframe.

Theo rushes at him, and my father calls him names so ugly I can't even repeat them, and I know there will be no cleaning the stains out of their relationship once this is over.

I try to get on my knees, but my head goes round and round. I press my hands to the floor and push up, but something under the bed catches my eye, and I know I can't be that lucky and my father that oblivious.

I pull out something the size of a shoebox and scream, "Stop!"

My father and Theo both turn and look at me.

"Is this it?" I ask. "Is this the fucking box you're losing your mind over?" I taste snot on my lips and blood in my mouth. Arthur might be an old man, but he still carries in his veins the blood of a brute.

His forehead creases, his brows cast dark shadows over his eyes. "What'd you do with it?" he growls.

"I didn't do anything with it. It was under your bed the whole time."

I think he's coming for the box, but he's aimed at me. "Where'd you hide it?"

He's an animal, and I'm crazy enough to not care. I get up and scream in his face so loud it makes my ears ring and my head pound. "I didn't do anything with it, you fucking monster!"

I throw his precious box to the floor and enjoy seeing whatever's inside fly out, littering the floor.

My father bends down, frantically scooping up what looks like cards and letters and notes and fuck him I don't care. He's crying into his hands and holding a butter-colored envelope to his chest.

"I'm sorry," he cries. "I'm sorry I hit you. I didn't mean to."

Theo and I look at each other, then around the room.

"You okay?" he whispers.

I nod, licking blood off the corner of my mouth. "Maybe you should go."

"I can't leave you two like this."

My father's slowly working his way into the fetal position on the floor, sobbing while he clutches the box in his arms.

I brush hair out of my face and wipe tears from my cheeks.

"We're all right. Please, just go."

CHAPTER 30

I make my father dinner. I didn't poison it, but I spent the entire time making it thinking about all the ways I could. Does that make me a bad person? Maybe. Maybe I don't give a shit because I'm too busy nursing a migraine and a swollen lip and a heavy heart.

I walk into the hallway and stop. His pink walls make me want to scream. I stick my finger in the mac-n-cheese and smear a large dollop along the wall. Too bad I can't punch a hole through it without hurting myself and taking all the fun out of it for my dad.

When I open his door, he's sitting up in bed, eyes forward, shoulders slumped.

I sit the tray on his lap. "Eat."

"I'm not hungry."

"Then don't eat it. I don't care."

The air's thick with unspoken words and wounds too fresh for niceties. I turn to leave, but his voice brings me to a halt.

"I'm so sorry I hurt you."

My body trembles as I silently weep. If I let him see me now, he'll know my pain and what kind of power he wields. If I don't, his ignorance will remain my burden.

I turn around and our eyes meet, and for a moment I see myself in the broken man lying on the bed. My pain is an extension of his. I recognize his tears, because I've cried them many times, and I know they're no ordinary tears. They're the culmination of a life of sorrow and dismantled dreams come to the surface, ready to meet those they've disappointed. They carry with them all the vile agony bottled up in one's soul. They taste of bitterness and torment, and if you don't get rid of them they'll choke you from the inside.

"I didn't mean to do it," he says, not even wiping away his tears.

"And I suppose you never meant to when I was little, either, right?"

His chin trembles. "This isn't the same. I thought I was doing the right thing back then. I was raised to believe children needed to be punished."

"Hit."

"Punished."

"Abused. You don't have to hit a child to punish them, Dad. There are hundreds of ways you could've taught me lessons. All I learned from you was that if I didn't like something, I needed to hurt it. No talking, no working things out. Just hurting. And Mom? What about her? Did she need to be punished, too?"

He looks away so he can't see the truth written on my face. He wears his denial as openly as I wear my honesty.

"I didn't know what I was doing," he says. "I was young. My generation was taught that there wasn't a whole hell of a lot that couldn't be fixed by exchanging a few punches. Boys fought and were friends the next day. I fucked up, my dad would nail me one and I'd never do it again. You acted up in school and the teachers slapped you with a ruler until you forget why you ever thought chewing gum in class was a good idea."

"Excuses."

"Maybe," he says. "Maybe they are, but that doesn't mean I'm lying. All I knew how to do was use my hands, whether it was for work, for war, for fighting, or for disciplining my wife and children. Hell, even the church taught me it was my duty to keep my family in line by any means necessary. Not to was considered a sin."

I laugh. "Using the teachings of the church as a guideline for parenting was probably your first fuck-up."

"They weren't all bad, Bryce. That's what you don't get. I didn't sit around conspiring against you. My intent was good, the church's intent was good. But we were misguided. My entire generation was misguided."

I lean against the wall, arms crossed in front of me. I'd like to think I'm witnessing a confession, but there's something about impending death that can make someone a phony bullshitter.

"Is this just you atoning for your sins before it's too late?" I ask.

"No. This isn't about anything other than me trying to apologize. I was wrong. Do you hear me? I was wrong on so many levels, but something tells me it's too late for apologies. I tried with your brother. I never laid a finger "on him. Even if I can't remember everything, I remember that. I was trying. But with you I just—"

"You call taking everything out on one kid and not the other *trying*? That's a fucking joke! And you never hit Scotty because I never gave you the chance. Think about it, Dad. How many times were you alone with him? How many times do you remember even seeing him when you were in a bad mood, huh? Can you recall even once when I wasn't there, standing in front of him or ushering him to our room? I took a lot on for that kid. For him and Mom. I remember going to bed in tears, so sore from a beating. You used to tell me you'd whoop my ass till I couldn't sit, and man, you weren't kidding. But it was worth it because I knew the pain you caused me was nothing compared to how much I would've hated myself had I let my baby brother take a beating. And Mom? I shouldn't have wasted my time protecting her when she did so little to protect me, but I hated seeing you hit her. I swear, you'd hit her and I'd feel it more than when you'd hit me. So I painted a giant X on my chest and got in your way so you wouldn't notice they'd gotten away without a scratch on them. I never thought I'd be in this position again. I'm not some pathetic woman who needs a man to show her love the way Daddy used to, who hangs on to the hope she feels in between beatings, when Mr. Wrong promises it was the last time. I promised myself I'd never let someone put their hands on me, and, until tonight, I'd kept that promise."

My father watches me so intently, like he's never heard me speak before. I guess he hasn't. Not like this. He's never seen himself through my words and accounts of the past. I imagine his appearance is startling to him, like waking up after an accident only to find that you've been hideously maimed.

How could anyone love me when I look this way?

"I never realized," he whispers. "All those years I was so busy never seeing past my own problems, I never realized you had become me."

"Don't ever say that to me," I tell him.

"Sit down and open the notebook, Bryce."

"I'm not you, and I won't sit here and listen to your—"

"Please get the notebook!"

"You do realize it doesn't mean anything, right?" I ask. "They're just words on paper. They don't have more meaning because I write them down."

He stares at me with eyes so sullen I can't imagine they've ever seen the light of day, and I never knew the mixture of love and hate could be so powerful. I want to hurt him like he's hurt me and then dress his wounds.

I slowly make my way to the other side of the room and bend down, rifling through the broken items on the floor for the notebook and pen.

"Here," I say. I sit in the chair and don't even notice that it's plaid anymore. It's just a part of my world now. "Start talking. I've got dishes and laundry to do."

He nods and sits back. "My mother was sick the whole summer I was fourteen. I don't know how many infections she had that year, but I feel like we were constantly sending her to the hospital for one thing or another. She was home on bedrest half the time. The rest of the time she spent in the hospital. As you can imagine, your uncle and I were pretty lost without her. That woman took care of everything. Laundry, cooking, cleaning, sewing, helping with school. My dad was a hard worker, but he was as useless as tits on a boar at home. If he couldn't shoot his dinner, he'd starve.

"With Mom gone, Dad delegated chores to Jerry and me. I got lucky. Dad gave me all the outdoor jobs to tend to, but your uncle got stuck with all Mom's work. Being the youngest, he didn't know what the hell he was doing. Poor kid was only ten. Every time he'd ask Dad how to do something, he'd get smacked upside the head. 'Use the goddamn brain you were born with,' was my dad's usual response. It's no surprise your uncle just stopped asking, and I was no help. He'd come to me and I'd just give him more of the same.

"My dad came home from work one night in a bad mood. Your uncle was in the kitchen doing something, I don't remember what, and next thing I hear my dad calling him a fag. 'You a little faggot now? Only queers wear pink, you little faggot.' My brother had done a load of laundry and didn't know not to throw my mother's red dishtowel in with the whites. His shirt came out pink, but he was too afraid to tell our dad. Guess he hoped he wouldn't notice.

"I came out of my room and saw him push my brother to the floor. He threw a rag at him and told him to get on his knees and clean like a woman. 'Wanna be like your mother, I'll treat you like her, pussy.'

"Jerry started crying, and I remember being so pissed at him for it because he was just making it worse on himself. It didn't dawn on me that he couldn't help it. When my dad raised his fist in the air and Jerry screamed, I knew it was going to be bad. That was the first time I ever laid a finger on my dad. I grabbed his fist and held it there, and he spun around and looked at me like the Devil. That was also the first time I stopped giving a shit about what the man thought."

I stop writing and watch my dad as he speaks. His jaw's set, his brows low. I can almost see the determined fourteen-year-old boy who just learned he has two legs of his own to stand on. I want to know this young man, but he becomes the villain in his own story, and how could he not have known better?

I look back down and write his words even though I want to change the ending to a happy one.

"My dad told me to get my hands off him. My voice up and disappeared on me, but I shook my head, and I'll never forget what he said next. 'If your mother were dead I'd kill you.' I don't know now if he meant it, but when you're a kid, you believe what your parents tell you. Still, I held on to his fist until he asked me if I was willing to pay for my brother's crimes. I nodded. He pushed me down the hallway, into my mother's room. She had one of those tables with all her perfume and makeup on it. He grabbed her tube of red lipstick and threw it at me. 'Wear that to school tomorrow. You think it's okay to be a fucking pansy, you'll wear it, and don't you let me find out for a damn minute that you took it off.'

"Being a woman was the very worst thing you could be in my dad's eyes. That's the first time I ever wanted to cry in front of him, but I knew he'd make me wear a dress, too. At first I remember thinking there was no way in hell I was going to go through with it, but that's when I realized it was my brother or me. I was fourteen. I only had a few years left in school, but Jerry...

"The next day, my father drove behind me while I walked to school wearing my mother's red lipstick. When he came home at the end of the day and saw the black eye I'd earned, he told me I looked pretty for a fag. Forced me to wear lipstick all throughout the dinner he made me cook while he drank his fucking beer and called me Katherine. In that moment, I knew what it was like to be my mother, and I remember thinking she'd be better off dead."

I don't know what to say. My father's story is dangling out there, nerves exposed and bloody. I hate the man who created the man I try not to hate, and I'm glad I never knew him. He's all that's wrong with my father, but my dad's a big boy and didn't need to wear his father's shoes just because their feet were the same size.

"How am I supposed to react to that?" I ask. "I won't sit here and tell you my heart doesn't break for you, but your father's sins don't erase your own. So you had it bad. You either grow from your past or you become an echo of it. All I know now is that you intimately knew the pain you caused us and did it anyway."

"I cared. I just didn't know better. It's like sitting in a room full of people speaking a different language. You want to join in, but if no one ever taught you to speak it, you're shit outta luck. I wanted to be better than my dad, but I didn't know how to, and I was afraid of what it would mean if I tried."

"Afraid of what? Why? What's so scary about not being piece of shit?"

"I was afraid of who I'd be instead."

"That doesn't make any sense, Dad. That's what makes life an adventure. Not knowing who the hell you're going to be but knowing you don't want to relive your past."

"You don't understand, Bryce. It's not that simple."

"It is that simple. It's the simplest thing in the world."

He rubs his forehead and sighs. "I didn't want to hurt you. I didn't want to hurt any of you. I'll go to my grave being sorry, Bryce."

I bite down hard, swallow my emotions. "No, you won't. You'll forget all this before then."

His eyes gloss over, his Adam's apple thrusts up and down between words. "Then let me tell you now how "sorry I am. I didn't know what was happening earlier today. I knew who you were, but I didn't. Everything felt...different. I knew your face but couldn't remember anything about you. Same with Theo. I was so scared, Bryce. That was the most terrifying thing I've ever experienced, and all I can do is sit here wondering when it'll happen again. Everything just fell away. All I knew was that I needed to find that box, because it was the only thing grounding me to my past. I didn't mean to hurt you. I didn't know what was happening. I can't take back all the things I did to you when you were a kid, and I can't take back today. If there were a way to fix it, I would. I need you to believe that. I can't forgive myself, but I hope you will."

I feel his apology scrub some of the grime from the corners of our relationship, but it will never wash all the dirt away. His words have weight, but so did his words when he told Jackson to leave my side, and when he made me feel stupid for believing in my dreams, and when instead of telling me he loved me every day, he sent me to bed with welts that told me he didn't.

I'm a product of my father's making; he's a product of his father's making. I don't know if there are enough words and forgiveness to change that, but hate requires more energy than love, and I'm so fucking tired.

"I'm going to try to forgive you, Dad, because I deserve to live without all this shit I carry around, and I think maybe you do, too. I'm sorry for what happened to you when you were a kid, but I'm more sorry that you were too weak to not mimic your father, because I sure could've used a dad who loved me." I lean forward and hold his attention.

"I don't think you want your father's legacy to continue, so one of us needs to break the cycle. I don't "know why you were so afraid to be your own man, but I'm not afraid to be my own woman, even if that means I need to forgive you for things you haven't even admitted to. Maybe one day I'll tell you what those things are, but right now I need to stop talking before I stop making sense to myself and start hating you."

I get up and sit the notebook on the chair. I can't look at my father anymore without seeing red lips and a black eye and a sad boy who sold his bravery for his father's blueprints for life. May my grandfather burn in Hell. I've got a mouthful of sour spit meant just for his grave, and if I don't earn a ticket to Heaven, I'll find him in Hell and settle the score, because you can't burn a fucking diamond.

"Thank you," my father says when I turn to walk away.

I feel his hand on mine and turn around just as he pulls back. I want to reach for him, but I need to wrap my arms around myself for a while and cry till the little girl in me falls asleep in my arms.

CHAPTER 31

The house is quieter than I can ever remember it being. No wind, no rain, no snoring coming from my dad's room. It just sits here like a giant void, echoing my father's story about my grandfather. I come from a long line of savages. Put your ear to my chest and you can hear their war cries. No wonder the call of the wild stays in my gut and niggles at me when life gets too calm.

I stand in front of a small shelf in the living room and scan the few books my father has lined on the middle shelf. You'd think a man who had lived through war wouldn't want reminders around, but all the books are about that stinky swamp and the men who died there. All but one.

I bend down and pull out a book with light-blue writing on the side that reads *The Sights of Victoria*.

I remember Shana telling me about seeing my father at a pink hotel in Victoria. I haven't given it any thought since that night. If my father cheated, so be it. All's fair in love and war, and my mother certainly waged one hell of a battle. Part of me would like to think my father knew the touch of a woman who saw past his scars to the man I know so little about. To live a life without love is like never having learned to breathe. I've felt Jackson's skin on mine. I've taken him inside me and screamed *I love you* till the air left my lungs and I crumbled into his arms. For what it's worth, I suppose I can die content. Can my father?

I take the book to the couch and open the first page. There's a date marked inside, but nothing else. I run my finger along the ink and wonder if it means something. The pages are thick and a few stick together. They smell like a bookstore that's been boarded up for years. I hold it to my nose and breathe in.

I turn a page over, and another. Dated photos reveal a place not unlike here. The coastline is majestic—stony structures grasping at the clouds and land hidden beneath so many pine trees you can't imagine there being room to walk. There are photos of historical buildings and railways and parks. All the things that turn a main street into a town and a town into a city and a city into a bustling vacation spot for weary Americans looking to escape their material world and the in-your-face media coverage telling them what color Kim Kardashian's shit is.

Page after page, I imagine my father there, holding the hand of a woman he traded us in for. Someone soft and made of flower petals. Easy to fall into, easy to inhale, easy to squash at a moment's notice, when the wife says it's time to hurry on home.

Midway through the book, I turn a page over, and looking back at me is a pink two-story hotel that stretches along a swath on the shore of Victoria West. It's nestled deep in the trees and looks to be inspired by the designs of early Spanish American settlers, which strikes me as odd.

"Casa Mar," I whisper. "What do you know about my father that I don't?"

Just as I ask, I hear my dad whimper. I get up and press my ear to his door, but all I can hear is the rustling of his sheets. I ease the door open and listen to his breaths. He seems to have settled, but then I hear him cry. He tosses and turns and talks to the dead, and I wonder if his dream knows I can hear it.

I walk to his bed and rest my hand on his until his breathing becomes steady and his snores deepen. I want to listen at his ear and wait for secrets to crawl their way out in his sleep and tell me all the things I'm not supposed to know, but his subconscious mind stands guard.

"Good night," I whisper.

I shut his door behind me. When I step back into the living room, I grab my laptop and sit down with the bottle of tequila Shana and I lost to. It will no doubt fight to defend its title, but it has no idea how hollow I am tonight.

I spin the cap, flip open my computer, and stare dumbly at the cursor. My mind morphs memories into moving pictures, and I can still see my father knelt down on the side of the road, crying and clutching the earth, fingers dug into the soil. My breathing picks up. My body's reacting to something it already knows to be true, and this is what intuition is. My fingers hover over the keys, and my hands work without consorting with me. Words appear in the search bar.

"Accident on Madleten Lane, Steelson, WA."

The search renders several listings, all of which seem vaguely connected to the city but not the road my father's house sits on. I scroll past the first page and click on the second.

Site after site leads me farther away from my search. I search again, this time adding "car accident" to the end. Sites blaze along the screen, a few leading me to an article about a semi jackknifing on Highway Two, which is near us, but no dice.

Click. I type again, this time adding "body found." I hit the enter key and take a hearty swig from the bottle and keep the fire in my mouth, letting it burn my cheeks. When I read the very first link, I swallow and my mouth hangs open, my fingers trembling. I click the site and watch a page load slower than I'm used to. The article is from the city, the heading in bold letters that pack a punch.

"Pedestrian Found Dead of Suspected Hit & Run..."

I scroll down and pick the bottle back up but only hold it in my hands while I stare at the photo of a middle-aged man wearing a polo shirt, smiling at the camera. He's got a nametag hanging around his neck, but the letters are a blur.

I hear my voice break the silence as I begin reading the article. I press my fingers to my lips, mumbling each word that leaves me eerily certain I know what's coming next.

"Yesterday, the body of David Yodeen was found along Madleten Lane, with injuries consistent of vehicular impact. Police canvassed the area and interviewed several neighbors who reported hearing no disruptions. We're confident an ongoing investigation will lead local authorities to the person responsible for the accident. David Yodeen is survived by his mother and two sisters."

I read it again and again and again. The words are all there, but I can't make them make sense. It doesn't say where along the road they found him, but it's not every day dead men pop up along the streets of our idyllic city on the lake.

I rub the side of my pounding head and close my eyes. I slap it hard, but my dad's words won't stop ricocheting off the sides of my skull.

I'm so sorry I left you.

How did I not know about this? I would've heard. This city's big enough to not know your neighbor's birthdate, but it's too small for a secret this big.

I search the article for a date and find it in the upper right corner. I drop the bottle and bite my fist and watch the date fade away as tears fill my eyes.

"My God," I whisper. "What did you do, Dad?"

I get up, slap my laptop shut. I want to run down the street and dig along the side of the road till I find my father's skeletons. I look at his bedroom door and take a step toward it, then away. I want to believe in coincidences big enough to rock me back and forth and tell me it's all going to be okay, but there's a man in that room who battles the dead in his sleep, and there's a tragic story sitting on my computer that sounds an awful lot like family history.

I grab my phone, look at the time. Fuck it.

I text Jackson, my thoughts spinning so fast my fingers can barely keep up.

"What'd my father tell you? You better start talking. Now!"

"Ask him."

"I'm asking you."

"It's late, Bryce. Talk tomorrow?"

"No. Now. Tell me, or I swear I'm coming over."

"I can't. I told you, not my place."

"I swear to God, Jackson. This isn't a joke."

"Trust me, I don't think you're joking, but why can't this wait till tomorrow?"

"Because if I don't find out now why my dad was crying on the side of the same road they found a body on the night my mother died, I'm gonna lose it."

I watch the three dots move from left to right as he types. I wait only a few seconds, and then his text appears.

"I'll be right over."

CHAPTER 32

I open the door when I hear Jackson's truck pull up. He watches me as he walks towards the house and nudges past me in the doorway. No hello, no smile. Just pensive eyes and undecipherable body language.

I close the door and point to the table. He sits, eyes glued on me while I take the chair across from him.

"What happened to your face?" he asks.

I don't answer. My hands are pressed firmly on the table, my composure teetering on the edge of Jackson's unspoken words.

"Tell me what he told you," I quietly say.

"First tell me who did this. It was him, wasn't it?" His eyes dart to my father's bedroom door. I can see the muscles in his neck twitch.

"You knew where he was that night. He told you something," I say.

But he only lifts his chin, looking down at the girl with all the questions.

"You didn't come over here just to sit there and not say a word, Jackson."

He puts his hands on the table, too, but then pulls them away. He's biting down hard, like he's trying to break his silence in half.

"I don't know," he finally says.

I sit straight, my eyes boring into his. "Not good enough. Try again."

He draws his lips into his mouth, like he has to so they don't run off with all the words he's trying to suppress.

"Fuck you, Jackson. Don't be a coward. Tell me what you know. Does my father have something to do with the story I found?"

Has someone ever told you their every thought with only their eyes? The lines on Jackson's face strain as he frowns against the pain of holding too much in. He finds me, rooted in my seat. His eyes meet mine and hold me there just long enough for me to see what his lips won't betray, and I hear him so loud it hurts my head and makes my stomach churn.

"No," I whisper. "Why? What happened?" I'm crying. I'm shaking. Snot runs from my nose into my mouth and I should care, but everything inside me is coming out, and you can't stop a storm once it starts.

Suddenly everything's too heavy. I lean forward and my head drops to the table, where my tears continue to fall and coat my cheeks. The story's bigger than Jackson's silence, but I can't ask any more questions right now. My voice is curled up in a ball, hiding in the corner where the truth can't find it and make it seek answers my heart can't absorb.

Jackson gets up and stands behind me, his hands on my back. He lifts me from the table and I let him. My bones are made of grief—not nearly strong enough to hold me up but powerful enough to kill my resolve, and I fall into him, letting him carry all my wounds for just this one second.

He lifts my chin and looks down at me. We're in the same place. He's the only other one in the little room with no light, and he guides me to his side, where he'll watch over me till the sun comes up.

When I kiss him, it stings and I like it. I open my mouth, and it's messy and unbridled and provides the right kind of passion for my brand of misery. It's an ugly night for untamed things, and his mouth moves against mine, our lips doing all the talking, making sounds only we can understand. We devour one another and all our broken pieces, because they taste good and we haven't been fed in so long.

I push him toward the hallway and then into my room, crying into his neck. "Stay."

He reaches down and slips his fingers under my shirt. When it comes off my body, I feel more protected than ever. I take his shirt off and feel his skin against mine, and I know nothing can ever touch me so long as I'm coated in this exquisite longing.

I kiss him deeply, relishing the only flavor I've ever craved. Jackson's hands remember me; mine remember him. He knows how to touch me, how to bring me to my knees and silence the demons. They hold on tight, but the moment deafens their screams and forces them deep into my belly.

I don't feel the rest of our clothes come off, but I feel my skin prick to life with the quick intake of air my lungs know to take just before Jackson comes into me and I go under water and never come back up, and what a sweet way to go this would be. And then I'm home, and I know why an addict needs her fix.

I squeeze around Jackson with every part of my body and hold on for dear life, because the next time he leaves, it'll kill me.

CHAPTER 33

I sit back in the chair, feet propped on the foot of my dad's bed, watching him sleep as though he hasn't brought the whole world down in one fell swoop.

I lightly kick his foot with my toe and see his eyes part.

"We need to talk, Dad."

Hand raised to his eyes, he squints and furrows his brows. "What's the matter with you. What're you doing in here?"

His tone is icy. He pulls himself up, grunting as he sits back. "We have nothing to talk about. I don't want you here right now."

"What a difference a day makes, huh?" I ask. "I can barely keep up. Yesterday you were full of apologies, today you're kicking me out of your room. Guess the shelf life on kindness around here is pretty short."

He looks at me with disgust, like I'm something unclean. Funny, because I feel like I scrubbed seven years of filth off my skin last night.

"How could you?" he asks. "How could you do it?"

"Do what?"

"I heard you last night. Woke up to the sounds of you and that piece of shit… I can't even say it."

"Then don't." I drop my feet, lean forward. "I'll say it for you. You woke up to the sounds of us making love."

"Shut up."

"Absolutely tearing one another to pieces just for the sheer fun of it."

"Enough!"

"Why, Dad? Because I'm your daughter and how dare anyone have me? Or because it was Jackson? Wait. Don't answer that. I already know. Because it's Jackson, and you decided a long time ago we weren't going to be together. You saw to that, didn't you? Had me believe the last seven years were all his fault, and that he didn't love me enough to stand by me. You'd still have me believe that, but you're slipping, old man, and your secrets are falling down with you."

He flinches so quickly I almost miss it.

"What? Did you really think I'd go the rest of my life without finding out?"

"Finding out what? What did he tell you?"

He sounds more nervous than he looks. My mouth is a loaded weapon. One shot and he's dead. We both know it, and he stares at me like I might fire.

"Is there something for him to tell? Is that why you hate him?" I ask.

"He's bad for you. I wasn't the one who left you alone. I didn't walk out when things got too hard."

"And neither did he! But what I still don't know is if you believe your own bullshit, or if you're just a better liar than I thought. Tell me, Pops. Was it all planned, or were you acting on a whim when you told my boyfriend of four years to leave the hospital when he came to see me? Who was that for? Because it certainly wasn't for me, you selfish bastard."

He's shaking all over. His fists are balled up, but he's not going to do anything about it this time. I can tell by the fear overriding his rage.

"Did it ever occur to you that Jackson and I are meant to be together? That what you did back then would just postpone the inevitable? Was hurting me in the process just the cherry on top, or did you feel a twinge of guilt?"

"I wasn't trying to hurt you. I was trying to protect you."

"How so? How did pushing the man I love away protect me?"

"Because we always hurt the ones we love, Bryce!" He gets up and moves his legs off the bed. I almost reach out to catch him when he stands up and wobbles, but he rights himself. He leans on the mattress, panting each word.

"Look at your mother and me. Look what we did to each other. He was just a kid, Bryce. I barely knew how to handle what you had done to yourself. How was he going to? They had you so hopped up on drugs in the hospital, I knew you wouldn't notice that he was gone. Better then than later, when people weren't watching over you."

"So you forced him away then so he couldn't walk later, and I couldn't…what…kill myself?"

"It made sense. You don't know. You weren't there. I was trying to keep my daughter around. After losing your mother, I—"

"Don't even say you *couldn't lose me*. You had no fucking use for me. I got out of the hospital and left home, and you never even said goodbye. So why not tell me then that Jackson hadn't walked out?"

His mouth hangs open, cavernous, all the words dried up.

"That destroyed me, Dad. Jackson was the only person I had. I loved him so much. He was my best friend, and you changed every single plan we made. The entire course of my life got rearranged."

"Your mother did that."

"You both did that."

"He would've hurt you, anyway. I'm telling you, that boy would've run the minute he realized what he was in for. I know a little something about being with a woman so complicated you stop knowing right from wrong." He collapses onto the bed, holding his hand to his chest. His eyes are red, and his ribs expand with each breath.

"I thought I was strong enough," he says. "I thought I could battle your mother's problems and keep both of us afloat, but in the end, I killed her."

"I am not Patricia!" I say. "You see me and you see Mom, but I am not her. That night didn't make me weaker, Dad. I have the scars to prove it. I walked out of that hospital stronger than I'd ever been. It wasn't your job to decide who was allowed to love me."

He watches me with nervous eyes, probably waiting for me to leave, because even bad guys know when they've crossed the line.

I take a deep breath and stand as tall as I can. "You broke my heart, Dad."

The bottom of his eyes well up as he looks away, a sound like a caught bird squeaking from his throat as he silently weeps.

"I didn't want him to hurt you like I hurt my wife."

"He wouldn't have."

"That's what I thought about myself, but you don't know what you're capable of until it's too late." Now his cries bounce off the walls of the small room. "You don't know that he wouldn't have killed you."

"I can't stand your bullshit. Stop being such a fucking martyr! How about you own up to the things you did do and stop wallowing around here, talking about how you killed Mom."

"I can't."

"Why not hell not?"

"Because I killed her, Bryce! Because she came home that night, and I had one goal in mind."

"Really? Did you force-feed her all those pills?"

"No, but I might as well have."

My father's words stand in my way so I can't see around them. They're a wall keeping me from reading his eyes and expression and all the things that might make clear what I can't grasp simply with his words.

My voice comes from somewhere far away—a place totally unfamiliar to me. "What are you trying to tell me?"

He frowns, slowly shakes his head. "She came home that night and we got into it. She could barely stand up she was so stoned. I tried to leave the house, but she wouldn't let me. You don't know what it's like constantly being reminded of every wrong you've ever committed. Every mistake, every mean word…just every fuck-up. I heard it "all that night, and then some. I didn't know how many secrets your mother had been keeping.

"It was no surprise that I'd ruined her life. She constantly reminded me. I know you probably don't remember that. Your mom was pretty good about bottling things up when you were around, but I got to hear it every night, like some goddamn bedtime ritual. I'd say goodnight and she'd tell me how miserable I made her and what a coward I was. She wasn't even wrong."

"Get to your point. What happened that night?"

"I heard it for the last time. I wanted out and told her so. She didn't seem to mind the idea of a divorce, but when I told her she'd have to leave, she threw everything at me she could. The marriage, me leaving for Vietnam, my..."

"Affair?" His eyes go wide as he takes a breath he never exhales. "Shana said her family thought you were cheating. I guess they saw you at some hotel in Victoria once and you were pretty fucking obvious."

He rests his elbows on his knees and grabs each side of his head. "Yes, my affair. Your mother had known for a long time. That night, she told me it was my fault Scotty was dead. That if it weren't for me, he'd still be alive, because I was off with someone else when I should've been taking care of things here. That was the first time she'd ever said that, and I didn't need to hear it more than once to know it was true. Didn't make me hate her any less, though. She was the one here. She was supposed to be watching him, wasn't she? I can't remember everything, but...wasn't she?" He looks up at me with fire in his eyes and hatred on his lips. "She should've kept our boy alive, but she was too busy shoving a goddamn needle in her arm, and then Scotty was gone. Until you reminded me "how he died, I had forgotten some of this, and now I wish I hadn't asked.

"I hated her, Bryce. In that moment, I'd never hated anything more, and all I remember is wishing that it had been her instead of Scotty. So I pushed her and pushed her and pushed her. Told her it was her fault our son was gone. That if she had loved him, he'd still be here. I broke every picture of Scotty we had on the walls, and when she begged me to stop, I grabbed her stash from the dresser and threw it in her face and told her if she really loved Scotty, she'd go look for him and apologize for killing him."

I try to see my dad, but the remorse hanging around him is so powerful, I want to look away so it doesn't change me. But his words are already seared into my memory, the look on his face forever branded on my life's tapestry, and I know for the rest of my days I'll carry this day around my neck like a label that instead of reading "Burden" will read "Casualty of War."

"The last word I ever said to her was 'no,' when she asked if I'd ever loved her," he says. "She didn't say another word. I didn't know if she'd really do it, but when she took the bag into the bathroom and locked the door, I went outside so I wouldn't have to save her if I heard her struggling."

"Jesus Christ," I whisper.

There are times in your life when you forget the world is spinning and that anyone other than you exists. I want to hold on to the walls before I fall off and sink into a place with no exit, but I'm already there, just me, my dad, and his words still slicing through the air, severing any illusion of normalcy we'd previously held on to.

The house is tainted and we're tainted and our love for one another is tainted by our hatred for our past selves. It'd be easy to say the man in front of me is the Devil, but it's worse than that. He's just human, and somehow that scares me more. The Devil has no conscience. What's Arthur's excuse?

"I don't think I'll ever forgive you," I say. He only nods, as if he expected it. "There's more, though, isn't there?" I ask.

A simple swallow. That's all it takes, and I know my father's holding back.

"I found an article, Dad. Someone was killed down the road that night. You told Jackson something about it, and that's how he knew to find you there the other morning, right? What happened? Was that someone mom knew? A boyfriend? A dealer?"

He slowly rises from the bed and approaches me. I move back, he steps forward, hands out, reaching for me.

"Please, Bryce."

He's bent over, losing strength. He grabs for my hands, but I let him fall to his knees, crying tears that mean nothing now, begging for love he alone has stripped me of, and asking for forgiveness that's not mine to give.

"I'm sorry," he wails. "God, I'm so s-sorry."

My voice is loud. "What'd you do?"

"Forgive me. P-please forgive me."

He lunges for me and takes hold of my hands. I pull away but he holds tight, and all I want to do is get away from him.

"I don't deserve to live," he cries. "Please help me, Bryce. Please h-help me make it finally stop."

I rip my hands away and jump back. He crumples on the floor and instead of hearing his sobs, I hear my mother thrashing around in the bathtub, crying out for help, and instead of rescuing my father from his own misery and helping ease him through moments he wishes would be his last, I say a prayer that they'll go on forever, one endless stream of agony made just for him.

"I hope the memory of my mother plays on a loop till the day you die," I say. "And if you forget what you did to her, I'll be here to remind you. Even when you sleep, I'll whisper in your ear all the horrible things you said, and when you beg for me to help you end your life, I'll draw a nice bath for you and dangle a razor just out of reach."

I turn around and grab my things, dialing Jackson as I feverishly pack my belongings. When he picks up, I tell him I'm leaving.

"I'm done here. My father can burn in Hell."

I hang up and throw my shit outside, slamming the front door behind me, and I get in my car, where I won't have to save my father if I hear him struggling.

CHAPTER 34

I get on the freeway without remembering how I got here. The last twenty minutes are a blur. My head feels like a snow globe someone vigorously shook, and now the snow's beginning to settle so I can see the picture more clearly. But I don't want to see it. The words I spoke to my father cling to me, and I know the doctor was wrong. I do have cancer. Only not the kind that ends your suffering. My hate, my resentment, my father, whom I'm a replica of. These things infect me with something horrid and make me spew venom in the eyes of my maker—the man who killed everything I loved in one night. Arthur stood in that house and cursed someone with death. I stood in that house and promised I'd never let him escape what he'd done. We're arms connected to the same beast, and stooping to his level only made us both ugly.

I press the gas pedal down hard and scream so loud it drowns out the road noise. I scream until my head feels like it could float away and my vision goes dim, and my fist finds the middle of the wheel, and fuck all if my father never taught me how to throw a proper punch. I beat on the horn and say all the curse words I know.

The horn sounds when I punch the wheel again, and my knuckles crunch into the plastic. The person in front of me slows down. Jesus, don't mind me. I'm just back here suffocating on all my sins.

Everything inside me betrays me. Long ago, I built the strongest wall around myself and watched it grow higher and higher. Now there's a horse inside my chest, and men pour from its belly, wielding swords and cutting away the casing around my heart. Every emotion I stifled since the night of my mother's death have found one another and made an alliance, and now I'm standing alone, with battered fists and no army to hold back an assault.

My eyes fill with so many tears I can't see the road. When there's an exit, I get off the freeway and pull over. I open the door and jump out, trying to shake my hands free of the misery they hold on to, but it's coming from deep within, and I can't escape it.

Leaning my head on the door, I take several breaths and try to calm myself before the wannabe Washington hood rat waiting at the bus stop down the street thinks I'm an easy target and takes my keys. Or worse, asks if I'm okay. If someone approaches me right now, I'm not entirely sure I won't detonate, taking them with me.

The bus screeches to a stop and I almost don't hear my phone ring. I look inside and stare at it like it might sting me. It's Jackson, and I'm just now realizing how strange it is that this is his first call since I left my dad's house thirty minutes ago.

I answer the call, but my hands shake and I drop the phone. Again, I reach for it but hesitate to place it to my ear even though I can already hear Jackson calling my name, and I know from his tone that this is one of *those* calls.

"Jackson? What is it?"

"Get back here. They're putting your dad in an ambulance right now. He tried to kill himself."

CHAPTER 35

I lean against a wall and watch my hand go from empty to full as Jackson replaces it with fresh cups of tea every hour. I don't speak and I don't cry and I don't feel much of anything. My eyes remain on the floor, because I don't want anyone to see me and I don't want to see them. I have one job right now, and breathing's only harder when eyes are met and words are spoken.

Jackson touches my back, and I should tell him to leave the hospital, but my name's not Arthur. His hand feels warm through my shirt. My upper lip sweats and I might vomit, but I keep drinking hot tea because if I don't keep my lips busy doing something else, I might rush into the room my dad's in and beat his chest and scream into his ear until he wakes up and apologizes for doing the unthinkable and making me feel like it's all my fault.

"Can I get you anything else?" Jackson asks.

I hold the empty paper cup out to him and he takes it. He needs a job, needs something to do to help. That's how he is. Being useless is his greatest fear next to losing me. Being needy is my greatest fear, but I seem to be facing a lot of fears today, so what's one more?

"Just don't go," I whisper. I can feel his eyes on me, but I look past him.

"I'm not going anywhere, Bryce. I promise."

I believe him.

~

I run to the bathroom twice an hour to get rid of all the fluids and stare into the toilet, listening to the demonic, high-pressure swooshing as I flush over and over to drown out the sounds of the hospital. As if the pages and loud beeps and cries of small children aren't bad enough, someone here keeps playing elevator versions of The Carpenters' greatest hits over the loudspeakers. I'm in a place meant for healing, and yet they ear-rape you with melodramatic songs about birds that suddenly appear.

I wash my hands without looking at the bitch in the mirror who left Daddy's house so she wouldn't hear him struggling. It doesn't matter that she never thought he'd actually do it, because the blood still pumping through his veins is already on her hands, and words as ugly as hers can't be taken back.

~

My place on the wall waits for me, and I hold my hand out and wait for Jackson to put another hot cup of tea in it, only he doesn't, and then I hear my name.

"Bryce Price? Can you please come with me?"

When I look up, a nurse too exotic for these parts smiles at me and places her hand lightly on my shoulder.

"Your dad's awake. He's asking for you."

Suddenly I don't want my legs and eyes and ears. They can drag me, kicking and screaming, but at least I won't hear him and see him.

The nurse holds the door open while offering me another somber smile. She watches me walk in and then leaves, and now I want a mother to take my hand and walk me to the edge of my father's bed, where I can look up at him and be quiet while the adults talk about things too serious for my virgin ears and too heavy for such small hands to grasp.

There's a curtain pulled halfway across my father's section, and I slowly step around it, expecting to see my mother's bloated face, but my dad stares back at me, seemingly fine, but with heavy eyelids and tubes running from his arm. There's no wall for me to lean against, so I put my hands behind my back and stand at attention. I don't want to touch anything and break it. At least nothing else.

"You're still here," my father says, his voice raspy.

"So are you."

We wait and watch each other, silent and contemplative. I can see in his eyes that he's surveying me as much as I am him. My phone dings, and I pull it from my pocket and silence it.

"How'd you get that?" he asks, pointing at my knuckles.

"I got in a fight with my car. It won." I nod at him. "I'd ask what happened to you, but Jackson already told me. I took you as more of a leader. Not some copycat who had to follow in his wife's footsteps."

"We don't know for sure that your mother didn't just overdose. Besides, pills seemed easy. I didn't want to leave a mess behind."

"And you thought there'd be no mess?"

My eyes lock on his. He should look closer at my hands and see that the stains from my mother's death are still there, as faded as they might be.

"You could've drowned yourself in the lake and there'd still be a mess," I tell him. "But there you go again, thinking only about yourself."

"You're mad. You said I could open up to you about anything, but then when I did, you got mad."

"And when I got mad, you punished me by trying to kill yourself." His head raises slightly, his lips thin. "Well done. I wasn't carrying around quite enough baggage. Guess you took care of that."

"I wasn't trying to hurt you, Bryce. This wasn't about you. It wasn't punishment for getting angry."

I want to laugh, but my body doesn't know how to make joyful sounds anymore. "Then what was it about? Guilt? Because you're a weak, cowardly old man with nothing to live for but a daughter who was trying like hell to find some path to you."

His eyes gloss over as the muscles on either side of his jaw work to hold back tears he must know I don't want to see.

"Are you disappointed it didn't work?" he whispers. Now he won't look at me. Probably assumes he knows my answer and doesn't want to see regret splashed across my face.

"Look at me," I say. "If you're going to ask something like that, look at me. You created this mess, now you face it."

I can see him swallow as he looks up, and for the first time since arriving at the hospital, I want to cry. But I don't.

"I'm disappointed that you hated my mother so much. I'm disappointed that you hide behind lies and won't tell me who the hell you really are. I'm disappointed that our family seems to know nothing but sorrow. I'm disappointed in the man you've been, and I'm disappointed that when I look in the mirror, I see pieces of you I picked up and kept while I wasn't paying attention. But most of all, I'm disappointed that our relationship is one in which you need to ask if I'm disappointed you're not dead. You didn't do this because you can't live with your illness. You tried to take your own life because you're too weak to live with your regrets, and that is most regrettable."

He nods, blinks away more tears. "But that doesn't answer my question. Are you disappointed it didn't work?"

I take a deep breath and clear my lungs of all the emotions that threaten to come to a boil. "No, Dad. I'm not disappointed."

The door to my right opens with a loud *click* and a woman with thick eyebrows and a chiseled jaw that doesn't match her beady eyes walks in and picks up my father's chart. Her coat is crisp white, aside from the one speck of blood she probably doesn't know is on her side.

"Are you his caretaker?" she says in a heavy Indian accent.

"I am," I tell her.

"So you're aware that he shouldn't be left alone, especially for lengthy periods of time. Someone with these types of symptoms needs to be supervised."

This woman must've missed school the day they taught the fresh-faced doctors what empathy means. She's nothing but cut steel and a permanent scowl.

"I understand my father's illness, but I don't see what that has to do with anything."

My father passes me a warning glance as the doctor zeros in on me.

"Might I suggest you thoroughly research the symptoms of Alzheimer's? If you're unable to provide proper care for your father, maybe the job would be best left to someone more attentive."

My mouth opens but nothing comes out, and then I see it. Just another of my father's lies. I should've recognized it sooner.

"Can you please explain to me what happened?" I ask the doctor.

"Your father mistook the pills for Tums and when his heartburn didn't improve, he continued to eat the remainder of his tablets. Medications need to be kept out of reach. You should be regulating his medications and administering them when needed. You father could've died today. This is very serious."

My gaze flits between the doctor and my father. I'm shameful and irresponsible, and if the doctor doesn't stop looking at me like I got caught with my hand in the cookie jar, I'm going to squeal like a pig and dirty up her pretty coat with the truth.

"I understand," I say, and I don't know what was harder. Swallowing my pride or knowing that there's still a soft spot located right in the middle of my heart for my father. And now I understand what he meant when he told me my mother made him weak.

"Your father needs to stay overnight for observation. You can pick him up tomorrow. I don't expect to see this happen again," the doctor says, still watching me like I watch the moms at the store who let their toddlers climb in and out of the carts by themselves, apparently without the slightest inkling of concern for their skulls and how they can go splat.

"You won't see us again," I tell her, and then I turn around and leave before the good, honest girl I used to be breaks free and points out the plot twist in my dad's tall tale.

CHAPTER 36

I stare at the unopened bottle of vodka I bought on the way home. Home, home, home. That word's almost funny now. I'm glad I don't know word-for-word what its definition is. I can imagine what the dictionary says, but at least I don't know exactly what I'm missing.

Homes are meant to have photos from Christmas mornings on the mantel, handmade Halloween costumes stashed away in closets, and marks on the wall, charting the growth of children who spent their childhood days climbing trees that didn't break and getting boo-boos that Mommy kissed away and running into the arms of a father whose only wish at the end of each day had been to kiss his wife and children. Unlike my father, I understand the language. I just can't speak it.

I twist the cap off the bottle and bring it to my lips. The pink walls stare back at me, and I want to burn them to the ground. I stand up and chuck the bottle at the wall—shattered glass flies everywhere, but the smell makes it farther. I know what alcohol does to paint, and I want this house to match the ugliness I feel inside.

I watch the liquid run down the walls, changing the color of the paint as it finds its way to the floor, leaving dark spots on the carpet. Now I have nothing to drink, but the house needed it more. I've had breaks here and there, but this old girl has been with my family since the beginning, and she's seen it all.

I slouch in the chair and spin the cap on the table, crying into the silence, cringing at the thought of being the house's last survivor. Only I don't know that she'll let me go that easily, and I don't know that I care anymore.

My head's full of iron and my eyelids are, too. When I let my forehead drop forward, someone knocks on the door, startling me from my fog.

"Come in," I shout.

The door opens and Jackson walks in, looking far too good for a place this bad.

"Why isn't the door locked?" he asks. "Don't just tell people to come in."

"I knew it was you."

"Doesn't matter. It's dangerous."

There's no reason to laugh, but I do, because I have nothing else to fear, especially from strangers outside these walls. Jackson looks at me sideways, and I wonder if he wants to run this time, away from the girl with no wings, the song with no lyrics. I'm just one long, sad note reminding him that life sometimes comes in only gray, and some people never shake hands with Happily Ever After. I thought I saw her once, but she ran away before I could see the color of her hair and touch her glowing skin.

"What're you doing sitting in the dark?" he asks.

"I'm getting drunk. Or...I was going to get drunk. Now I'm just sitting here."

"Thinking about what?" He sits next to me and touches my hand. "You don't need to do this alone."

"Do what alone? I don't know what I'm doing. Is there something to do, 'cause if there is, tell me."

"No," he says, and then I look at him, because honesty's the only real thing I can cling to right now, and I want him to serve it in giants heaps on my head.

"There's not a damn thing to do, Bryce. There's just time to watch tick by, and then, at some point, you'll realize you're okay again. But you don't have to watch the clock alone."

"You've had a lot of practice waiting around, haven't you, Jackson?"

"For you, yes. And I'd do it all again, even if it was just to sit here with you tonight."

"You never told me how your date went. You sure you wouldn't rather be there?"

He sighs. "I realized halfway through dinner she wasn't you, so I cut the evening short and told her I had to work early."

I feel guilty for the smile tempting my lips, and I didn't even need to drink for my belly to feel warm. Jackson says all the right things and looks at me the right way and holds me together despite the parts of me that try to come undone. But I shouldn't notice these things. Not tonight, as my father lies in a bed of thorns he grew for himself, and I sit here and betray the night's many miseries by smiling in a house where you can still feel my hateful words if you go in my father's room. But that's what love does. It transcends all pain and makes you a fool, and I would know, because I've been a fool since the day I caught Jackson ogling me from behind his textbook in Mr. Craft's biology class.

I sit on both sides of the fence and feel my heart get torn in two by the love I feel for the man who smells like lumber and the hate I try not to feel for the man who tried to leave me forever today. I didn't know a heart could break while the man you love holds it together. I hear my father asking me if I'm disappointed he didn't die, and the heartache takes root.

"How can you hate someone you love so much?" I whisper. "You wouldn't believe the things I said to my dad. If he'd died today, I never would've forgiven myself. I'll still never forgive myself, because no matter how much I want to love him, I'm no good at it. He keeps giving me reasons to hate him, and I keep collecting them. Now I have so many, I feel like a fucking hoarder. I should throw them away. I want to. But I've grown attached to them, and in some sick way they give me control by giving me reasons not to get close to him. I don't think I'll ever forgive him for the things he's done. I know I won't forgive myself for not being any better than him."

Jackson gets on his knees and pulls my head to his chest. It's warm there, and his heart drums in my ear. At least I know what home sounds like now, but I think the sound is too impossibly sweet to be all mine.

"You've got to find a way to forgive yourself, Bryce." His deep voice gently rattles his chest. "I'm sure you and your father have both said awful things to each other, but you're still here, and I've got to believe that's more powerful than the words you say in anger. You've been here for him, as hard as I know that's been for you. Your "father is the way he is because his regrets outweigh his successes. No one's all bad or all good, but some of us choose to only see our failures. If you can't see the good you've done, keep me around and I'll remind you."

I shake my head and cry into his shirt. The promise I made my father repeats in my head—the promise to always be here to remind him of his failures. I want to stand in the mirror and throw sharp things at the woman before me and remind her of all her sins, but instead I let a good man stitch my wounds closed.

Still, despite the strong arms holding me, I carry my father's loneliness around my neck like a locket without pictures. I know he's in a room where the sick go to get better and the less fortunate go to die, but where do the defective go to become whole? Because I didn't see that wing in the hospital, and if they don't find my dad a reason to keep going and sew it into his chest, he's going to get out and write his own ending.

"Why's he there?" I ask. "Why'd he do it, Jackson? Tell me what you know before it kills him."

He cradles my cheek and presses me into him while he kisses the top of my head. "You have to forgive him, Bryce."

"How?"

"Because he deserves it." He leans back and holds the sides of my jaw, looking into my eyes with a certainty that scares me. "Because, like I said, no one is all bad or all good, and he deserves forgiveness, more than you know. So forgive him, and then ask him to tell you who he is."

"But I don't..." My words get lost somewhere between our lips, and I think maybe Jackson is trying to save me as much as he's trying to save my father from my judgment. "Okay," I whisper. "I'll try."

I lean forward and kiss him softly. I don't think I deserve to feel this connected to another person, but I know Jackson would tell me different, and tonight I'll rely on his thoughts because my own are scattered in a million dark places, and I don't have the energy to pick them up. Jackson's body speaks the only language I can understand, and I want to exchange a thousand words while we silently lose ourselves in each other.

He kisses my neck, and I reach between his legs and run my fingers along him, but he pulls away. I feel the rejection in my bones.

"What is it?" I ask, but he says nothing.

He reaches in his pocket and pulls out a ring box. When he opens it, my lips and brain go numb, and I stop breathing. My heart tries to reach between my ribs and take hold of the ring, but my hard shell won't let it out.

"I know this is really bad timing," he says. "But I want you to know that in the worst of times, I want nothing but to be by your side, Bryce. Even when things are falling apart, being with you is still a kind of heaven the rest of the world would kill me to get to if they knew it existed. I didn't leave you back then. I will never leave you, so long as I'm breathing. I ask nothing of you but to be my best friend and say yes to forever." He sets the ring box on the table. "But I also know you, and I know tonight isn't about hasty decisions, so I'm going to leave this here. I'm probably crazy for thinking you'll say yes, but if you decide to wear it, you let me know and I'll drive over here any time, day or night, and put it on your finger." He takes my hand and holds it to his chest. "I'll stay if you want me to, but I'll understand if you need some time."

I look at Jackson and finally see it. It's not that one of us can't be whole unless the other is broken. It's that we can't be a whole unless we put our pieces together, as one complete picture. We were built for one another, but I have to smooth my edges before I can fit snuggly beside my best friend without hurting him all over again.

"I can't say yes right now," I tell him.

"I know."

"I might not ever be able to say yes."

"I know that, too."

"Shana told me you went to see me in the hospital back then. I'm sorry for hating you for so long. But I've always loved you."

He stands up and looks down at me. "It's okay. It wasn't your fault. I would've hated me, too. But you've still got to forgive your father for this, Bryce."

I kiss him goodbye and tell him to go, because he's right about me. I need time to get my house in order, and I can't do that with him around. Things are going to get messy, and I can't rebuild myself while I'm worried about him.

I lock the door behind him because a smart man told me it's unsafe not to, and suddenly maybe I've got something to live for. The ring box is on the table. We stare at one another with mutual fascination, and I wonder what it would feel like to wear Jackson's oath around my finger. I pick up the box, but I don't dare touch the ring. Trust me, diamonds remember your touch, but more than that, they remember your absence, and I don't want it to resent me if I run the other way.

I put the ring box in my purse and walk to the bathroom. There are no pieces missing from the bathtub, but if I close my eyes, I can see my mother's hands whittling away. I get in the tub, because tonight's meant for rebuilding, but my mother's standing in the middle of my construction zone, dripping water all over my subfloors and stressing my frame. We're going to have it out tonight, and even if it kills me, I'll find a reason to forgive her.

I lie down in the cold bathtub and close my eyes, and for the first time, I pull the cover off the cage my mother's memory has been hiding in, and I throw it bits of seeds and fruit and wait for it to eat from my hand.

CHAPTER 37

We drive away from the hospital just in time to get home and make dinner. My father watches the rain tap dance on the window and traces his finger along the beads dripping down the glass. I haven't asked how he's feeling; he hasn't offered to tell me. I'd prefer silence to his pleas for death. I can't emotionally afford to hear him say he hasn't changed his mind. If I have to bury him in the rain, no one will see my tears and that I loved him.

"What do you feel like having for dinner?" I ask.

He keeps his eyes on his window. "Nothing. They fed me supper already."

"But it's only five."

"Supper started at four. I figured I'd let you have a night off. Didn't know if you had plans."

I smirk. "Was that a dig, or are we having a conversation?"

"No dig. I just figured you and Jackson might have plans."

"He's saved your ass twice now, Dad. You'd think you'd loosen your hold on that grudge." I grip the wheel and take a deep breath. "But, no. We don't have plans tonight. I told him I needed time to consider his offer."

"What offer?"

"He asked me to marry him."

His hand falls to his lap and he slowly turns to look at me. The lines on his forehead deepen, and this isn't how I envisioned this day when I dreamed of it in high school.

"I know you hate him," I say. "So no need for congratulations or anything. You know me. I probably won't say yes, so you can breathe now."

Arthur's a man with words but no way to say them. He's a mime again, and I know what those sad eyes mean. He slowly shakes his head and looks at his hands.

"Can you stop by the house and then take me to the pier?" he asks.

"What do you want to go to the pier for?"

He rubs his forehead, deep in an internal conflict that couldn't be more obvious if he played both roles and screamed his lines out loud.

"There's something I should tell you," he says. "I don't want to be cooped up in that house when I do."

My mouth goes dry, and there's that horrible palpitation I used to get when I ran up the stairs to my apartment too fast. Only now I slow down, because the pier's not going anywhere, nor are my father's secrets. And shit! Why can't my palms stop sweating?

"What do you need from the house?" I ask.

His voice comes out quiet and low, and I realize he sounds guilty before he's even made a confession.

"The box. The one under my bed."

"The one you thought I took?"

He nods, looks away. "That's the one."

Now I look away, too. I don't want to see my father's face. I don't want to see what's coming. Just shoot me from behind and close my eyelids once my heart stops.

~

I balance the shoebox in my hands and lock the front door. As I make my way back to the car, raindrops mar the top of the box. My father's staring straight ahead at the dashboard, and when I get in and set the box on his lap, his whole body seems to tense, and my God, what's in there that he's so afraid of?

Pulling away, we drive in silence, my father taking heavy breaths like a kid waiting in line for a rollercoaster. It's funny how fear changes your perception of reality. I watch the thick clouds slowly cruise along the sky and think I've never seen them so dark, though I know I have. And the rain. It seems to fall in slow motion, which I know isn't possible, but it hesitates before falling to the ground, where we humans taint the Earth's surface with our secrets. The weight of my father's silence gives everything a dark hue. Even the pine trees look black, and the lake has turned to onyx.

I park and put my keys in my pocket, and now I clutch the handle and wait for the old man with no words to remember how to speak.

"What do you want to do, Dad?"

He swallows again and again, wrestling something down his throat while the box trembles in his unstable hands. "I want you to tell me you love me," he says. "Before we get out of this car and I make you hate me, I want you to tell me you love me, just so I'll know you did at one time."

"I love you, Dad. Always have."

He gives one nod and then opens the door, waiting for me to walk around and meet him. When I do, he holds the box under one arm and takes my hand with the other, leading me through the rain and to a place where I'll learn to hate him, but I don't think I can, because his hand feels kind, and no one's all bad.

I grip his hand tighter and watch the back of his head as I follow behind him and we make our way to the empty bench under the covered pier. He waits for me to sit, and then he positions himself beside me, the box on his knees.

He watches the lake, and I offer my silence. This is a ritual, a dance of sorts, and I know if I push him, he'll let go of my hand and close his heart, and I hate when my father's just a wall.

When I turn to watch the rain fall on the lake, I hear him, but I don't look. Not yet.

"The night your mother died… There's more to it than you know, Bryce. I told you your mom knew about my affair. It was no secret. We tried like hell to work past it. Fixing what I had done became the impetus of my life, and I swear to you, I spent every breath trying not to love anyone other than your mother, but I wasn't strong enough. My affair…it had been going on for a long time."

"How long?" I keep my eyes on the water.

"Since before I married your mom."

I drop his hand and look at him because I don't want to miss the moment I meet my real father.

"What?" I breathe. "You said you loved Mom. That she was the most magnificent thing you'd ever seen."

"She was. That wasn't a lie. But I met someone else, someone I fell in love with. Not because the things I told you about your mother weren't true, but because they were. She was never made for me, and I certainly wasn't made for her. I wanted to love only her. How could I not? She was amazing, Bryce. I shoved my feelings down and buried them so deep that I almost forgot how to feel, but I had met someone who made me believe I was worth loving, and…you have no idea how many years I wished that person had been your mother, but it wasn't. I tried to end it before the wedding. I told the love of my life I was going to marry your mother, and I walked away with no plans on going back, but then your mom found a letter from… I was careless. You said you watched our wedding video. You saw your mom's face, how nervous she looked. Something happened that morning. She found a letter written to me from… We used to exchange these silly notes, and that morning your mother found the very last one. Or, it was meant to be the last one I ever received.

"I told your mom everything right then. She was devastated. I told you she was a flower, but not after that. I thought she'd leave. I actually hoped she'd leave. But she said she loved me too much and wouldn't give up on us. She thought she could fix me, but I was never broken. It's taken my whole life to see that nothing was wrong with me. I just married the wrong person, and our entire family paid dearly for it. I wasn't strong enough to stand up for who I was back then, and so I tried to become what I was supposed to be.

"I was faithful to your mother for a long time, but then our relationship started unraveling. We were never the same after she found that letter on our wedding day.

"She became disconnected, and then she had an affair, too. Boy, she showed me."

"And you ran back to the other woman?"

"Not exactly. I mean…yes. Once you spend so many years hurting each other, your skin gets thick, and you barely feel the pain anymore. Your mom moved further away from me, and I fell deeper in love with someone else. You can spend a lifetime tearing the people you love to shreds and not even realize the extent of the damage you're causing. It all seemed to go by in a flash, and before I knew it, your mother was an addict and I was the husband that ran off to a hotel in another country every chance he got while his son died and his little girl carried the load all alone.

"That's why I left for Vietnam right after the wedding. Your mom thought some time away would do me good and clear my head, but I came back and was no less in love than when I left. Then we had you and your brother. It was supposed to make everything complete, but it just made everything hurt more.

"All those weekends I went away, Bryce, I wasn't working. I was trying to find a bit of happiness, and I did, just for a moment. But I'd come home on Sunday nights and go back to being the miserable bastard you always knew. You can't imagine the self-loathing. I hated myself so much that even breathing felt like a battle."

I don't know how long I've been holding my breath, but I'm lightheaded. I wipe my tears away and ask, "So what happened?"

"You know what happened, until the night of your prom. I told you your mother and I got into a fight that night. That part's true, but what I didn't tell you was why. When your mom came home, she found me in our bed with—"

"Dad, no."

His eyes get red. He bites down hard and seems to search for his words. His voice comes out heavy, sorrowful.

"She found us together. At first I wasn't even sorry. She'd had so many men in our bed, any illusion of sanctity was long gone. She betrayed our marriage so many times. Every man she brought into our home, every betrayal, every lie… She killed me little bits at a time, but I had no right to be angry. I'm the one who destroyed everything before we'd even exchanged vows. I guess I killed her little bits at a time, too. I was so deep in my depression, I didn't know how to get out of my own hell, so I just kept her down there with me. That night she caught us, I felt relieved thinking that maybe I could finally talk her into a divorce, but she wouldn't leave, and she threatened to tell you everything. She knew that was the one thing I couldn't do. I couldn't tolerate the thought of you knowing."

"Why?" I ask. "What would've been so wrong with me knowing something made you happy, even if it wasn't Mom? I wouldn't have hated you. I hated what you did to Mom, I hated how you treated us. Had I known you were capable of being happy, I would've understood. God, why'd you marry Mom in the first place? You could've married this other woman."

He picks up the box and places it on my lap, and then he does something I've never seen. He looks like a child, and suddenly my approval is the elephant threatening to break the pier with its sheer weight.

"Every letter's in there," he says. "All but the one your mother found and burned on our wedding day. Open it and read one to me."

"Dad, you don't need to do this. Reading letter's from your girlfriend isn't going to—"

"Just read one." He opens the lid and pulls a letter off the top of the pile. "Doesn't matter what it says. Just read it, Bryce." And then he closes his eyes and waits.

The paper holds something so heavy, I can feel it on my fingers. I want to stop before it reaches the rest of me, but just like my father, it begs to be understood, and I don't have the strength to disobey orders right now.

My hands shake as I pull the folded paper from the envelope and almost smell the agony pouring off my father. His eyes are still closed, but he flinches as I hold the paper up to read.

I squint and hold it closely. The letter is short, the words neat, but already something's off, only my crowded brain can't decipher what it is.

And then I read.

By the time you read this, you'll be back home, which means I'll be counting down the days till I can see you again.

Don't be mad, but I watched you sleep this morning. I know you hate that, but I needed something nice to think about on the long drive home and couldn't think of anything better.

I hate the time and distance between us, Arthur. One of these days I'm going to convince you to make it right. Until then, I'll just keep loving you in small doses.

Oh, and we can get a dog if you really want one. It can stay with me during the week. But I get to name it.

Till next time.
Love, David

My eyes hang on the last word. I move my lips, trying to say the name, but my body won't listen when I tell it to breathe. The tears pouring from my dad's closed eyes can't be real. I'm imagining his silent sobs and the words on the paper and the shock holding my voice captive.

"Oh my God," I finally whisper. I look at the paper again and read it until the words are locked forever in my mind, where I can go back to them whenever I need to remind myself that this wasn't a dream.

I put the paper down and watch my father so I can put a face to this moment.

"David?" I ask. "David is the man you're in love with?"

His eyes finally open, only they aren't the same. They're shattered in tiny specks of brown and gray, and now I finally see the tears they've spent a lifetime holding back.

"Was," he says. "Was the man I was in love with."

CHAPTER 38

The silence between us is palpable. If I knew what to make of it, I'd shape it into something I could understand, but it's too large to wrap my arms around. The last twenty-six years have been a lie. They were never real, so what does that make me?

I drop the letter in the box and clench my fists at my sides. My fingers are numb from the cold and all those alien words, and I don't know where to file them in my mind.

"How?" is all I can say.

My father only offers a shrug, as if a house hasn't fallen from the sky, pinning our history under its weight.

"I've always been this way. I don't know why."

"I don't mean how are people born gay." He flinches when I say it. "I mean how are *you* gay? The bigotry and distain you've had for… The way you've talked about…" My brain is still processing the information my heart can't make sense of.

I try to rub away the pounding in my temples, but it only makes it worse. My words are muddy and slow. "The things you said about Theo. My whole life…the way you talked about people like him. I just don't understand. I'm trying. I really am. But it feels like you just introduced yourself to me, and you look nothing like the father who walked me out here."

"I know. I'm sorry, Bryce. I realize how shocking this must be, but I couldn't carry these secrets around anymore. I realized a lot while lying in that hospital. Whether it's by my hands or not, my time's coming to an end. I don't have the luxury of hanging around, pretending to be someone I'm not. More than that, you deserve to finally know the truth. When the ambulance arrived yesterday and I thought I might not make it, my only regret was that you never knew who I was. I don't expect you to get it, but I ask that you listen before deciding you hate me."

"How can I hate you when I don't even know you?"

He looks at me with something close to despair in his eyes, and for the first time I see how much my opinion means to him. Now guilt settles in with the cold. He's been telling me since I came back that there were things about him I didn't know. I just never imagined that it was more than just things. That it was everything—my whole universe and everything within it.

"I guess you're right," he says. "You can live with your own lies for so long that you lose sight of how big they are. I owe you an explanation, Bryce. I don't know "that you'll understand, but if anyone will, it's you. You always had more insight than your mother and me. It takes me years to wrap my head around the things you seem to get without even trying."

I sniff, drying my eyes with the back of my hand. "Then tell me."

A frown, a fidget. He doesn't know where to begin. "Being me"—he folds his hands together and watches me intently—"being me wasn't okay. Not in my home, not with my father, not with my generation, or even this town. You know what things were like when I was a kid because you've seen movies and read textbooks, but to live it was something else entirely. Some call it a simpler time, but not for me. I used to start every day by getting on my knees and praying that I'd be cured. Then I'd go to sleep resenting God for letting me go another day without his mercy. Being gay wasn't just something people thought was disgusting. It was a crime. Here, in this town, you could be arrested for loving the wrong person. But that was nothing compared to what God had in store for me. I used to have nightmares about burning for an eternity in flames that never died."

"So you knew when you were a kid?"

"Yes. But I thought my dad was right, and the church, too. I thought I was sick and that it would go away if I prayed enough. It wasn't until I met David that I knew I couldn't ignore it anymore. I lived in perpetual fear. Do you know what it's like to be afraid of yourself?"

I can barely stand the look in his eyes. I shake my head and make myself keep looking. I bore witness to his atrocities. I'll be damned if he dies without someone bearing witness to his admissions.

"I'm glad," he says. "No child should live that way. The safest thing for me to do was hide who I was and wait "for a miracle. I told you about your grandfather. He would've killed me. Living honestly was never in the cards. Hell, I didn't know it was something people even did, living openly gay lives. The thought would've been ludicrous to me back then. So I did what I was supposed to and met a beautiful girl I knew I could love and waited for that love to grow into more, but it never did. I did everything right. Got married, had kids, went to war and got blood on my hands, but then I came home and waged another war with my wife, and then with you.

"I studied every man I knew, imitated every macho movie. I shut you out, because men who spent too much time with their little girls were funny. I fought so hard to deny who I was that I became the stereotype I hated most. I became my father. A big brute who slapped his family around and made fun of those who were different. It was easier to hate what I couldn't admit to being than admit to hating who I'd become. That's my greatest sin. I wanted to be the part I played so much. It didn't matter that I was destroying everything. I wanted to fit in, and having to work ten times harder to do it made me a monster."

"Like a magician," I say.

"What?"

"You were a magician. Sleight of hand. Keep your audience so focused on one area that they don't see what's going on right in front of them. You used your marriage and kids to trick the world into thinking you were just like them."

"No, Bryce. I used my marriage to convince myself I was average."

"But it doesn't work that way, Dad."

"I know that now. I just didn't back then. Leaving for Vietnam, coming home and playing house with your mother...it was all designed to heal me. But you and your "brother weren't mistakes. You weren't a diversion. The second you were born, I wanted nothing but to stay by your side forever. You're my little girl. What dad wants to let go of his daughter's hand? But I saw the way your mom watched me when you were a tiny thing and I'd play with you too long or laugh too flamboyantly. I think she was afraid of how soft you made me, and what that meant I was becoming. So I stopped, and then I shut you out. Scotty was nothing to worry about. Your mother never looked over my shoulder when I was with him. Fathers are meant to spend time with their sons. I loved that boy with all my heart, but I never stopped missing you. You have no idea how many times I wanted to take you out for dinner, just to get to know you, or ask what you were going to wear to your dance and take a hundred pictures, but by then a part of me had died. The only time I remembered I was alive was when I got to see David. When I'd come home...it's like my soul would disappear and I'd just run on autopilot until the next weekend, when I could breathe again.

"You were the only bright thing left in our home," he says. "I'm not expecting forgiveness, but I'm begging you to believe me when I tell you I adored you then and I adore you now. There will never be sufficient words to tell you how sorry I am. Not ever. I let you live in the misery I created, and that's unforgivable. I used to think God had punished me for what I was. Now I think he's just going to have to love me, since he made me as I am. But it's your forgiveness I pray for most. I've lived a cowardice life. I didn't want to forget all this before I had a chance to tell you. There are already pieces missing from my memory. I didn't want my regret to be one of them."

I've had a response for everything in life, but not for this. My words sense my inner turmoil and even they don't know if they can weather the storm.

My father paints a picture so brutally honest I owe it to him to consider his pain, but my own pain is standing in the way, crying for me to ease it. I try to picture myself as a baby and the smiling father pinching my cheeks and laughing at my gibberish coos, but I don't have my own memories to tell me this ever happened. I've only the look my father gives me now, and I know I see great love there, but I also see every wound my heart sustained.

"I don't hate you, Dad. But I don't know what else to say right now. This is the first time you've ever been beautiful. You wear your honesty well. I just wish you hadn't snuffed the life out of everything around you to express it. I want to forgive you, but there's more, isn't there? That morning you took off... The article I found. Jackson said you told him a story. What was it, Dad? Before I can forgive you, I need to know what I'm forgiving you for."

"I don't need your forgiveness for this part, Bryce. I need my own forgiveness." His expression hardens; he lifts his chin. He's wearing a kind of strength designed to hide weakness. "Like I said, your mother came home and found us the night of your prom. David took off right away. We had met earlier that night and I drove him to our house, so he didn't have his car. Your mother and I fought, just like I told you, and I went outside. Once I calmed down a bit, I came in to talk to her, but the bathroom door was locked. I kept pounding on it, screaming for her to open it. I'd never been so scared in my life. You'd think war would be scarier, but no. I wasn't lying to you when I said deep down I didn't believe she'd do it.

"I threw my body at the door and the damn thing came down. When I didn't hear her scream, I knew. I reached in the water and pulled her halfway out. I swear to you, I tried to save her, Bryce. I sat there, beating on her chest, screaming at her to breathe, but she wasn't coming back. Next thing, you and Jackson came home early from the dance. You were laughing about something, telling him to be quiet so he didn't wake us. I looked at the door and can still remember telling myself to close it so you wouldn't see. Just a kick of my leg, but I was frozen. Just couldn't move. That's when you came down the hallway, and before I could react, you saw her. The whole goddamn thing still plays out in slow motion in my head, and I want to puke whenever I see you pick up her body and scream at her to wake up. That's a memory I'd gladly give away.

"I tried to talk to you. I grabbed your arms and tried to get you to look at me, but you weren't having it. You ran out of the bathroom and were out the front door before I could think about what to do next. Calling the cops probably would've been the logical step, but all I knew was that you needed me. The look on your face before you ran out... I've carried that with me every day, Bryce. It was the most terrifying thing I'd ever seen. My only goal was to find you, so I got my keys and drove off down the road.

"Everything was foggy. It was so dark. You were wearing this long dress, and I kept scanning the sides of the road for a girl in a long dress. I was homed in on that one thought. Every minute that passed by left me in a panic. I remember pressing the gas pedal and thinking I needed to slow down in case you were near the road, but I can't recall if I actually did. Everything was so confusing.

"When I got to the top of the hill, I came down too fast and swerved. I tried to correct it, but I thought I saw someone on the side of the road. I was looking to my left, trying to see if it was you or a deer, and when I looked ahead again, it was too late. That's when it happened."

My father's voice cracks. His mouth opens and he gasps for his next breath with just enough lunacy in his eyes to tell me he might unravel. He grips his knees and leans forward, crying the kind of tears that screech from your throat and leave you breathless. I reach out for him, but midway I find myself paralyzed by his torment. My breaths come faster. I don't know how to ease this kind of suffering, and I'm afraid to touch him even though I want to remind him I'm here. But then he talks and takes the rest of the air along with him, and the world goes quiet around us.

"I killed him," he sobs. "I killed D-David. I didn't see him. G-God, I didn't see him. I don't know where he came from. He shouldn't have been there. He should've been gone by then, but he must've stayed to see if I'd come looking for him."

My hand finally finds my father's, and I swear his agony radiates through me.

"I didn't know what to do," he says. "I got out and held him, screaming for someone to help me, but we were too far away from any houses, and I had no way to make a call. Two horrible accidents in one night, and all I could hear was your mother's voice in my head, the way she used to say bad news always comes in threes. Then I panicked. I knew you were going to die, Bryce. In that moment, it wasn't even a question. I knew you were going to hurt yourself, and then I'd have no one. Not Scotty, not your mother, not David, and not you. I wasn't thinking. I just reacted. I couldn't save David. He was gone. But I "thought maybe I could find you. It made no sense to do anything else, and so I left him."

He holds my hand tight, and I feel him silently beg me not to let him fall under.

"I left him, and when I found you at that lake, covered in blood, I thought you were dead, too. When I got closer and heard you crying, I just held you. I couldn't let go. I remember thinking I'd never let you go. I couldn't lose my little girl. I wouldn't have survived it. I knew what would happen if I went back for David...if I called the cops. I knew what it looked like. Here your mother was, dead in our bathroom, and here was a strange man dead in the road a few miles from our house, late at night. Husbands snap all the time, and I knew no one would believe the truth. Especially not about David and me. It was only because I was friends with the chief that no one tried to put two and two together after I called in your mother's accident later that night. I didn't care about me, Bryce. I deserved to spend the rest of my days paying for what I'd done to the people I loved, but there you were, lying in my arms, bleeding all over my hands. You were going to need me, so I left David there and never went back. When you got out of the hospital, the guilt had already eaten me alive. When you left for Seattle, I didn't know how to care anymore, so I watched you go and have been living in hell ever since."

"It was an accident, Dad. It wasn't—"

"No. Hitting him was, but having him there was no accident. I brought David into our home, and as a result, he and your mother died. That was my punishment. I still don't know why God had enough mercy to allow you to live, but I'm so grateful. I could've lost you. That's why I refused to ever love someone again. I deserved a lot more "than living alone with my demons. It should've been me, Bryce. Not David, not Patricia, but me."

I grab my father's forearms and force him to look at me, and then I speak from a place where I lie in pieces but let someone else's suffering fuel my strength, because this moment isn't about me, and my father needs rescuing from the only person he trusts to reach in and pull him to the surface, and maybe I can save one parent.

"Look at me, Dad. What happened that night was more than awful. A thousand better decisions could've been made, but it was still an accident."

"But they're gone because of what I did."

"They're gone because of something they did, too. Dying doesn't absolve you of guilt. They played their parts."

"No." He vigorously shakes his head. "Their deaths are on my hands. I destroyed everything."

"You saved me, Dad. Do you know what I was going to do that night? I was going to wait till I bled enough to pass out, and just before that, I was going to crawl into the lake and swim as far and as hard as I could so I wouldn't have the strength to swim back. That was my plan, but then you saved me. And you know what? I'm glad you did. I never thanked you for that, but I thank you now. I'm here because of you, and it's because of your story that I will never take a moment for granted again. You made a terrible mistake that night, but then I woke up in a hospital with air in my lungs because you knew I needed you, and you found me. Just before the lights went out, right before I thought it was almost over, I remember feeling you scoop me off the ground, and for that one brief moment, I felt safe. I don't know that I can make you feel safe ever again, but for the first time in your life, let someone who truly knows you love you for everything you are. I'm not "afraid of your past. And I don't think you're sick or wrong or abnormal. I think my father knew love in his life, and I wish I could thank the man who showed you that you were worth it. David and me…we've got a thing or two in common. I think you're worth it, too, Dad."

"What I did…telling Jackson to leave the hospital when he came to see you… I didn't want to hurt you, but I was too selfish to think of anyone but me. I wanted you all to myself, to protect you."

"So that's how he knew where you were that morning. I don't get it, though, Dad. Why'd you tell him? Especially before telling me."

"I didn't mean to involve him. I was confused and…it just kind of came out. Doesn't matter now. I'm just so sorry."

Worlds separate my father from redemption. I can almost see the outstretched hands of his soul reaching for it, like a starving man to food. How the guilt didn't fill his lungs like wet concrete and stop him from breathing all these years, I really don't know.

"Did you ever give more thought to calling the police?" I ask.

"All the time. David's mother and sisters never knew the truth about him. They deserved to know what happened that night. Closure's the least a person can ask for, and I robbed them of it."

"So why not tell them now? They're not going to lock up a man in your condition."

He looks out at the lake, and I wonder if it can read his thoughts. Maybe that's why it's so deep and black—full of everyone's splintered pieces and unspoken words.

"I can't, Bryce. One day. I've always told myself one day, but…I feel like I just got you back."

"Okay," I say. "A simple thank you sounds so small, but thank you for telling me everything, Dad. But can I ask you a favor?"

"Yes."

"We don't know each other all that well, and I'm looking forward to getting to know you, so please don't do anything before I've had that chance. I won't tell you I don't get why yesterday happened. But please don't trade in the rest of our time together."

But he won't look at me. His heart's still hanging on the words "one day," and as much as I believe he wants to learn who I am, my love's no match for the lure of finality.

He puts his arms around me and holds me. If I look at him just right and forget that he won't promise me tomorrow, for the briefest moment, I almost feel safe.

CHAPTER 39

The light in the bedroom is murky, like being underwater with gray skies above, but there's no rain this morning. I get out of bed and look out the window and see the thinnest layer of flog blanketing the ground. Just enough to swallow your feet and leave you hovering above the earth, grazing its tarnished surface with your toes. I grab my knit sweater off the foot of the bed and throw it on over my pajamas. It'll be no match for the cold today.

The faint hum of my father's snores fill the hallway, blending in with my heavy sigh of relief. I tell myself I'm braver than that, but I spent all night with my ear against the wall, afraid my father would find a way to free himself of his guilt in the middle of the night, and I never want to wake up in this house alone.

There are things to be done before either of us can clean the past from our hands. As much as I wanted him to, Daddy wouldn't promise to stick around to help me blow out next year's birthday candles, and I can't even be mad. For once he fed me truths, and I'll never sit at a man's feet and beg for scraps of lies from the dinner table. Still, his honesty causes me a new kind of pain I want to rid myself of but won't, because this hurt mean he loves me, and I love him.

I pause at his door and run my fingers along it while putting his breathing to memory so I'll have something to listen to when the day comes that his misery delivers a fatal blow. We're in the eighth round, and I applaud my dad for still standing.

I grab my phone and silently open the front door, closing it behind me and making sure it's locked. The air is dry, the wind heavier than I thought, and it whips my hair around, taking all the life from my gypsy waves. It tickles my lips and gets in my eyes, but I leave it there as I walk to the road and breathe in the smell of my lavender shampoo.

Gravel crunches under my rain boots, and I think I love that sound—the way you can hear and feel each step you take, like they have meaning, purpose. It sounds different than the solid thud of concrete. Despite the hole the city left in my heart, I woke up craving the sounds of Mother Nature and the brush of her icy hand upon my cheek. The city's too loud for the alarms in my head.

I wrap my sweater as tightly around myself as I can, stressing its seams, and I try to remember where the small valley was where I found my father. Maybe I'll sense it, because now I know that what happens in a place does define the land, and in my mind, that particular bit of land will forever be defined by my father's agony.

~

The clock on my phone says I've been walking for fifty-seven minutes. My feet remember this road and the blood it took from them when we last met. It can remember my flavor—I can remember its touch. But now it's something else entirely that pains me.

The gigantic pines densely packed on each side of the road cast shadows that keep it dark and cold on the black vein I walk along. The enormous roots nearly touch the asphalt, like sharp fingers clutching at a foreign object Earth's soul knows isn't meant to be there. We leave bruises behind in our wake, like the blemish left just up the road, where my father tried to wash it clean the other morning with his tears. But they just weren't powerful enough. Some blemishes need to be cut out and burned until all that's left is a memory. Others soak into the soil and become part of a place's subconscious. The only thing strong enough to cleanse that is a sacrifice.

I walk up a small hill and suddenly feel it, the change in the air—a different energy, a soft whisper. I crest the hill and see below the very spot where my father sealed his fate and left his heart behind, and God, how I wish I could pick it up and take it home to him. But this isn't about rebirths. This is about atonement for a sin my father didn't mean to commit—a sin that even reaches my hands, tainting my fingertips.

As I near the small valley, I slow down. You don't just barge through someone's door without first knocking and waiting to be invited in. This place is sacred, and so I stop and wait until I know being here won't disrupt the state my father left it in.

After a moment, I kneel down and gently place my hand on the dirt next to the road.

"I'm Bryce. I'm Arthur's daughter," I say, my voice as faint as the fog at my feet. I don't know that there's anything to believe in, but two men died in this spot—one gone forever, the other seeking a way out. If ever someone were going to be out there listening in the ether, I'd like to think it would be now.

"Maybe you can't hear this, but if you can, I want to thank you for loving my father. I think you should know that he's never stopped loving you. Not even for a minute. But something tells me you know that.

"I know you didn't choose to give your life for me, but had it not been for something foolish I did that night, my father wouldn't have been on this road, and you'd still be here, and maybe you'd be together. Your death was just as much my fault as it was my father's. I feel stupid asking for your forgiveness. Wherever you are, surely you've evolved past human emotions. But I ask that you forgive my father and me, and even my mother, and maybe every person who played any part in keeping you and Arthur apart. I'm sorry, David. I'm going to do what I can to make it right. It might be the biggest mistake of my life, but you and my dad deserve to finally put that day to rest."

I close my eyes and breathe in deep as I slowly stand and turn around. The walk back home is going to be harder on every part of me, and now I cry for all the moments lost with my father and for the moments that will never be. I cry what will be the first of many tears, and I take my father's guilt and swallow it into my belly and make it my own, because maybe that's not what we're meant to do for the people we love, but it's what I do. And then I pull out my cell phone and make the call.

"Yes, I have information about a hit-and-run case. I'd like to set up a time to meet."

CHAPTER 40

"Dad? You up?" I ask.

"Yeah. In here."

I follow his voice into his room and find him sitting in his plaid old-man chair. For the first time, I get it. It suits him well. He gives me a half-smile and holds up the notebook.

"I was trying to write in here. I don't want to forget yesterday."

I nod, look away.

"What is it, Bryce?"

I play with the hem of the blanket, rubbing my finger along the worn edge. "It was wrong to ask you to stick around for me," I say. "Seven years ago, you wanted me "around at any expense. Fast-forward, and here I am, wanting to keep you around at any expense, even though I see how you struggle through every minute. Growing up, I never knew why you were so unhappy. I can't tell you how many times I thought that if I were that miserable I'd just end it. That's what people do. We make allowances for ourselves that we'd never make for anyone else, because we think with our hearts, and as right as that is, it's also selfish."

"Bryce, I won't tell you it's easy. Nothing about my life is easy, especially now, but I want to be here for you. You need me."

"But I don't."

I look in my father's dark eyes and wish only for my own silence, because selfless decisions are the hardest to make. But I was wrong. I don't want to collect broken people and keep them around for my sake.

"I want you, but I don't need you," I say. "There's a difference. I'm not trying to hurt you by saying this, but I learned how to live without you a long time ago. I didn't sleep at all last night. I was too busy weighing your pain against my selfishness, and guess what? Your pain is much greater than my need to keep you here. Yesterday meant more to me than you'll ever know, and I promise to never forget it, Dad. Never. I've always loved you, but somewhere in the last couple months, I learned to like you, and yesterday…yesterday I learned to respect you, not out of fear, but because I admire your strength and drive to do what you thought was expected of you your whole life. You and Mom failed. I failed. We all inevitably do. You're just the poor bastard whose failures and mistakes took away almost everything he loved, and you've been biding your time ever sense. The Alzheimer's…that's just one more stake to your heart. I "get that now." I lean forward and take both his hands. "Of course I want my dad around. And I know you want to be here with me. But I want your suffering to end more. I can carry some of the burden, Dad. It's time you had a break. You asked me to help you, and I said no. I'm not saying no anymore."

"I can't ask you to do that, Bryce."

"You're not asking. I'm offering."

The air streams out of his lungs in one long sigh, and his next breath seems to fill him with a kind of relief that brings color back to his eyes and a beat back to his heart, and this is when you know you're doing the right thing. No man or woman was meant to live under a boulder, heaving for every breath. The gratitude in his eyes speaks straight to the part of me I'm afraid will die along with him, but I let my fears get lost in his peace, and I don't think I can even see them anymore.

He leans forward and kisses my cheek. I feel his stubble and hold him there, and I take from this moment what should have been given to me so long ago. I will remember my father's skin and the way it smells, and how his touch no longer fills me with fear but with compassion for splintered things that still shine. When I think back on this moment, I will try to remember that for a second, it was perfect. And then I kiss my father back and take in his smile as he sits back, looking like a lighter version of himself. I don't even mind how heavy my heart is now that I've taken a bit of his sorrow on.

"I have only one thing to ask of you," I say.

"Anything."

"Tell the police. Tell them everything that happened, and let David's family have the closure they need. It was my fault you were out there, Dad. Tell them, and make it right. Don't take this with you."

"I told you I can't, Bryce. Not now. I just—"

"I already called the police. I set up a meeting at the station. I give you my word, I won't let them arrest you. It won't happen that fast. You tell them, and we'll come home and do what needs to be done."

His relief evaporates, and some sort of horrible grief seems to infect him.

"You're not going to prison," I tell him. "I'll keep my promise to you before they even have what they need to arre—"

"What've you done?" he whispers. "Jesus, Bryce. What've you done?"

"You're scaring me, Dad. It's going to be fi—"

"It was Jackson. He was driving, Bryce. It was Jackson who hit David that night."

His words...I don't understand them.

"What?" I whisper.

"Jackson killed him."

I can't breathe. God, I can't breathe. I collapse to the floor and feel the air leave me as I begin to understand my father's meaning. I'm unaware of everything around me now but the pain in my chest, burning my lungs as I struggle for air. But then that eventually fades away, and all I'm left feeling is the weight of the diamond ring I placed on my finger this morning, right after whispering, "I will."

CHAPTER 41

I pound on Jackson's door—the thing standing between me and the last truth I can bear. I don't know if I'm crying or screaming or calling his name, but he answers quickly and stands back, staring at me like he doesn't know what to do with the wild thing on his doorstep.

"Are you okay? Hurry. Come in," he finally says, pulling on my arm and closing the door behind me.

"Why didn't you tell me?" I sob, trying to catch my breath. But it's no use. "What the hell happened? Why didn't you tell me you were there? You killed him. How could you not tell me you killed him? Please help me understand, my God, please help me!"

Jackson's hands drop to his sides as his mouth falls open, his lips moving as he mutters something I can't hear.

"Tell me now!"

"I'm glad he told you," he says.

"Glad? You're glad I just found out the man I love killed someone?"

"It was an accident, Bryce. I've been telling your father for years that he needed to tell you everything. It wasn't my place, but I wanted you to know. I wanted to tell you so many times."

"Is that why he told you to leave the hospital? Was he afraid you were going to say something?"

"Maybe. Probably. I don't know. But that's why he's spent every minute since then hating me. That's why I came over on your birthday. Once I found out he had Alzheimer's... I just thought he needed to finally tell you."

"Why were you even there that night?"

"When you ran out, your father and I went looking for you. No way I was going to let him drive like that. He bawled his eyes out the whole time, rambling about how much he loved you and how sorry he was for lying to you for so long. I don't even think he realized I was there. He just said all this stuff about hiding this man from you guys and how badly he had screwed it all up. It wasn't until the next day that I put the pieces together. My only concern that night was finding you, but it was foggy. I couldn't see anything, and...he came out of nowhere, Bryce." He drops to the couch as tears settle in the corners of his eyes.

"I was a damn kid, not even out of high school yet, and I had taken someone's life. Your dad thought he was going to lose you. Frankly, so did I. I was standing in the road, losing my shit while your dad held this guy, and the next thing I know, your dad's telling me we need to go.

"That finding you was the most important thing. He told me to take my car home and clean it. He kept saying, 'Clean it well, Jackson. Don't leave anything behind.' I couldn't even make sense of what he was saying. Everything happened so fast. I dropped him off at your place and left. That's when he got in his car and drove out to the lake and found you.

"I swear, Bryce, I was seconds away from going to the cops. There was no way in hell I could live with myself. I had my keys in my hand, and when I opened the door to leave, your dad showed up, telling me you were in the hospital and how I better not call the cops. I told him he couldn't stop me, so he clocked me. I didn't give a shit. I would've fought your old man all the way to the police station if that's what it took. But then he said it would kill you. That's when he told me what you had done to yourself. He said I was the last thing you had, and if the cops didn't believe us, or if anything went wrong, you wouldn't survive me being taken away. Before I knew it, I had a rag in my hand and was scrubbing blood off my car. As much as I wanted to tell the truth… I believed him, Bryce. If I could do it all over, I'd do it differently, because I know you're strong enough to handle it. I just didn't know that then."

"So I'm to blame for everyone's fuck-ups? I'm the excuse you and my father gave yourselves to hide something so heinous?"

"No! It wasn't like that. It was done. Putting you through more hell wasn't going to bring David back."

"You're a liar!" I yell. "You said you wanted to tell me, so what happened? Where did that boy go? All these years and you never said a word."

"I don't know." He rubs his forehead. "When I showed up at the hospital the next day, your dad looked at "me like he hated me. It didn't matter that it was an accident. I knew then that he'd always see me as the bad guy. The reality of what I had done settled in, and that's why you never heard from me again. It took two years before I could stand looking at myself in a mirror, four years before I could work up the courage to apologize to your dad without falling apart, and after all this time, I still can't forgive myself. You try to live as perfectly as you can and make right everything you've ruined, but it's always there. You were the only thing that stood out in the middle of what had become a living hell for me, Bryce. By the time I'd learned to function again, I'd lost you, and the more time that went by, the harder it became. I know you don't believe me, but it wasn't my place to tell you. Not about your dad and David. How was I supposed to tell you what I'd done without telling you about them?"

"So you two just buried this secret? Just learned to live with it?"

Before I can react, he stands and is in front of me, looking down at me with regret I can't stand to see on the man I love.

"One year ago, Bryce. The last time I sat parked in front of the police station was one year ago, and the only thing that kept me from going in and telling them the truth was that I knew there was no way in hell your dad wouldn't be arrested right along with me. I couldn't do that to you two. As much as you've thought you hated him in the past, I couldn't take away the man he loved, his freedom, and what was left of your family. I don't know how to apologize for something this big. I know there's no making it right, because I've tried. I'm sorry. From the bottom of my heart, I'm sorry. Can you forgive me? Knowing what you know now, can you ever forgive me? Or will you always look at me the way your dad does?

"Because I can't handle seeing you look at me like that, Bryce. Not you."

I can't speak. My hands are bloody and my nails ripped back from trying to dig for answers buried too deep below a surface Jackson and I have barely begun to scratch, and still, every cell in my body screams for me to hold the man made of lumber, who's crying tears he's probably cried a thousand times before, and begging to be loved in a way he knows only I can love him. But what he doesn't know is that I pulled the trigger and killed the darling life we could have had. I'm barely breathing, and before long, Jackson won't be here to hold me together anymore. He'll be in a place without dreams, full of men who learned how to hate before they learned how to love.

I hold his face and pull his forehead to mine and breathe in the air that lingers between our lips, and now I can forgive him if he can forgive me.

"I'm sorry," he says against my lips.

"So am I."

"What do you have to be sorry for?"

I stand back and raise my left hand. "I didn't give you a chance to put it on before answering," I say, shaking from head to toe and doing all I can to not fall over.

His hands find my waist and he pulls me in, but I push him away and shake my head and try to wring the love from my heart and the agony from my soul.

"I called the cops, Jackson." My voice is just above a whisper, but it's still too loud. I don't want to hear what I already know is coming. I don't want to hear words that match my pain.

"I didn't know it was you," I say. "My dad took the blame, and I…I thought I was doing the right thing. We're supposed to be there in a couple hours to make a written statement. They're going to find out it was you. I'm "wearing your ring, and they're going to find out it was you."

My heart flatlines in my chest, but my lungs betray me and somehow take another breath even though life is sour and stings. It holds me down and rubs mud in my face, and just when I've fought my last fight and haven't any life left in me to keep going, it asks me to hold on for one more kick to the gut.

I tremble and cry but make neither sound nor movement. Jackson is my reflection. We both stand still in the carnage, blood dripping from our wounds as we watch each other fall away without saying goodbyes our hearts can't bear to utter. I'd rather be the quiet to his pain and let his strength be the picture I take me with. I could've told him I loved him a thousand times over the years. Now I rip my heart from my chest and give it to him, because the damn aching thing was never mine to begin with. I had it all wrong. He was always the rightful owner.

"I have to go," I say. He grabs my hand and speaks to me without words, but there's nothing in my chest to feel with anymore.

CHAPTER 42

Am I still me if everything that made me the woman I am is falling through my fingers and disappearing before my eyes? I reach out to touch the afterglow left in their wake, but I blink and it's gone. And I thought I knew loneliness. Silence in the absence of the ones we love has a thickness to it that coats your entire existence and holds you in place like a web does a fly. It's heavier than the chattering of a thousand strangers and deadlier than your worst nightmare, and the harder you fight it, the quicker it swallows you. Isolation is poison in my veins and ice water to my heart.

The steering wheel glides under my fingers as I turn onto my father's street. All of me is left in the little house two miles from here, with a man inside with his arms full of all the parts of me that belong to him. He can hold on to them, and maybe one day build a better version that doesn't know how to betray him with her honesty. I'm just scraps now. Just enough skin, bone, and muscle to stand and walk and open the door to face a promise my heart made but my loneliness and guilt try to stop me from keeping.

"Bryce?"

My dad is sitting at the kitchen table in his robe, a mug in front of him and an empty glass beside it. I can feel his eyes on mine and mine on his, but whatever used to give me my voice is gone.

"I was worried. Did you go see Jackson?"

I pull out the chair next to him and sit down, trying to remember what I said to Jackson, but I only know that I lit a match and held it to the house that held our love, and now all the pictures I paint will be in ash and shades of what could have been. Certainly the rest will come to me in my sleep for the remainder of my days and play on what little life is left in my shell. I'm already resigned to drowning in tears that will never end, even when, like my father, I grow old with solitude and wake each morning with remorse laying beside me, hogging all the covers and elbowing my ribs.

I talk, only because I remember the sounds to make, but their meaning escapes me.

"He knows," I tell him.

"What did he say?"

"He said everything he could say."

"He wanted to tell you sooner, Bryce. He always did."

"That's what he told me."

He nods and slowly spins his mug around on the table, a faint cloud of steam billowing from the top.

Before I can see what's in it, he slides it away from me and holds his hands out.

I lay my hand in his and watch as his eyes redden behind heavy lids.

"I can't imagine what you're going through," he says. "Your whole world's been turned on its head."

His next words come out a bit mumbled, and I can't tell if it's from impending tears or if he's just tired. "I wish I were strong enough to stick around and try to make it right. Promise me you'll try to forgive me one day. It doesn't need to be now, but promise me you will try."

Can he really expect me to keep my promise? Can't he see that I've already paid too great a price today? If I sell the rest of my soul for his peace, what will keep me going?

"I don't think I can do it, Dad."

His head lazily tilts as he smiles at me. "It's okay. It wouldn't be fair to ask you for this, too. Not now."

"Then what does that mean? What're you going to do?"

I hold my breath and wait for an answer I'm not sure I want, but I can see by the content look in his eyes that he's already gone. It's just a matter of logistics now. Asking him to stay would be like asking someone who just escaped the walls of prison to go back inside and forget what freedom tastes like.

"I'm going to sit here and enjoy my daughter," he says, "and then I'm going to finish my tea and take a nap."

I watch the way his lips fumble around when he speaks and how his setting eyes seem to have no idea it's still morning.

"Are you okay?" I ask. "Why're you so tired? Did you take something?"

"Just the rest of my pills."

I close my eyes and sigh. "There were only seven left. What did you think that would do? All that's going to happen is you're going to get sick and that doctor of yours is going to throw you somewhere where sheets don't get washed and the food looks like paste. Seriously, Dad."

"I just need it to make me sleep. That's all it has to do."

"Why? What do you mean?"

He slides his mug over but puts his hand up so I can't touch it.

"Our neighbor Mrs. Lorton has a green thumb."

"I've noticed. Her house looks like a giant fairy garden. But why does that matter?"

"Did you know she grows beautiful ornamental plants?"

"No."

"She used to come over here all the time, always with a planted pot in her hand, offering me one thing or another. I don't remember when it was—sometime after the fire, but she came by with this beautiful pink flower that reminded me of the place where David and I spent our weekends. It was my home away from home. The only home I ever shared with him.

"Mrs. Lorton told me I could have it but that I'd have to respect what it could do. I didn't know anything about oleanders. I just liked the color, but when I found out that this little pink flower could end the show, I fell in love with it. Even took it to the hardware store and got the color matched up. You've been asking about the walls. They make me think of David, and in case I forgot I had it, I hoped they would remind me there was a way out once the symptoms got too bad."

"When I dried the flowers out in the garage, I didn't know if I'd use them. They lost all their beautiful color.

"Guess it doesn't matter now, though. They'll serve their purpose. The pills just make it so I don't have to be awake for the finale. From what I read, it won't be pleasant."

I look at the mug, filled to the brim with poison and promises, and I stutter, my chin trembling.

"Let's not leave anything unsaid, Bryce."

His hands are warm on mine, and I don't want to feel the cold air when he takes them away. His lap's too small for me to crawl into, and God, why can't life come with a reset button and enough self-forgiveness to loosen the noose around my father's neck?

My breaths come in short bursts, tears coat my cheeks, but I won't let go of his hand so he can wipe them away, because I know they'll be the last tears he'll ever dry.

I'm trying to be strong and not fill his last minutes on this Earth with desperate pleas, but the little girl in me wants her daddy to make the scary monster in the closet go away and never come back. Instead, my father's holding its hand and letting it lead him away, leaving me the girl with no mommy and a daddy whose path will be hard not to follow.

I'm all alone. I want to scream it as loud as I can so he can hear the echo of my words even in death, but my pain recognizes his and keeps the little girl at bay.

My future has in store for me a lifetime of lovely things I could have had and a view of my unfurled dreams as time makes them brittle and the ravages of age turn them to dust, and my heart will learn a lesson my father's has already learned. I will know what it means to truly lose the man I love. I can't ask my father to keep surviving this.

"Who will I have left?" I whisper. "There's no one."

"That's not true."

"It is, Dad. My whole family will be gone."

"No"—he shakes his head—"you'll have Jackson."

He pulls two envelopes from the pocket of his robe and lays them on the table. One bears a woman's name and an address, the other blank. He holds up the one with the name and says, "This is for David's family. I wrote it years ago and never sent it. The other is a confession. I want you to give it to the police." He bends his head down and holds my chin as I cry on his fingers. "You know why I didn't report David's death after it happened?" I shake my head. "Because I knew what it was like to have lost the absolute love of my life, and I didn't want you knowing that pain. I screwed up, Bryce. I've done a lot of bad things in my life, but protecting Jackson wasn't one of them. I know I turned him away, but that was only because I could see how broken up he was about what he'd done. He was lost, Bryce. At the time, you wouldn't have survived his guilt, and he wouldn't have survived your will to get out and start anew. I didn't stop you from leaving when you got out because I knew both your problems would've eaten the two of you alive. But now he's ready, and I think you are, too. You're going to need him, so let him love you. He can handle it. You take this letter and let me do what I was trying to do back then. Let me protect you two."

And then I break.

Sobs build in my chest, forcing their way to the surface, and I cry my pain and lose the last of my composure in a house made of my bones, and in a place that tells my story. I throw myself at my dad and wrap my arms around him, holding on so I don't forget that in this moment, he was good.

"I d-don't know how to say goodbye," I weep.

"Of course you don't," he says. "Neither do I. We've never done it before, but if you hold my hand, I'll hold "yours, and I promise not to leave until I absolutely have to."

I look into his eyes, the same color as mine, and leave nothing left unsaid. "You're not your father. You're not like him. The story you told me...the man he was—"

"What story?"

"You don't remember?"

"No."

"It's okay," I whisper. "It doesn't matter now. I just want you to know that you're brave. I know you were afraid to be your own man because of what that would mean, but you're beautiful, Dad. And when you stepped out from behind the version of yourself you'd been hiding behind, you pulled me out from behind the woman I'd been hiding behind, too, and you made me beautiful. I don't know how to thank you for trusting me."

"I'm sorry I waited till it was too late to tell you. I love you, my sweet girl. Always know how proud I am of you. If you remember nothing else about me, remember that I'm sorry. For everything I've done, I'm sorry."

I shake my head and frown. "I'll remember right now. I'll remember when I was scared and you held me. I love you. I love you so much."

And then I kiss his cheek and let him hold me before we say goodbye in a house that's known its share of sadness and now its share of love.

CHAPTER 43

I get out of my car and stand in the rain. It's not till now that I notice I'm still in my pajamas. Luckily the water doesn't care. It'll hug you tight and show you the way to the bottom.

I walk out onto the pier overlooking the lake shaped like a dragon and think I want to feel its fire on my skin and in my hair, and I'm so numb I won't even cry. But it's the water I want to wash away my tears. My afflictions are too great for a bathtub. I need something that can hold all my weight and not overflow when I never stop crying.

The water below is glass, but I can break it with my sharp edges. I stand on the end of the dock and bend down, dipping my toe in the frigid pool under my feet.

The water stays on my toe and seeps into my pores, and I think I hear my mother say my name. It's rude not to answer.

Sitting down, I lower myself into the lake, first to my waist, and then I let go. My skin perks up against the icy water—my nipples ache. It hurts so good I can barely breathe.

My brother splashes somewhere around me, and his cries of joy carry on the slight breeze and sting my eyes with every punch of its memory. I want to tell him I hurt and make him carry half the load he was too little to carry before, but in my mind his hands are still so small, and I don't want to see them worn and calloused.

I lie on my back and do my best to float, but my lungs don't want to hold enough air. Layers of gray clouds slowly drift overhead, gazing at me. The rain's heavier now, but I don't close my eyes. Water below me. Water above me. Nature baptizes me in her palm while I drop my pain like acid into her waters and don't even care that I'm now a blemish on her glassy eyes. It's not enough to wash it all away. I need to go under.

Air out, water in, I exhale and lie suspended just under the surface and watch the rain fall, stopping just before it can reach me. Arms outstretched, I let the deep pull me down and lull me into a place too serene for my sorrows to thrive, and for one glorious moment, I wish I were brave enough to stay where the light doesn't reach and the water knows nothing but the sterile cold that disinfects all who inhabit it. How could I not? This place is like the arms of an old lover, a touch so soft, a smell so familiar. The trees encircle the lake, like outstretched arms waiting to receive me. I want to get lost in her icy depths and settle on the sooty floor, where my tears will blend into her celestial body and my pain will be stricken down with each inhalation of brackish water. When her weight takes from me my last moments of life and the scars the world left on my heart vanish into the inky darkness, my weary soul will find solitude in her boundless womb.

I feel myself fall in slow motion and my vision begins to dim. But just when reality is almost out of reach, my skin warms, and a soft whooshing whispers in my ear. I don't know if it's real or just a product of my traumatized mind, but I feel a presence beside me that feels too much like my mother to be anything else.

My mind plays for me a scene I've already met, and I see my mother combing her hair in front of the bathroom sink. I look up at her and tug on the side of her dress, asking where she's going. She doesn't answer, but she smiles at me so sweetly it makes my cheeks warm. Her pink lips form a heart, and she blows me a kiss while wiping a tear from her eye.

"You're my favorite thing in the whole world, Bryce," she says.

Her fingers graze my cheek and I sink into her touch.

"I love you, Mommy."

"I love you most."

My eyes snap open, and I reach for the surface of the water. The burning in my lungs floods my eyes with bright spots I can't see through. I frantically kick but make no progress. I don't want to die. I might be a product of two dysfunctional people, but if you turn me over and read my label, it now says "Loved". My parents loved me wrong, but Mommy loved me most and Daddy was always proud, and I don't want to hide behind hollow versions of myself and, like my dad, take love in small doses on days that only start with S.

I've got a life to start living, but I can't reach it, and now even my next breath feels too far away, and shouldn't it still be hurting?

Legs limp, arms sapped of strength, I scream at my eyes to stay open, but they close out the light and wrap me in darkness, and I know I don't want to die, but all the colors are gone and…

~

I feel water rush by as something powerful hauls me to the surface. I try to see what's happening, but water blinds me and I can't breathe.

"Cough! Now!" someone screams at me, but I can't take the breath I need to in order to cough. My lungs are going to explode even though they're empty.

"Now! Come on. Breathe!"

Big arms wrap around my torso, moving me through the water. Just when it feels like I might die, my throat opens and I cough so violently I feel something pop in my neck and I think I broke something.

"Again!"

I take a short breath that feels like knives in my chest and cough as the arms continue to pull me to the edge of the lake. Once more, my eyes flood with specks of light as I continue to cough and strain so much that my throat burns and I taste blood in my mouth. And then I hear myself gasp before I feel the first full breath fill my lungs and clear the fog from my head.

"Jackson?" I cry. "Jackson?"

He's pulling me onto the shore and has me in his arms, and now I see his face and try to reach for him because I need to feel him to make sure he's real.

"Why?" he gasps, "W-why, Bryce? How could you? What if I hadn't known you'd be here?"

I want to tell him I wasn't. I swear, I wasn't trying to. It was just so warm down there, and I wanted to be close to my mom, because she looked at me like I was her everything and she loved me most and I forgive her, but I can't speak. My body's so cold, even my tears aren't warm. I shake my head, but I don't think he can see it through all my shaking.

"Dammit, Bryce." He holds my head to his chest and wraps me in his arms, his sobs blending into mine. "Don't you ever leave me," he weeps. "You're not allowed to, you hear me? You're not allowed to leave me. I won't let you." He chokes on his words, and when I reach up and touch his tears, they're warm on my skin. "If you ever leave, it'll kill me."

I try out my voice and don't know if he can hear me. "I'll never leave you," I say, my throat raw, my voice strained. "I promise, I'll never leave."

CHAPTER 44

My father's headstone stands out among the rest. It's a light stone with flecks of pink no one can see, but I know they're there, and it makes me smile when I come visit him.

I walk along the plush hills of the cemetery and see his name in the distance. My arms are full. Light-pink peonies and one worn box.

I reach his headstone and set everything beside it while I try to get comfortable even though it's getting harder to find a position that doesn't leave my hips aching and my back throbbing. I lean against the headstone, panting from the summer heat that's left everything so green it's hard to remember winter takes it all back, and I place a kiss on my father's name.

"Hey, Pops," I say. "Looking beautiful today, as always." I grab the flowers and lay them beside me. "I brought you peonies. They're the color you like. They're my favorite. These aren't as pretty as the ones we had at the wedding, but I went to that fancy florist with the orange roof and got the best ones I could find. I see lots of carnations on the other plots, so I say we got 'em beat."

I trace my finger along my swollen belly and curse my bladder for being so needy.

"I'm officially in my third trimester," I say. "I feel like an alien host. I try to describe to Jackson what it's like when she kicks, but I don't think I'll ever be able to put it into words. It's like trying to describe blue to someone with no sight. How do you do that?"

I sit in silence for a moment and watch a small bird pick things from the grass as it hops about, flitting its wings in the sunlight and making me think of precious things and new beginnings, and I wish my father could meet my daughter.

"I'm happy, Dad. Like, crazy happy. Happy in that way I used to resent when I saw it in other people and just thought I wasn't built that way. The only thing missing is you and Mom and Scotty. I wish you were here so you could see that people like us were meant for more than surviving storms. I'm still prickly, but Jackson's worked on me. Between him and the baby, I'll be the perfect stone for skipping before she's born. Well…maybe not perfect, but I'm aiming high."

I grab the box and set it on my lap, running my hand across the top. I keep it under our bed, just like my dad did when he was alive. It reminds me of what I have and that, even when the blessings of life blend into the monotony of each day, every moment is something special and each second a symphony I almost deafened myself to. If nothing else, this box, these words, they deserve to be in the presence of love, in a home where "I love you's" aren't in short supply, and where I'll keep my father and David's relationship alive, even if it's just in the memory of my father's smile when he said David's name.

"Thank you, Dad," I say. "Maybe you're tired of hearing it, but thank you. If it weren't for you..." I sigh at myself. "Sorry. I'm all tears lately. Being pregnant has made me seriously uncool. Anyway, had it not been for you, I would still be alone, trying to figure out how to get out of my own way. This little girl owes her grandpa a big thank you. It's because of the lessons I learned through your loss that she's got a mommy and daddy who will always love her most, no matter who she is or who she loves or what she wants to do with her life. You broke the pattern, Dad. Maybe it took you a lifetime, but the day you told me all your truths, something in our family's destiny changed. My daughter's not going to have to fight the same battles, because you and I fought them first, and for that I will be eternally grateful. You helped give her a good mama. I'll make sure she knows that."

I dab my eyes and flip open the shoebox. "Okay. Enough tears for one day. I promised you I'd read another letter last time I was here, and I'm a woman of my word."

I pull out an envelope with my father's name strewn across it in cursive. I open it and pull out two sheets of paper.

"Ready?" I say. And then I lie down on the earth that blankets my father and begin reading to him all the words that made him the man who taught a woman with sharp edges how to love.

Acknowledgements

Thanks to my amazing editor Ashley Davis (A.K.A. Mistress of Collegiate Badassery) for catching what my hurried mind doesn't always see and for supporting me. You're my homegirl, even if we're both pasty.

I want to thank the extremely talented Keri Knutson of Alchemy Book Cover and Design for another ridiculously awesome cover! You're both a kick-ass artist and a kind friend.

I also want to thank my best friend and the love of my life, James, and our two lovely, beautiful, stunning, amazing, and utterly perfect daughters for allowing me the time to put words to paper and the support needed to give them meaning. Without you, this would truly be impossible. You're my all, my everything, and the passion that fuels me, and I still love you more.

Last but certainly not least, I want to thank my readers. Some of you have been with me since Irreparable Deeds, and some of you are new, but you all mean a great deal to me, even if you think I totally suck. Thank you for giving my words a home. For that, I will forever be grateful.

About the Author

Sloane Kady is the best-selling author of two novels and several short stories. You can find her debut novel and suspense thriller, Irreparable Deeds, on Amazon, along with several anthologies featuring her short psychological horror stories. Sloane is currently working on her third book.

Sloane Kady is also an avid artist who's not afraid of bright colors and radical expression. Her work has been featured in several shows and is available for purchase.

Sloane resides in the Seattle area with her husband of 16 years and their two lovely daughters. When she's not writing, she loves spending time with her three favorite people. She's prone to sporadic pine tree sniffing, and she finds beauty in honesty, even if its edges are sharp and it stinks of something ugly, dangling from the underbelly of society. After all, too many things coated in candy only rot your insides, and sometimes salt is the best thing for an open wound.

Stay up to date with Sloane Kady at www.sloanekady.com.

J. Daniel Stone writes from NYC, where he was born and raised. He is the author of the urban horror novels *The Absence of Light* and *Blood Kiss*, and the collaborative, stand-alone novella *I Can Taste the Blood*. In 2016 he was selected by readers to be included in *DREAD (The Best Horror of Grey Matter Press)*. He writes under a pseudonym to keep the wolves at bay.

Find him on Twitter and Instagram @SolitarySpiral